EDEN RISING
THE CLAIMED COVENANT

BY

JH DEMOND
&
TJ BERRY

FOX FIRE PUBLICATIONS, LLC 2024

<u>*Acknowledgements*</u>

JH DeMond,

To my real-life Gwen and Gavin, who listen to all of my kitsune stories and show me all of the cute foxes in the world. To my parents for their love and support. To my husband for his inspiration and encouragement.

To TJ Berry, who opened up a whole new world that day he walked into my office and asked for the names of two characters by the end of the day. And to the strong women in my life who reflect in all of our female characters: Trish, Sharon, Wendy, Stephanie, and Linda.

TJ Berry,

First, thank you God for giving me the strength (and creativity) to complete this journey. It was a labor of love, but it was laborious to cross the finish line. Thank you to my partner, best friend, co-owner of Fox Fire, and my beloved co-author, JH DeMond…the babies are all grown up now. To my family and friends who've supported me, thank you and I cannot put into words how much your love and encouragement means to me. To all the readers, who've made this journey with us, I hope you enjoyed the ride and that these characters have found a place in your hearts…but don't worry, there's more to come.

Fox Fire Publications would like to thank SelfPubBookCovers.com/RLSather for our cover art.

Chapter 1: Beach

Angela

"Oh, look at him," I say about the teenager, riding by on a grungy skateboard with cutoff camo-green shorts and that stupid spiked helmet. I take a deep breath. He smells musty with a hint of not showering in about three or four days…and still my mouth is watering. "I could probably eat him, and no one would miss him at all."

"Perhaps," Duchess hums, still scribbling away in her little journal. "But then he'd be your first kill…or worse, you'd turn him, and you'd be stuck with that idiot as a sire-son."

"You didn't even see him."

"I didn't have to."

I glare at her. "Has anyone ever told you your French accent is stupid?"

"So is your New York accent." She hasn't looked up from her book once. I kick some sand at her. "Ay…" She lifts her head and points her pen at me. "…I've been here with you in this self-imposed exile because…"

I slam my hands on the painted cast iron table. "…because you sold me…your own sire-sister…out to En Quosque." The metal groans under my fingers. It feels like rubber…and not just the texture.

"Only because I'm not in love with anyone…and their next target would have been Maggie or Raven…and would you really like for them to steal our sire-mother's love for father…and then kill Vance? Because that's what they would've done."

"Of course not."

She returns to her journal. "Then clearly you are not the monster that you believe yourself to be. The monster who called me up and… How do you say? …guilt-tripped me into joining you out here. The monster who caused you to move across country to begin with."

"I am."

"You're NOT. If you were, you would've eaten that idiot without a thought…or even mentioning it to me so that I could 'talk you out of it.'"

I lift my hand and stare at it. The same hand that I used to drive a wrought iron spike into Devon's chest…up to my wrist. The same hand that I used to squeeze the trigger on Bal… I sigh. …repeatedly. Click. I jerk. Click. Jerk. Click. Jerk. "I am…I haven't felt…anything since…" My finger twitches on its own. Click. "…since…"

"Balthazar." I look at her. She sweeps that big dangly curl out of her face. "It's okay, little sister. You can say his name…" She returns to her book…again. "…and you can stop attempting to comfort yourself while simultaneously placing a barrier between the two of us."

I look down at my arms, crossed over my silk wrap, doubling as a belt. "Stop psychoanalyzing me."

"Stop giving me a reason to."

"Hey," comes from behind me. I turn and glare at the two shirtless tanned, blood bags with more product in their hair than I have. "You ladies out here by yourselves?" the one with Gumby hair and a blondish streak moving up the center asks. They smell like Coppertone...sunshine...sea water...way too much cologne to cover up the smell of sea water...and delicious, delicious blood. I swallow a lump and smack my lips as my mouth fills with saliva. The monster wants a bite.

"No," Duchess purrs while staring at her book. "We were out here because we were waiting on two shirtless idiots to come along and harass..." She lifts her head. "Oh...you're already here."

"Bitch," the other one snarls, and they walk away.

I turn back to her and motion to B Positive and A Negative walking away. "What about them? I KNOW nobody would miss those two...except maybe each other. They're so clearly gay for each other and don't realize it because they're so ultra-hetero."

"We could've..." She pauses to put the back of the pen against her chin. "Ah...but then we'd never get the smell of that ridiculous knock-off body spray out of our clothes. It'd be like a human eating too much curry." She drapes her tongue out of her mouth and resumes writing. "Bleh."

I shake my head and turn toward the sun, still high above the ocean. Still not used to seeing it over water in the afternoon instead of in the morning. LA's a lot like New York. Just as crowded...just as dirty and used...but everything's lower here...so you can see all the 'used' parts.

I stare at the family...two moms, a son, and a daughter...playing with squirt guns further along the beach. I miss my moms...Raven and bio-mom...I haven't talked to either of them much since I came out here...since he told me to 'Run...go and find yourself again'...whatever that meant. Still hungry though.

I lower my shades. "Do we still have more of the pig's blood in the fridge?"

"No, sorry...I threw it out...it was starting to coagulate. I picked up some more cow...and sheep." I groan. "I thought you liked sheep."

I sigh. "Better than goat, I guess."

She laughs. "Ah, it's about time you showed up. I wondered how long it would take."

"What?" I catch his scent before I hear him. I clench my jaw...out of all the people...human, wolf, vampire, daemon, and everything else on the planet...there are exactly two people who'd be the last people I wanted to see…Nate…the guy who I was in love with, who En Quosque stole my love for…the one who told me to run…and… I turn to "Natavius." …the wolf who professed his love for me, trying to get me to stay. "If I missed the baby's christening then too bad."

"You did, but that's not why I'm here."

"Oh," Duchess purrs. "How is little Anara doing?"

"Clearly, you've been talking to Nate, not Alana." My spine stiffens, and my head starts to pound. Just from hearing his effin' name. "Kya Anara Dumont is doing well…" He looks at me. "…due in no small part to her godmother."

"They named me godmother?" He nods. "So, they make me their MOH at their wedding…and now, I get their kid if something, God-forbid, happens to them?" It's like they're trying to torture me.

"Pretty much." He holds his fist out to me. "Godparent crew…" I frown. "No?" I shake my head. "But I am…the godfather."

"That's good. Something happens to them; you can have her."

Duchess slams her book closed. "She's all yours." I glare at her. "I've had to put up with this…this caca for the last three weeks, Natavius. You can have her. I'm going back to Paris…or perhaps, Milan…I need to do some shopping."

"You're leaving? Seriously?"

"Yes, sister…as you've been telling me for weeks now…'you don't need me.'" I open my mouth. "You're right though. You don't need me." She tips her head toward Natavius. "You need him…and from the way he looks at you…he needs you too." She wraps one arm around me and gives me a squeeze. "I will miss you though. I was finally getting used to your odd morning routine."

"Yeah, I'm weird." I hug her back…with both arms. "I'm still mad at you though."

"I know."

"But I still love you."

"I know. And I love you too, sister." We separate. "And if Maggie or Raven ever decide to talk to me again…I'll tell them too." I smile. "Au revoir." She walks away taking her phone out. "We're on…I'll need the item delivered…"

I come back to Natavius, who's still staring at me. I frown. "You cut your hair," he says. "May I?"

"Surprised you haven't."

He shrugs and plays with the part that frames the left side of my face. He leans out so that he can see how much shorter it is in the back. "I like it."

"I don't care." He nods and stops playing with my hair. "Why are you here?"

"Why do you think?"

I shove him aside and walk toward the beach house. "Then you might as well head back to New York…and tell Nate or Raven or whoever sent you that I'll come back when…"

"I came because I wanted to see you." I stop walking. I knew that was the reason, I was kidding myself thinking it wasn't. "Nate is my best friend…has been my best friend for the last two hundred years. It took me two years before I was scouring Middle America for him. It took all of three weeks before I hopped a plane to come find you."

I sigh. "What do you want me to say, Natavius?" I turn to him. "I just don't…see you like that…and thanks to En Quosque, I probably never will."

"You're wrong." He taps his temple. "Remember, I was a member of their little club…so I know that they need a very specific love from you…the true love…pure love of a vampire."

"So, why would you or anybody else settle for less than that?"

"Because that doesn't mean you can't love it just means…" He groans. "…being with you is not settling."

"So you say now," I say, turning back toward the beach house…pfft, beach house…more like crappy second story apartment that Duchess rented for us…crap, she never did tell me who her blood connect is. I wonder if this is her way of telling me to go back to New York. "But after one hundred years of spending time with someone who's dead inside…"

"You're not dead inside."

"Yeah, I am."

He grabs me by the shoulder and turns me back to him. "Why are you talking like this?"

"Because…it's true. Now, let go of me…the Raiders are playing the Giants, and I don't wanna miss it."

He lets go. "Fine, then I'll come up and watch the game with you." I frown. "I like sports." My eyebrow goes up. "I don't mind watching sports?" My mouth twists up into a pout. "Alright, sports are so boring that I could probably make paint drying seem more interesting…" He throws both arms forward. "…I mean, the guys on the field move sooooooo slow…and why do they even call it 'football?' They carry the ball way more than they kick it!"

I laugh and give him mental points for knowing that the sport was football. I clear away the amused look on my face. "Fine…whatever…and the people don't move slow…" I point at his nose. "…you just move too fast."

He huffs a laugh as I turn back toward the apartment. "Ugh. So, you guys have been staying here?" I nod, staring at the pale blue duplex with white trim. "Better question…Duchess, actually stayed here?"

"She's not nearly as pretentious as you'd think." He nods. I key into the heavy metal storm door on the first floor. "It's a nice little two bedroom…beach adjacent…" I come back to him. "…that she HAD to have. It has a nice view and quiet downstairs neighbors who don't ask questions about the two girls on the liquid diet."

"That's good." He scratches the back of his head as I march up the stairs. He follows, and I can't help wondering if he's staring at my butt. I glance back and see that he has two eyes full of khaki shorts. I clear my throat. "What? You've got a nice butt…and you know it."

"First of all, it's better than 'nice.'" He chuckles while bobbing his head in agreement. "And second, that doesn't mean you get to stare at it." He lifts his hands innocently. I shake my head as I reach the landing outside our door with its little B just below the peephole. "So, as you can see…I'm…"

Natavius catches my hand on the back swing. He steps up behind me…I feel his warm breath on the back of my neck. "Ange…?"

"I'm not coming back," I moan. "I'm done." I take my hand out of his and open the door. "You can come in for a little while before you head out…but I'm not…" I frown…and sniff because I don't believe what I just smelled. It's human…earthy…but with a lot of metal…mostly silver…and an overabundance of noradrenaline and lots and lots of adrenaline.

"Vampire hunters," Natavius whispers into my ear. His breath smells like cinnamon, but without the harshness. It's warm without making my skin feel moist. His voice is manly without being overly authoritative or too forceful. The tips of his left middle and pointer fingers barely tap the back of my hand. His skin is like warm silk.

I'd look at him, but I don't need to be reminded of how gorgeous he is with his big brown eyes, naturally sun-kissed skin, and hair like black silk. He's perfect…but somehow, I don't think of him romantically…the way he wants me to…the way he told me he loved me, hoping it would make me stay in New York.

I nod. "…going back to New York with you," I say louder. I push the door open and walk in. He holds in the doorway for a second and then follows me. I put my bag down and glance around the room. I tilt my head back and listen…I hear the rhythmic breathing of six pairs of lungs…and the slightly accelerated thumping of five heartbeats. I reach underneath my silk belt. I wrap my hand around the dagger that Raven gave me.

"WHOEVER YOU ARE, I SUGGEST YOU COME OUT NOW! YOU DON'T WANT ME TO FIND YOU!"

Two men come out of the kitchen to my left with their automatic assault rifles, complete with laser sights, pointed at me. Another one comes out of the hallway on my right, leading toward my bedroom…he better not have gone through my underwear drawer. I just switched from thongs to French Cut…and those things are expensive. Another…I glance over my shoulder…woman, hmph…comes out of the living room closet behind me.

"She's not alone," the panty-raider says.

"Is it the other vampire?" kitchen-dweller number two asks.

The woman points her gun at Natavius. "Nope. He's got a heat signature…heartbeat…and smells like a wolf."

"Wolf and a vampire?" kitchen-dweller number one gripes. "It's a freakin' epidemic."

"There are only four of you," I say like a complaint.

"With guns," closet girl chimes.

"Yep," I say. "And all I have…" I pull it out. "…is a knife…" I pull the second one that I had custom made of wrought iron to match Raven's next. "…or two." It doesn't feel right. It's a little heavier than hers is, but it's balanced well so it doesn't bother me much. "And still," I continue. "There are ONLY four of you."

"I know right," Natavius chimes. "I could…"

"I got this," I say, tilting my head back toward him. He frowns. "It's not like I've been out here just lying on the beach, working on my tan." I cut my eyes to the kitchen-dwellers. "Big sis and I have been training…non-stop…every day." He frowns.

The air turns electric around me…the hairs on my arms stand on end…I feel a little tickle on the back of my neck…I turn to the hunters as they start squeezing their triggers, and everything freezes. I move toward the kitchen. It feels as if I'm walking instead of the full sprint it used to feel like.

I tap the clip release on kitchen-dweller number one's gun and pull the clip out of his. I spin and drop the mag out of kitchen-dweller two's gun, too. I step back. I really focus and jab number one three times in the ribs with the butts of my weapons. I do the same to two. I jump and throw my new knife at the panty-raider, handle first. I sigh while coming down, and everything returns to normal.

The kitchen-dwellers fall before their magazines do, and the knife pegs panty raider in the center of his forehead, dropping him so hard that his legs kick out from under him like a cartoon character. I glare at closet girl. She looks around curiously, before settling on Natavius. He points at me. She looks at me…wish I could see the look on her face…but these vampire hunters seem to like dressing like ninjas with cops' riot gear.

"I didn't kill any of them," I say, moving slowly over to my new knife. I pick it up. "If you want to keep it that way, take your goons, get the hell out of my apartment, and never come back."

"We would," a woman's voice says from the kitchen. She steps out wearing their usual black gear, plus a trench coat but minus the mask and goggles. Her hair is so black that it looks purple. It hangs behind her in a huge, anime-style ponytail. "But you haven't been properly catalogued, Angela Price." I frown. Natavius steps forward, and I hold my hand out to him. Closet girl lifts her gun, and the woman extends her hand the same way. She comes back to me. "…sire-daughter of Raven Gregory…biological daughter of Maria and Michael Price."

"It sounds like you've catalogued plenty," I complain.

"Not even half. We need to know your abilities and your limits."

"Why?"

She pulls two short swords from behind her back…each curved upward at the tip and downward at the handles. "Because it is what we do."

"Um, Ange?"

"I need this, Natavius." She twirls both weapons. I do the same. "Like I said, I haven't just been lying on the beach out here…every minute I wasn't in class or at work…I was training…when I wasn't sleeping."

"Or drinking blood," closet girl says.

"No comments from the peanut gallery," Natavius says, pushing her gun down. She tries to resist, but he holds it easily.

"Then let's see the fruits of your training, girl," the boss-lady says and glares at me with crystal blue eyes, down a long slender nose with full on pouty Mediterranean lips. She takes a stance with one blade in front and one above her head. Crap, my apartment's too small for this, so I'll have to end it quickly. I inhale deeply, and the room slows. I run toward her…but she's not stopped…she's not even moving slow…she's moving as fast as I am.

My blade collides with hers, and it feels like I hit a brick wall…you know before I became a vampire. She brings the other down. I drop back. She misses me, and I lunge at her again. She blocks with one swinging upward…while bringing the other up immediately behind it. I lean back, and two hairs fall away from my forehead. I sweep at her legs. She jumps up but kicks off my entertainment center and pushes forward.

I roll out of the way, and she slices up my futon with both knives. She crouches on the arm, springs up, taps the wall with her left foot, and comes at me again. I roll again and throw the knife in my left hand. She deflects it…there's a breaking thump sound…and then keeps coming at me. I jump to my feet…deciding to switch tactics. She stabs at my chest. I lean back and catch her right arm between my left forearm and chest. She stabs at my midsection, but I already have my knife there to block the hit. I spin and toss her…nowhere. She managed to get one foot down and maintained her balance somehow.

She stops, spins, and kicks me with the heel of her boot in the stomach…my teeth gnash together…the back and front of my stomach feel squished together…my spine jerks, and I lose a lot of air. I stumble back. If Duchess hadn't hit me there like a dozen times over the last three weeks, I'd have puked up blood.

I lift my hands because I know she's not going to let up. She springs off the coffee table…and kicks the knife out of my right hand. I manage to spin, then catch her ponytail with my left hand and pull back…hard. She bends with it and brings her right arm up with the blade aimed at my arm. I let go and jump back. The blade whispers past my arm.

I drop into a kung fu stance…yi ting…like Nate taught me. My right fist and left leg out front… I take a deep breath, have to stay calm…have to be ready for anything.

"WHAT THE HELL JUST HAPPENED?" closet girl asks. "I missed everything, but it looked like you two were all over the place."

"They were," Natavius says, sounding angry.

The woman stands, both swords still ready with one of her feet up on my coffee table. "Are you sure you want to refuse your friend's help?"

I nod.

"Even if it means I kill you?"

"If he wasn't here, you'd kill me anyway, right?"

She sighs and lowers her weapons. "No." She slips them behind her back and stands. "Bond," she barks.

"Yes, ma'am," closet girl snaps with a salute.

"Start collecting the others and get them out of here." Bond…formerly known as closet girl…snaps off her salute and goes over to panty-raider. She lifts him and tosses him over her shoulder. She hurries out, and Natavius holds the door for her.

"And you…Angela…"

"What?" I grumble.

"You are far too young to have given up on life already."

"You don't even know me."

She nods. "I know that in most reports of catalogued, formerly good vampires going rogue, that's the case…" She glares at me. "…that they lost whatever it was that kept them tethered to whatever humanity they held on to." I scoff and look away. She stands in front of me…she's almost a full head taller than I am.

"What's your problem?"

"No problem at all." She removes her right glove and offers me her hand. "Sorry for the way that I entered. My name is Sera Marković; I'm one of the Order's training coordinators." I shake her hand hesitantly. "You can call me Marko…everyone does."

"Marko…? You're Jamie's…sister's…mom, right?" She nods.

"You're awfully chummy," Natavius says. "For someone who tried to lop her head off two minutes ago."

"I finished my assessment." I frown. "She passed." She walks toward the kitchen. She takes a piece of cloth from my table…it's her trench coat. When did she take it off? She tosses it and then slips her arms into it. "You know, in all of the fights I've been in…you're the first person who's been fast enough to grab my hair." She nods. "I may have to think about cutting it. Speaking of cutting…here." She offers her blades, sheathes and all, crossing each other in an X. "Consider them an assessment gift. They're a little sturdier than yours, and they're made of a steel, wrought iron, and silver alloy." I hesitantly claim them.

Closet girl rushes in and grabs Kitchen-Dweller One. Marko grabs Two and tosses him over her shoulder effortlessly. "Also, sorry about the mess." She offers me a card. "Call this number, and they'll replace any of the damaged furniture as well as reimburse you for any damage done to the apartment." I take the card. "Ciao." She walks out of the apartment and closes the door behind her.

"Okay," Natavius says. "What the heck just happened?"

I stare at the little card with the name *Ezekiel, ltd.* in the center and a ten-digit phone number below that. I fan myself with it…wafting its jasmine-scent toward me…no, it's Marko's. I didn't notice it while I was fighting her…but it's like a body lotion or something she wears.

"Natavius?"

"Yeah?"

"You could've taken her, right?" I look at him. "I mean, you're fast enough to beat her, right?"

"Yeah."

"Could Raven…? …beat her, I mean."

"Yeah." He closes his eyes, and his fingers move through that black silk he calls hair. "Probably." He looks at me. "Why? What's up?"

I stare at Marko's blades, crossing each other. I squeeze the leather belt attached to their sheathes, and it groans. "I think I found a reason to go back now."

He crosses his arms and nods. "Okay." He nods again. "Okay, but we have one more stop to make, before that." I frown as my left eyebrow arches.

#####

Chapter 2: Marriage

Gwen

"I have to go," I whisper to my husband, Alex…the man of my dreams. Maybe not my dreams, but he's everything I could've ever wished for in a mate. He's kind, loving, brave, and complements me in so many ways…not to mention he's so cute with his chestnut-colored hair, forest green eyes, and that cute little dimple in his chin…made even cuter by his experimenting with facial hair in the form of stubble.

"I know," he purrs, leaning into me at our intimate table.

"Ugh," Kai groans, moving to stand. "I'm gonna go get some hot chocolate…and maybe, something to help stop me from barfing." Alex's very blond cousin…my cousin-in-law moves toward the counter.

Alex laughs, and his warm breath caresses the nape of my neck. I pant as my mind instantly takes me back to two nights ago, when we… I giggle as my cheeks inflame.

"What?" he moans, collecting a handful of my red hair. I shake my head. "Fox-face," he purrs, commenting on my kitsune or fox fire side. "I know you better than that." I hum softly. "Please," he adds, pulling me, chair and all, closer to him.

"The leaf," I whisper, bringing him back to two nights ago as well…when obāsan sent us a leaf pertaining to our newly minted nuptials.

"Oh, that," he huffs.

#####

Two nights ago…

"I love you," Alex says, holding me closer on my daybed. I blush thinking about the last time we were here…together…and how that came to an unfortunate, fiery end.

Not now! We're married, and my obāsan removed the seal that protected my…ahem…virtue. "I love you, too…husband."

He frowns. "What's wrong?" I shake my head as my lower lip protrudes a bit. "Gwen?" he hums, brushing his nose against mine. He can read me like a book, and I love that about him.

I sigh. "I got a leaf from obāsan."

"A leaf?" he asks with a frown. "Did she teach you some new trick or something?"

"No, it's…a message written on a leaf…infused with fox magic, so that it only seeks out and can be read by the person it's intended for."

"You ended on a preposition," he complains.

"Look who thinks he's so smart," I whine. He smirks, proving that he listens to and retains everything I say.

"So, this leaf," he continues. "It's like…ultra-secure text message?"

"Exactly!"

"So, what'd this one say to make you look so worried?"

I bow my head and come back to those beautiful, tender eyes of his, drinking in my face. "Tsukino-san…Toshiro's father is contesting our marriage."

"What? How? Why can't that loser just get a life already?" he growls as his eyes flash amber. "I mean, we helped…" My eyebrows arch. "…*you* helped his family hold on to their position, so what's his problem?"

I heave a heavy sigh. "I don't know. Perhaps, he feels he should still be the patriarch of his clan."

Alex nods. "So, what'd the letter say? How's he contesting our marriage? Is it…?" He holds a clawed hand over his heart. "…because I'm a skinwalker and not a full kitsune?"

I go over obāsan's fiery message, and my cheeks feel enflamed all at once. I open my mouth, and nothing comes out, because we've brought up this subject before…just before we left Nanbu and even the last time, we were on this very bed…although, we didn't actually talk about it at that…

"Gwen?"

"Um, no. It's…ahem…that's not…the problem," I stutteringly hedge out as a response.

Alex bobs his head. "Is it because of my kitsune bloodline…? Am I not *noble enough* for him?"

I roll my eyes. "No. In fact, because you're the emperor's second cousin…your mom, being his first, means your family ranks higher than mine…or his for that matter, even if their original bloodline claim was legitimate."

"Okay," Alex whispers. "Then what is it? What's the problem?"

I move my right hand over my left in an explanatory way. "We haven't…" I clear my very dry throat again. "…made it…um…official, yet." I huff. "Our marriage, I mean."

Alex shakes his head. He lifts his left hand, holding mine. "We have rings…we did the ceremony…"

"No," I moan. "I mean…*official*…"

He shrugs. "What? Did we need more witnesses?"

"No!" I sigh into a groan. "Do you…see how we're…lying on my bed, relaxing…holding each other…on my bed?" Alex nods. "Well, we…you and I…should've already…*not* been *just* lying here…on my bed…together."

He scowls and shakes his head subtly. "Oh! Ooooooooooooo," he moans.

"Yes," I say as my face feels warmer to the point that even my ears heat up.

"Well, you know…" He motions to me. "…like I said in Nanbu…I've been…um…waiting on you." I nod. "And if you want, I can keep waiting on you."

"Really?"

"Yeah. I mean, I've wanted to…you know…since the first time I saw you…"

I frown, and all the attraction I felt for him evaporates. "From the first…!?" I shake my head. "…you didn't even know me then!"

"Gwen," he whispers with a sexy bass filling his voice, blotting out my anger. "Deep breath…it's okay. I've loved you from the moment I first saw you, too." He caresses my cheek. "You're my wife. I love you. And you're the only person I want to do…that with…" His thumb sweeps across my lower lip, sending the most amazing tingles through my body. "…now and for the rest of my life."

I smile. "I never really thought about it." I nibble my lip, sucking up the electric tingles that his touch gives me. He arches his eyebrows and mouths, *Never?* "No, not that…I've…" Blush. "…thought about *that* a few times, but…" I motion between us. "…we're married. We're going to be together for the rest of our lives."

"Yeah, that's what I'm saying," he starts.

"Then…" I tug on his t-shirt. "…why don't we…start the rest of our lives, now…you know?"

He frowns, and his heart skips a beat. "What about your foster parents? Won't they…?"

"They won't be home for another hour or two…"

"Okay, but…Gwen, are you sure?"

I caress his cheek this time, while pulling his shirt toward his head. "The only time I've ever been surer, was when I was staring at you…" He smiles. "…and said, 'I do.'"

He leans in and kisses me passionately.

#####

Present

"What are you two talking about?" Kai interrupts our shared memory.

"Nothing," we both say at the same time. My eyes meet his, and he laughs, causing me to laugh. "Nothing at all," he whispers, as his fingers dance along my inner thigh…just like that night…that was so perfect…so beautiful, so…

"Then why are you guys staring at each other like a couple of freaks?"

"I…umm…"

"Hey, Kai," Alex jumps in. "It looks like Em put out more of those sweet rolls you like!"

"The ones as big as my face?"

"Yep!"

"Damn, there's a line!" He looks at his phone. "And we're supposed to meet Jamie and the other witches in a little while."

"Then you should get in line now," I reply, offering him some cash.

"Yoink," he snaps, while snatching the bill and moving away from the table simultaneously.

We laugh. Alex's laughter dies off with a sigh. "What? Did you not like…? I mean…we were…"

"No! Noooooo! I loved all of it…when you rubbed my…" He emits a stuttering sigh.

"Okay, because when you kissed my…" I shiver.

"And when you did that thing with…" He grips my thigh firmly under the table. I move closer. "…we-we…should talk about something else," he says in a breathy whisper that caresses my cheek, taking me right back to that amazing night.

"Agreed," I return with a matching volume and weighty breath. "What were you thinking about just now? Before we…" I swallow a lump…and slide my chair a little further away from him. I replace my thigh with my hand under the table.

"I was just thinking about what happened yesterday," he answers.

"You mean when you stopped by…and climbed through my window?" I hum, leaning forward again.

#####

Yesterday

"I'm sorry, loser," Meghan says, folding yet another of her cute sundresses. "I wanted to make sure I had enough to last the entire week that Stephen and I'll be spending at my aunt's place."

"And your aunt…Maria…?" She nods. "Her daughter Angela, your cousin, is a vampire?"

"Apparently, an especially special one who can walk in daylight."

"How is that possible?"

Meghan sighs. "Well, her mom was extra tight-lipped about that part."

"Good!"

"Good?" Meghan asks.

"Could you imagine if some of the vampires we've met were able to walk in the daylight?"

"Good point," she returns, while zipping up the largest of her three bags. I turn to the other six bags out in the hall.

"Are you sure you have enough?"

"Well, Stephen and I are going to tour Columbia and NYU while we're there…so that's two days…and then we'll do some sightseeing, so that's another three days…we leave today, come back on Monday."

"And how many outfits did you pack?"

"Only twelve," she says of her five-day trip. My eyebrows go up. "Pfft, fine! Fourteen!"

"Uh huh," I return in my best North Carolina accent. "And why did you have to leave from my place?"

"Because, loser, I wanted to raid your closet to make sure you didn't have anything especially cute that I wanted to borrow!"

"You didn't take anything!"

She snickers. "You don't pay as much attention to me as you think." I frown. She moves over to my bed. "I stole back my shorts that are like capri pants on you…my silk white sleeveless top…my…"

"I get it, I get it," I say, moving to the closet. I survey all the blank spaces she left in her wake.

"So," she starts again. "How's married life treating you?" Springs creak as if…

I turn to her quickly. She's sitting on my bed…exactly where Alex and I…and I… "Um, Megs…would you mind…not sitting there?"

Her brow comes together, and her head cants to the left and moves forward. "Well," she groans, peering around the room. "There's nowhere else to sit. You don't have any chairs in here."

"I know," I return, walking toward the door. "I'll go get you one, just…don't…"

"…and since when don't you want me sitting on your bed?" she asks suggestively, while rising from her seat.

"I…um…it's…just that…," I trail off, tucking my hair behind my ear and fidgeting, so much fidgeting.

She walks toward me, examining my face, my hands, and my shifting stance. Her mouth falls open as she takes several shuffling steps closer. "Gwen…is your bed…sacred ground now?"

I gasp. "No." Yes. She leans in closer. "Yes," I murmur.

"OMG, Gwen!" she says, claiming both my hands. "YOU AND ALEX FINALLY!" I nod as my cheeks feel warmer. "How was it?" she asks directly in front of me.

"I'm not going to talk about it…" *AMAZING!* "…except to say…" I take a deep breath as the feeling of Alex and me…and all those amazing tingles we share, washing over me only times a thousand. "…I honestly didn't think I could love him anymore than I did…" That feeling returns all at once. My eyes drift closed, and I shudder. "…but now I do. I really do."

"Wow," Meghan breathes. "The first time Stephen and I did it…I thought I was gonna break him." She tosses her hair. "I was too busy trying not to hurt him to be all lovey-dovey."

"You…and Stephen have already…?"

She purses her lips and nods. "Now that I've got down how much…" She pauses. "…pressure to apply…we've been going at it like a pair of bunny rabbits."

I open my mouth to respond with a response my brain hasn't even prepared yet. Clink, clink, clinka, clink comes from the side window, and I feel him before I even peer out the window.

"And now you have to go," I say, moving her bag toward the door with one hand, while dragging her with the other.

"What? Why?" I turn to the window…and Alex, my husband, perched on the nearest branch. "Oh…that's why…"

#####

Present

"I remember what happened next," Alex interrupts. "…but that's not what I meant." I shake my head. "I was talking about what happened later that morning…at school," he adds.

"Oh."

#####

Yesterday (a bit later)

Alex and I file into Chemistry class hand-in-hand…taught by Mrs. Pritchard in the same classroom as Biology last year. Her hair remains tied back in a salt-and-pepper bun at the back of her skull. Her tiny rectangular glasses remain perched at the tip of her nose, defying gravity. The bell rings as Alex and I settle into the same seats as last year…minus Stephen to my immediate right. He took the afternoon class with Meghan and Jamie-Lynn.

Alex leans back, and I can't help playing in his silky hair, feeling those tingles climb my arm. He tilts his head back into my hand, and I just want to kiss him right here and now.

"Gwendolyn," Mrs. Pritchard calls, breaking me out of whatever I was imagining doing to my husband. "You cannot distract other students while I'm trying to teach class! Please refrain from touching Mr. Garner, Ms. Frost!"

"Frost-Garner, ma'am," I return before I can stop myself. Alex leans back and peers over his shoulder at me.

"What?" Mrs. Pritchard asks.

I take a deep breath. "My name," I start. "...it's not Ms. Frost anymore, ma'am. It's Mrs. Frost-Garner."

"Holy crap, she's actually doing this," Kai says, staring at me from the seat next to Alex.

I stand up. "Over the summer, Alex and I went to Japan and visited my maternal grandparents. While we were there, as a part of a custom in my family..." I put my hand on a very uncomfortable looking Alex's shoulder. "...Alex and I were married." I sigh. "So, like I was saying...not Ms. Frost, Mrs. Frost-Garner."

A low rumble of whispered conversations moves through the class. "Quiet everyone," Mrs. Pritchard demands. She comes back to me and then her eyes dart to my right. "Mr. Garner...is this true?"

He leans closer to me. "Gwen, I thought we weren't telling people about this."

I smile and rub his shoulder. "Alex...I don't ever want to keep any part of...what we have a secret, okay?"

Alex smirks and stands. "Well, when you put it that way," he whispers. He holds his hand up between us. "But I'm gonna need my ring." I reach for the necklace he gifted me this morning. I take it off, dropping the pair of wedding rings in Alex's hand. He puts his on while I replace the necklace. My husband then puts my ring and engagement ring combination on my finger. I smile as it settles into its natural resting place.

Alex turns to Mrs. Pritchard. "Yeah, Mrs. P...it's true. Gwen and I are married." He flashes his ring, and I do the same.

"GO TO THE PRINCIPAL'S OFFICE!"

"What?" I ask.

"Why?" Alex adds. "For...for being married?"

"Yes! Go!" Alex and I collect our bags and walk out.

After a brief, confusing lecture from Mr. Stanford, Alex and I sit in the waiting area. I lean against him and trace the lines in the palm of his hand. He rests his head on top of mine. I want to purr because of how good this shared energy feels between us. Admittedly, since we were, well...together, I feel it all the time...diminished, small...but constant and perfect.

"You two just had to tell people, didn't you?" Mrs. Garner says storming in.

"Sorry, Mrs. Garner."

"Mom...Gwen. Call me, mom...and..." She sighs. "...it's okay. Just tells me how much in love you are." I smile.

"Mrs. Garner," Principal Stanford starts, all smiles and his heart skips a beat at the sight of her. "I'd like to explain..."

"It's alright, Mr. Stanford. I figured that Gwen and Alex's marriage would cause problems for them at school, so I asked them to keep it quiet." She looks and then smiles at me. "Plans change though. I wanted you to know that her grandparents condone the marriage, I condone the marriage, and that I've talked the matter over with Gwen's foster parents...and they're...finally on board, as well."

Stanford clasps his hands together. "Then...I suppose there's nothing we can do. Nothing in the rules says that two students can't be married in high school."

#####

Present

"Sorry," I whisper to Alex's arched eyebrows. He leans in and kisses me.

"Gross," Kai moans before biting his massive, sweet roll. "And your ride's here, Gwen."

The trademark Jelly Bean Coffee bell rings as Gavin and Sora walk in. "Are you ready?" he groans.

"What's with him?" Alex asks Sora.

"He saw you two kissing from outside," she returns.

"Whatever," he groans and walks out. Sora takes the seat opposite me as she starts to laugh.

"Does she look alright to you?" Kai whispers, staring at his sister while leaning closer to Alex and me. "She looks a little...green."

Alex shrugs before coming back to me. "I'll be back before you know it," I tell him.

"Still won't be soon enough." I nod. He steals a quick kiss. "Love you."

"I love you," I reply, moving to stand...but he holds on to my hand...and I his...until I finally slip away.

#####

Chapter 3: Ultimatum

Alana

"Again, Angel Face?" I purr to my adorable daughter's vibrant eyes staring up at me. She gurgles into a giggle. "Very well. Once upon a time, there was a beautiful princess…held captive by her wicked father, despite the protests of her loving and less restricted older brother and sister. The princess was secure…she was safe…but unhappy…and quite lonely." She frowns.

"One day, on one of the princess's many secret excursions outside of her father's vice-like hold over her life, she encountered a hunter…set on ending her life…" She makes an O of her mouth, and her brow arches. "…but luckily, the princess encountered a brave and devastatingly handsome warrior…" Her large cheeks go up, and she blushes. Her arms move up and down quickly. She always gets so excited when I get to the part about her father. "…who came to her rescue. The princess quickly fell in love with the warrior…and the warrior shared her feelings."

She puts her tiny fist to her mouth and suckles on it. "After many trials and tribulations, the pair were finally united…after the unfortunate death of the hunter, revealed friend…the death of the princess's father, revealed blackheart…" I sigh. "…and the death of her brother, revealed angel from heaven."

My tiny angel yawns, and her eyes drift closed. Her spittle-covered fist moves up to her eye. "The warrior and the princess married…and were soon after blessed with a beautiful child…"

"Now, that's not quite right," Mosif says, lumbering over to us on his cane. I smile. "As far as I know, the child came into the picture before the warrior and princess were married."

"Yes, Uncle Mosif, but my daughter will ALWAYS hear this version." I lay her down in her carrier and pull the shield over her face, providing her some shade. I point at Mosif. "Clear?"

He huffs a laugh and holds both his hands up in submission. "So," he starts again, gazing at the serene setting. "Picnic in the park, huh?"

I nod and lean back on the blanket. "Yes. It's such a gloriously beautiful day, I couldn't resist." He nods and claims a spot on the blanket with me. I motion to the rolling hills, trees, and shrubbery nearby. "Our guard detail has promised to stay close but respect our privacy."

"I know. Spotted 'em on my way over." He looks at Kya. "She's the spitting image of you."

"Thank you."

He stares at me. "…and you're the spitting image of her."

"Thank you again."

"I meant…"

"I know who you meant." I nod. "Did you know her well? All I have to go on are the brief moments she implanted in my Nathan's memories and what my siblings told me about her."

"She was…" He scratches the whiskers at his chin. "…everything they say about her. She was warm and loving. She was beautiful…smart…funny even."

"No one has ever used the word 'funny' to describe her before."

"She never spent as much time just talking to anyone like Mosi and me." He shakes his head. "We all loved her…but nobody loved her as much as my brother."

"Was he…in…love with her?"

"What do you think, angel?"

"Were you…?" The corners of his mouth turn down, and he stares at his cane. "Did you and she…?"

"Never," he says with great weight and sadness.

I gasp. "Did Mosi and my mother…?"

"No, no, she only saw us as her friends…not like the other Aldiens. They saw us as tools…as weapons to aim at the daemons…the vampires…and even the fae, if need be."

"You make my ancestors sound so sinister."

"They were no more or less evil or good than any other race as a whole." I nod.

"They were not the best," an older voice calls behind us. I turn to it, leaping to my feet…one hand on Kya's carrier. An old man walks toward us, wearing a tweed suit…pale green shirt and dark bow tie. He wears a fedora atop his head and large, dark sunglasses cover his eyes. His pale, grayish skin sags under his chin and droops at his cheeks. "…no, that they weren't."

"What are you?" I snarl. "And how did you get past my guard detail?" I kneel next to Kya and take hold of the secret compartment on her carrier, containing my gun.

"Well, now…they're wolves, ain't they? Why would wolves stop a little old man out for a stroll?"

I sniff. He *is* human…not even an enhanced human, like the hunter's guild, but how is that possible? He knows about Aldiens. He takes another step. I point the gun at him and cock the hammer. "That is quite close enough."

"Ezekiel," Mosif moans, forcing himself to his feet. "What are you doing here?"

"Ezekiel? As in the Eye of Ezekiel Order? As in the human member of
En Quosque?" I renew my aim, and Mosif places his hand on the silver slide,
pushing it down. "What are you…?"

"Ezekiel's a lot of things," he says, removing his smoldering fingers from
the silver-made weapon. "…but he's not dumb enough to start a fight in the
middle of Central Park…in the middle of the day…with an Alpha…" Mosif's
head bows, and he releases his cane. The soft hairs moving along the backs of
his hands stand on end. "…even a former Alpha…" I feel it a second
later…the power emanating from this old wolf. He's almost as strong as my
Nathan…not quite as strong, but very dangerous all the same. He nods.
"…that'd be suicide for…your little cabal."

"Mosif, my old friend…have you turned against me?"

Mosif's fists clench tight, stretching the skin over his knuckles. "Well,
you were never on my side, so I guess we're even."

"What are you doing here?" I growl. "Because if you've come for my
child, I will kill you…human or not."

"If I don't first," Mosif grumbles. He winks at me.

"As if either of you could," he says confidently. "No, I'm not here for
that." He turns to me. "I'm here to talk some sense into you. Just…give us the
child…no one has to suffer…and when Eden returns…"

"Hell," Mosif says. "It'll be hell on Earth, only this time there probably
won't be an end to it." Ezekiel looks at him. "I heard stories…the few daemon
and fae who survived the last resurrection of Eden…Devi has the most vivid
memories…" Mosif's eyes go distant…into the past. "…she vividly
remembers forcing her mother to destroy herself to stop Eden the last time…"
He glowers at Ezekiel. "…so much so that the Fairy Queen's already named
her successor…because she doesn't want to suffer another bout of Eden's
rule."

Ezekiel comes back to me. "We will destroy you if we have to. Wouldn't
it simply be better to give us the child so that you don't have to die? You and
your beloved Nathan can live out the remainder of your days in peace."

"Not that I would ever contemplate giving up my angel, but my
grandfather has made it perfectly clear that no matter what…my Nathan and
I would have to die."

"Oh, that's not true."

"'A true god has no parents,'" I repeat his grim statement, just before he
slit my throat.

"So, you won't listen to reason?"

"Would you?"

"I did. I paid that price," he purrs. "Once." On that one word, over 2000 years of pain washes over me. He does know. He gave up a child for Eden's mad pursuits.

"Then you know…" I nod, while kneeling to put a hand on my daughter. "…you know that you are asking the impossible of me."

"I'm asking you to make a sacrifice…no more or less than I have…than your mother did…" I tremble. "…than we asked your father to make."

"My father was a monster. What do you know of him?" I snarl.

"Monster?" He laughs. "I know that rather than turn you, and the wolf over to us, he'd rather see you dead." I touch my throat, reflexively. "That's right…I saw him slit your throat…rather than give the two of you to us." He shakes his head. "He believed in your mother so much…"

"What are you saying?" I gasp.

"Your mother walked your father through every step of the last century…" I shake my head. "…your conception…"

"No."

"…your…birth…"

"No."

"…her death…"

"LIAR!" I snarl and before I even finish the word, my protection detail surrounds Kya and me.

"Ma'am," Jackson moans, offering Kya to me. I take her from her carrier and leave my gun in her place. Jackson returns the carrier to the blanket. "Is this man bothering you?"

"Don't get these young wolves killed, Alana. They've only just started their lives. The oldest of them has half your years. The rest…young even by human standards. Don't forfeit their lives."

"We're leaving," I say, holding Kya closer.

"I take it, that's your decision then?"

"It is."

"Very well." He places his hat on his head. "War, it is."

"You foresaw this," I say. "I know you did."

"I did. Doesn't mean I didn't have to ask." He tips his hat and walks away.

"Hah," Mosif groans. He drops down to one knee.

"Mosif?"

"Fine, fine…I'm just not as young as I used to be. I haven't changed in over three centuries…and that's the closest I've come in all that time…" He nods. "…at my age, it puts a terrible strain on the body." Two of my guards help him to his feet and a third offers him his cane. "Thank you, pups."

"Of course, Lord Alpha," they bark simultaneously…except Jackson. He wears a strange expression.

"Jackson? Are you alright?" I ask, petting Kya.

"I'm sorry, ma'am," he whispers. A tear slides down his face.

"What are you…?"

"ARGH," Mosif screams and drops to his knees again…with a spat of blood near the small of his back. One of the guards behind him has his knife drawn…and it's covered in blood.

"What…?"

"Give us the child," Jackson says with no emotion. I turn silver eyes on him. "That won't work on us…Anaras gave us our orders himself."

I gasp. I cradle Kya close to my heart as the guards surround us. "Then I'm afraid you leave me no other choice." I kick Jackson as hard as I can in the chest, sending him flying with the sound of snapping ribs. I break for that opening as the world becomes electric around me.

NATHAN! NATHAN, MY LOVE, WE NEED YOU! I peer over my shoulder, and our six…no, seven remaining guards are keeping up with us. Nathan thought it would be advantageous if they were able to move as fast as we can…clearly, that one came back to bite us in the ass.

Kya begins to cry as we reach the park's edge; she must sense my mounting fear.

"What's that? Are they chasing that woman?" a young woman asks.

"I think so," a young man returns.

I peer over my shoulder. They're gaining on us…and I don't want to move any faster for fear of injuring…

LANA!

"I'M HERE!" I yell, running toward a line of trees. The guards enter on my heels. Three of them leap into the trees above while the other four continue on the ground. I stumble…my ankle rolls, but I remain on my feet…colliding with a tree! Concern for my injured shoulder and ankle will have to wait. I check Kya, and she cries louder… "YOU WILL NOT TAKE HER FROM ME!" I snarl at our former comrades closing in on us.

"You tell 'em," a woman calls in a charming southern United States accent. The wolves, still on the ground, turn to a beautiful blond woman, who instantly calls to mind Angela.

Jackson stops and turns to her. "Do not interfere, woman."

"Oh, I'm gonna do more than that," she says, stepping forward with her pretty, pale yellow sundress swaying gently around her thighs. Jackson tips his head toward her, and the nearest wolf, Donnie, I think, approaches her. He reaches for her, and she instantly takes his wrist. Bones crunch as she gives it a squeeze. Donnie falls to his knees with a scolded puppy whimper, holding his fractured arm. She kicks him and sends him ricocheting off a tree. The others gasp. "Next," she says with a beckoning motion of her left hand.

Kya's cries break off into a gentle coo…and then she laughs. "Daddy's here?" She squeals and claps her hands.

Suddenly, the three tree climbers fall to the ground like lead stones. The other three look up just in time for Nathan to land on them. He tosses one effortlessly, toward the blond woman. She swats him as if batting a balloon away. He, like his fellow, bounces off a tree, before falling to the ground.

Nathan kicks one wolf in the face, sending blood and teeth flying away. "Ouch," the girl purrs, closing one eye.

"Nathan?" He puts his foot on the teeth-dispatched guard's chest holding him in place while lifting Jackson with one hand around his throat. "NATHAN?"

He turns honey and emerald eyes with black replacing the whites on me. "Do NOT kill them." He growls. "They are under Anaras's thrall. I think I can sort them with time…but not if you kill them."

He bows his head and frowns. He tosses Jackson and pushes down on the third's chest until he blacks out. "Happy?" he grumbles.

"Far from it." Kya giggles and claps her hands. "…and should we be concerned that our daughter takes such delight in you hurting people?"

He walks over to us and caresses her cheek. She grabs his finger and gives it a squeeze. "I'm just glad she's still able to take delight in anything."

"Well, that was scary," the girl says.

"Ange?" Nathan poses, his voice finally returning to normal.

"Nope, Meghan. Meghan Powers."

"Powers? As in, Anne and Matthew Powers?"

"You know my mom and dad?"

Nathan nods. "I knew your mother…I only know of your father." I stare up at him. "Angela's aunt and uncle." I nod.

"You know my cousin, Angela? Have you seen her? Has she come back to New York?"

"HEY," a young man yells, running up behind Meghan. He pants wildly as he comes to a rest next to her, hands on his knees.

"Slow poke," she mocks.

"You super jumped…not fair," the mocha skinned young man says back to her between pants. "Did you do this?" he asks looking around.

"We did," she returns, motioning to Nathan.

"Whoa," the boy says. "Doesn't he look like that big wolf in Japan…the one who asked you to be his mate?"

"Yeah, only a little shorter and not as muscly." Meghan bows her head. "Oh…but he's dead now."

"Dead?" I ask, petting Kya, who's preparing another bout of crying thanks to Meghan's emotions.

"Are you talking about, Alpha Quinton?" Nathan poses, his voice becoming somber. The boy nods. "He's my br...my fa...." Nathan sighs and so much pain washes over him. "He was my father."

"You're Nathan," the boy says. Nathan frowns, and we exchange a glance. "Alex talked about you a lot when he got back to Nanbu...and when we got back to Edenton."

"You're from Edenton?" Nathan and I query at the same time.

"Yeah. Stephen Harper," he says, motioning to himself. He motions to the girl. "And I'm sure you've already met Meghan."

"Damn," Nathan purrs. "Angela was right." I nod. "We have been circling each other for years."

"We should get some privacy," I suggest. "Perhaps, call a clean-up crew to gather these wolves and a medic for Uncle Mosif." He nods. "You're welcome to join us, if you're able." Meghan leans on Stephen and nods. I come back to my Nathan...and just stare at him.

"What?"

I shake my head slowly.

"We'll have to be careful," he whispers. "It seems En Quosque is getting even bolder."

"Definitely," Meghan concurs.

I nod, never taking my eyes away from Nathan. "What?" he asks again. "Do you wanna kiss me or something?"

"A little." He kisses me, causing another bout of clapping from Kya. We separate, and I can't help noticing that Meghan has her hand over Stephen's eyes.

Nathan tickles Kya, who has not stopped her happy giggles and squeals. "Yeah well, we'll see if you still think it's that cute when you're older." I sigh...because for some reason the image of me raising our daughter alone will not leave my head. I have my daughter...I have my husband...but for how long?

#####

Chapter 4: Sisterhood

Jamina

I yawn and throw my covers back. I don't feel different, but at the same time, everything is. I scoff a laugh. I'm sure I've changed too, but I didn't really have time to notice, with the missing mom, plot to destroy the world, dead father returning, evil mom returning too...oh, and let's not forget the pair of two-hundred-year-old brothers, who I fell in love with, who fell in love with me. I chose...and it seems like I get to keep him at least. I put my hand over my eyes. "He asked me to marry him?"

"WHO?!?!?!" Amira barks through my bedroom wall.

"NONE OF YOUR BUSINESS!!!" I shout back. "Stop eavesdropping!" Let's not forget that my very alive father had a daughter with another woman at about the same time my mom had me. Now, my pain in the ass of a younger sister, by only three months, but older is older, is living with my dad and me in my mom's family home. "Complicated."

"What is?"

"SHUT...UP...!!!"

"Rude," she replies from the bathroom.

I drape my legs over the edge of the bed and slide my feet into my fuzzy, bunny slippers. Dad laughed when I picked them out, because they're just like the pair I had when I was a kid. I can't help it. I get all nostalgic and crap around him.

I reach for my glasses and... "Ugh," I moan as my ears start ringing. I pant as the ringing subsides. My ears have been randomly doing that since I went after mom at their En Quosque/Ezekielite base. I wonder if Gothic Barbie cast a curse on me. That can't be it though. I've done several cleansing spells and even had Sara cast a few.

The ringing is still super annoying though. I take a deep breath...that plus the random heart palpitations, and my nose randomly picking up the weirdest smells.

I stand, and my ears start ringing again as the Crescent Moon Pendant and its Philosopher Stone center return to their place over my heart. Could it be this thing? I squint because this bout is more intense, plus it's the first time it's every happened back-to-back like this. I sigh. No, it can't be the Philosopher Stone...I've searched every proverbial inch of it with my spirit magic, and it's empty...except the raw power the supernatural beings, who used to be trapped in it, left behind.

The doorbell rings.

"I got it," Amira chimes, and I hear her big heavy footsteps, pounding along the floor and then down the stairs.

"Wait?" I whisper. "How did I hear that?" Amira's basically a ninja…she always walks light on her feet and, on top of that, we have thick beige carpeting all along the hallway and on the stairs. I frown.

The front door unlocks. How am I hearing this? The door swings in as I walk over to mine.

"Hello," Amira sings. "Who are you?" she says in a flirty way. "And please say you're here for me." I frown and hurry down the hall. "I could really use the workout," she adds as I reach the top of the stairs.

"Um," Quincy, my gorgeous almost two centuries old boyfriend, replies. "…do I have the right house…? Wait, yeah…" I move down the stairs. "…runes are still…" He pauses. "…who…?"

I reach the second stair from the bottom and spot Amira standing in the doorway, wearing tiny, blue boy-shorts and a mid-drift, yet low-plunging tank top.

"Amira," she says, extending her hand to him. "…and you are…?"

"Not here for you," I rumble, walking over to them.

"Tsk, whatever," she moans back, before returning to Quincy. "Bye," she issues with a finger wiggling wave. She walks toward the kitchen.

"Hey, babe."

"That's…" He moans with a point. "…your sister?"

"Yes," I return already annoyed with the fact that I'm wondering if my boyfriend thinks my sister is hot. I turn to her…ass almost hanging out backside. "…and PLEASE go put on some clothes!"

"I have on clothes," she mutters, before disappearing into the kitchen.

"Put on more clothes! Like A LOT more clothes!"

"Bite me!"

"You bite me!"

"DAD!!!" we bark at the same time.

"I can come back later," Quincy says, still standing on the porch with his right thumb aimed at his car by the curb.

"No," I say, taking his other hand. "No, come in…come in." He does. We walk around the sofa and sit…and suddenly, I realize that I'm wearing a very similar top to Amira, except mine actually covers my stomach. I haven't even looked at my hair and oh my God, my breath. I pull my shirt down, before smoothing down my hair with one hand, while covering my mouth with the other.

"Stop," Quincy murmurs, leaning into me, getting so close I feel his warm breath on my neck. "I've seen everything under that tank top…and I love it, by the way…" I fight off…aw, who am I kidding? I smile. "I love your hair, and no bout of morning breath could ever make me not want to do this." He kisses me on the cheek before cupping my face and kissing me on the lips.

He sniffs as we part. "Is that…old eggs?" he jokes. I smack his arm as he laughs, which makes me laugh. "Sara's back in town," he says with a solemn voice. "She has her entire coven with her, and Nate sent down some wolves to help her design…well, she and her coven will design, but the wolves will help carve out the seal around the voracious seal."

"Okay," I purr. "Let me go get dressed." He nods and steals another peck.

"I wanna go," Amira says from the kitchen doorway, jar of peanut butter in her left hand, two fingers full of peanut butter on her right. I groan. "Sounds like it might be fun…plus, you might need protection."

I return to Quincy. He shrugs. "It's your call."

I turn back to Amira. "Fine, but I'm in charge."

"Says who?"

"Says older sister privileges…" I bob my head unevenly. "…plus, I'm sure you don't even know what we're talking about."

"Sera forwarded me a well-documented file on this particular incident," she says, moving her arms behind her back and standing at relaxed attention. "Including details about the entity known as Eden, the organization known as En Quosque, and the fact that our former compatriots are involved."

I frown. "How?"

She takes the peanut butter from behind her back and dips her fingers into it again and then pops those two fingers and the accompanying peanut butter into her mouth. "Dad," she moans with a mouthful of PB. She smacks her mouth. "He's been telling Sera everything."

"Sara?" Quincy asks.

"Her mom, Sera," I reply. He nods. I throw my hand out to her. "Fine. You can come. And that jar of peanut butter is yours now."

"Yum," she chirps, dipping her fingers into it again and running toward the stairs.

Quincy motions after her. "Apparently," I start. "She needs a ton of protein to rebuild muscle and stuff if she gets hurt." He nods. "I'll be back down in ten." I give him a quick peck and run for the stairs.

"Don't forget to…" He makes a teeth-brushing motion. I start to flip him off, but I just shoot him a dirty look and run up the stairs instead.

I head straight for the bathroom…surprised by the fact that Amira wasn't in there already. I brush my teeth quickly…ahem and check to see if I need deodorant. I definitely do.

Amira walks through the still open door wearing dark jeans, boots, a dark t-shirt, and a black jacket. I motion to her. "How are you dressed already? Isn't that against pretty girl code or something?"

"Wouldn't know," Amira says, checking herself out in the mirror. She picks up her brush and moves it through her long, dark brown hair a few times. "And don't care. We were trained to be mission ready at the drop of a hat...or some other dumbass expression." She bundles her hair up near the back of her head like a ponytail. "Ugh," she moans, shaking out her hair before just tossing it and giving up. "I've had it...this stupid wind and this stupid humidity have messed my hair up so bad!!!" She throws her brush out into the hall. "Argh!"

"I hear you," I complain, brushing out my hair only to have the big, springy ginger-colored curls bounce right back into place.

"No, you don't," Amira snarls. She puts both hands in my hair and tosses it from side to side. "This mop stays put no matter what happens to it."

"Hey," I growl, shoving her away. "That's mean...and true, but still."

She wraps her arms around me and laughs. "I know, and I didn't mean it...okay, I did, but I didn't mean to be mean about it." She nods, rubbing her forehead against my temple. "You're my sister...and I love you, mop and all."

"I'm your big sister," I say to our mutually facial structured reflections. She nods with her light brown eyes staring at my dark, brown-eyed mirror image. "And you're my little sister."

"Uh, only by three and a half months."

"Three months or three years, older is older." She groans, but smiles. I put my hand on her forehead. "Yeah, well, you might be my little sister...but your head's pretty big, so..." She giggles and nearly falls into the hall as she stumbles away.

"Jerk," she chuckles back at me. "We were having a moment." I laugh again. "Now, get dressed so we can kick evil's ass."

"We can't kick too much evil ass," I say, stepping out. I head toward my bedroom. "If Sera's really gonna let you stay here with me and dad, we need to get you registered for school."

"Ugh," she moans from the bathroom. "Yeah, but I was homeschooled up through graduation...doesn't that count for anything?"

"Not if you don't have paperwork to prove it," I repeat what dad told her. My ears start ringing again...and bad...like the mother of all migraine inducing ringing noises. "Ugh," I groan, going down on my knees. I hear heavy footsteps thudding up the stairs. Lighter ones are moving away from the bathroom.

"Jamie-Lynn?" Amira says, kneeling next to me.

"Jamina?" Quincy says from my other side. "What's wrong? Are you under attack? Is it a curse?"

I shake my head as best I can, clenching my eyes shut tight, tears managing to break loose. "No...no," I pant. "It's something else. My ears…are ringing…and peanut butter," I rumble. "Amira, you didn't brush your teeth?"

"I did," she returns. "Mouthwash and all." She sighs. "It's in my room though…on my nightstand, but it's closed." I open my eyes as best I can and peer at her closed bedroom door with its skull and crossbones carved into the wood.

"What's going on?" Quincy moans.

"I think, I can answer that," dad says, but he sounds like he's yelling in my ear, and the start of every word felt like a clap of thunder. Footsteps scrape across the carpet and then dad's directly in front of me. "Jamie-Lynn," he says at a lower volume. I open my eyes and look at him. "Good," he murmurs, but I hear it as clear as day. "Trust me…you're gonna be fine." I nod as best I can.

"Give me your hands," he says, offering me his. I shake my head, not wanting to take them away from my head. "Jamie-Lynn, trust me. I can help." I swallow a lump and place my trembling hands in his. "Good." He looks down at my hands, and a cheek-puffing sigh comes from him. "I thought so, especially after you told me about the fight at En Quosque's base."

"What is it?" Amira asks.

"Jamie-Lynn is the daughter of a hunter and a witch…" He nods. "…a powerful witch. She's just as powerful if not more powerful than her mother…add to that a hunter's strength and stamina…"

"…and you've got bringing a ceramic frog to life when you only meant to animate it," Quincy says. "And setting fire to a shrub when you only meant to light a candle."

"Exactly," dad says. He lifts my hands closer to his chest. "So, your mother came up with these…" He caresses my thumbs with his. "…these bands are dampeners. They're usually used to help anxious wolves contain themselves. Or, to keep werewolves from reaching full strength during a full moon."

"What does that mean?" I ask, still hearing the ringing even if focusing on dad's voice helped quiet it.

"It means these have kept the hunter in you in check." I frown. "But during your fight with the hunters, it looks like they got cracked." I think back to the first hunter I punched with the taser knuckle as Alex called it. I remember hearing a click, but I thought maybe I'd accidentally broken his nose or something. "So, now they must be malfunctioning…"

"How do we fix them?" Amira asks, and I can hear her heart rate accelerating with the pace of her breathing.

"Her mom made them, so only her mom can fix them."

"Then what do we do, dad?" Amira snarls.

"This," dad says. There's pressure on my thumbs and then a crack...and then the ringing is gone. I stop grimacing and look around...I stare into dad's brown eyes with little flecks of green in them. I see the tiny freckles on his cheeks and moving across the bridge of his nose. Tiny beads of sweat forming along his hairline. He takes a deep breath, and I hear the air rustling around in his lungs. It's like I used my volume increasing spell, but...I didn't.

I turn to Amira and see how remarkably flawless her skin is. I see how beautiful and vibrant each strand of her hair is...I feel like I could count them because I see them so clearly.

"Jamina?"

I turn to Quincy...and gasp, I literally gasp. My hand reaches for his face fast...like crazy fast, but somehow it didn't feel like it. He doesn't flinch, though. His eyes dart down to my hand and back to my face again. I caress his. "What's wrong?"

"You're beautiful," I purr before I can stop myself. He smirks, and I know, I blush.

"How's that peanut butter smell?" Amira says over my shoulder.

"Like the jar's open, right under my nose."

Amira wraps her arms around me. "You're a hunter, like me!" she squeals.

"Easy," I moan putting my finger in my ear.

"You'll get used to it," she returns.

I go back to dad. "And you knew about this? Is that why you didn't want me to take them off?"

He nods. "Control was always an issue with you, Jamie-Lynn. Your mom figured that if you had less stamina, she would have time to teach you more control. When I got back and saw that you were still wearing them, I assumed..."

"Assumed what?" I snap.

"I assumed your mother had her reasons." He shakes his head. "I'm sorry, baby-girl, I really am."

"I'm your baby-girl," Amira whispers. I glare at her. "Well, I am," she whines. We both start laughing at the same time, and she hugs me tighter as Quincy rubs my back.

#####

Chapter 5: Meeting

Alex

"Seriously," Kai complains, slipping his hands into his pants pockets. I can hear his left hand caressing his small square of tiger's fur. His right hand moves across the key fob to his sister's jeep. He hunches his shoulder drawing his snugger than I would prefer blue t-shirt up. "She hasn't even been gone three hours," he continues, looking at me, dressed similarly, but with a looser black t-shirt and faded black jeans.

"I know, it's just…," I start, feeling as if my fingers can still feel her skin…as if that spark that passes between us is still doing its thing, right now…with her even on the other side of the planet. "…we fought so hard to get back to where we are and…"

"She'll be back by the end of the day!" he whines back at me. "Geez!"

"What are you guys talking about?" Jamie asks as we approach the small group of people standing in the huge, chain grocery store's parking lot.

"Nothing," Kai answers, before I can. He motions to me as if he's about to hit me. "He's just whining about his missing wife already."

"You're married now!" Jamie snaps. "Dang it!" she adds a moment later with two clenched fists raised toward me.

I laugh as I put my arms around her. She slips hers underneath mine and pats my back. "So, is this cool?" I ask, looking at all the random people…including the five women talking to Tony Blackshear, the really hot redheaded Latina talking to the tall guy in the suit, and Quincy trying his best to ignore a girl on the other side of him.

"Yeah," she replies. She throws her hand out toward Tony. "Sara put up a glamour to block us from prying eyes."

"You put a glamour over a glamour?" Kai asks. "Oh, fancy. So…glamourous." He smirks as Jamie and I groan.

"Hello, cutie!" a familiar voice says behind Jamie.

"What the…?" Jamie snaps as that girl pulls her out of my arms and steps into her place.

"I want next," she purrs, while putting her arms around me. I raise my arms to make sure that no one mistakes that I'm trying to hug her back. "What's wrong, cutie?" she says, peering up at me. "You don't like me no more?"

"It's you," I snap, recognizing her. "You're that girl who was killing vampires in Nanbu!"

"You remembered!" she hums and begins rubbing up against me. "I'm touched."

"You're gonna be touched!" Jamie barks, pulling her back by her jacket's collar. "Pushing up on a married man like that!"

"Married?" the girl asks looking from Jamie to me and back. I wish I could remember her name.

"Yes, very," Jamie returns with a little more attitude than I think I've ever seen her display. "Alex, I think you met in Japan, but just in case, this is my pain-in-the-ass younger sister, Amira Markovic-Baggett." She motions to Amira. "Pain-in-the-ass younger sister, this is my best friend since I was four, Alex."

"So, you really are his best friend?" she asks, pointing at me. Jamie nods. "And he's married?" Jamie nods again with a sympathetic look this time. "What about the other one?" Amira whispers in a secretive way while pointing her thumb at Kai.

"Gay," Jamie says simply.

"Damn!" Amira snaps and wanders off.

"Is she serious?" Kai asks.

"'Fraid so," Jamie sighs as her head bows.

"Oh…my…goodness…," a woman with brown hair with streaks of purple and a sweater that seems to be working overtime to contain…ahem…her says walking over to us. "…if didn't know that you were already in love with him," she says, motioning to Quincy Blackshear. "I'd swear you were in love with this adorable mop of chestnut-haired cuteness!"

Jamie just laughs in response to this. "Could you call the others over?" she asks.

The woman taps her forehead with her index and middle fingers. "Just did." The four other women and Tony Blackshear make their way over to us.

"Alex and Kai Garner, I'd like to introduce you to my friend and mentor…"

"D'aaaaaaaahhhh," the woman purrs with a huge smile on her face that feels like sunshine.

"…this is Sara Pond and her coven…" Jamie extends her hand to the tall, hot librarian type with glasses. "…this is Rebecca Graham…" She then moves on to the shorter, pale skinned woman who rivals Sara in terms of…sweater strength. "…Amie, that's A-M-I-E, Wells…" She moves onto the pretty woman with medium brown hair and dark, doe eyes. "…Jess Robinson…" Then she moves on to the natural red-head with shocking blue-green eyes. "…and Stephanie Wilford."

Jamie comes back to me. "Ladies, this is my best friend, Alex and his cousin, Kai." The women all nod, wave, or give some indication of a greeting.

"They're going to be the ones who complete the new seal around the voracity seal, while the rest of us…pretty much stand guard."

"Cool," Kai says.

"I know, right?" Sara replies.

"Oh," Jamie says as the guy in the suit and the unnaturally redheaded Latina approach us. "This is…"

"We heard," the man says, looking down on us with piercing…yeah, that's the word…because I feel like he's staring through me…piercing blue eyes. "Alex Garner. Kai Garner. I'm a member of your cousin's pack. My name is Dr. Vance Purdue, and this is another member of our pack, Kyra Martin."

Jamie leans closer to me. "She's that long-haired wolf who was with Nathan's adoptive sister."

"S'up," she says with a quick head nod. She then turns back to Dr. Purdue. "Midnight Watch says they have the designated area surrounded…" She looks to her right. "…if the witches are to be believed."

"We are," Jamie and Sara say at the same time. They look at each other and laugh. There's something weird going on with Jamie…and it's not just this whole world ending organization mess. It's not even the fact that just a few days ago she chased her mom through a portal or something with the intention of killing her. She seems…happy…but sad…like she's in her element, but at the same time…more nervous than I've seen her in her entire life…including when she stood in front of the entire school and recited the Gettysburg Address from memory in the fifth grade.

"This is so weird," Amira says, crossing her arms.

"I know, right?" I reply absently. Everyone looks at me for a moment as if I have something to add. I purse my lips, cross my arms, and shake my head.

"What do you mean?" Jamie asks her.

"This," Amira says, motioning outward. "Wolves, witches, skinwalkers…" She motions to herself. "…even hunters, all working together to stop these bad guys. That's…that's…"

"The power of a true Witch of Light," Sara says, putting one arm around Jamie. "Witches of Light have been known to bring races together in a sort of natural non-aggression-"

"That's nice," Vance interrupts. He motions to the open space surrounded by several people wearing black-on-black uniforms with police style body armor. "…and I hate to interrupt. Can we get on with it? I have a nervous wife back in New York who is worried sick about her niece and her youngest sire."

"Of course," Jamie says and turns to the open space. She looks at Sara, who steps up beside her. "Do you need me to do anything?"

"No hon," Sara replies. "All we need is for you to stand watch and make sure nothing bad happens to any of my girls…" She smirks. "…because I'm pretty sure that once we get started, all hell's gonna break loose."

"What do you mean?" Kai asks.

"I mean," Sara starts. "Nothing about this magic is subtle, hence the glamour I put around us, not because of the large group. Once we start casting this spell and placing this seal, it's going to be noticed…" She tilts her head toward the open space. "…especially if, Jamina's mother, and En Quosque's Witch of Shadow is in there, which I absolutely don't doubt that they are."

"Wow," I say. "You really are as good at spirit magic as Jamie said you were."

She winks at me, and I actually can feel my cheeks fill with red as a reaction. "And don't you forget it, hon." She returns to the open space and spreads her arms wide as if she's about to conduct a marching band. "Ladies, let's do this."

"Hell yeah!" Stephanie says with her fiery red hair and disturbingly blue-green eyes, slamming her right fist into her left hand.

"Right," Rebecca, the tall, gorgeous librarian-type to her left, says while pushing her glasses closer to her eyes.

"All right," the pale woman, Amie, says with a gentle toss of her dark hair.

"We got this," the other woman with soulful doe eyes, Jess, says with a slight tilt of her head.

All five ladies raise their hands above their heads, and then start chanting, I can only assume in Latin, before placing their hands on the ground directly in front of them. "Now, hon," Sara says having turned to look at Tony. He nods and takes his huge bowie knife from behind his back. He puts the blade against his palm and pulls it across it really fast. I flinch, he doesn't. He then squeezes out a few drops of blood between Sara's hands.

Sara looks to her left and nods. Quincy is standing next to the redhead, and he does the same thing only with a much smaller knife. Beyond him, Tony's already made it over to the librarian woman and is doing the same thing again. And they repeat like that until they make it back around to Sara, where they both do it again in front of her.

Sara throws her arms out wide, and says, "…et nunc cum sanguine Eden, hoc cubiculum permitte ut hoc oppidum iter facias et defendas. Loco alligatus est, in quo Angelus lapsus mortuus est. Obligatio."

"Obligatio." Stephanie repeats after her.

"Obligatio." Rebecca repeats next.

"Obligatio." and then Amie.

Jess ends with, "Obligatio."

As soon as Jess finishes saying the word, a gold circle forms at their hands, moving around the large open space. Suddenly, gold lines dart between the five of them, starting with two moving away from Sara's hand and then repeating with the others. Writing soon forms on the outside of the circle, along the lines on the inside, and moving along the lines created by the five-pointed star forming at their hands.

THOOM! Sounds out, causing Sara to raise her head.

"Here they come," she says, calmly looking back at Jamie.

"How much time do you need?" Amira asks, pulling her katana out of its sheath.

"Maybe another three minutes," Sara says, looking over their handy work.

"We'll give you five!" Jamie barks, and Amira smiles with that same weird gleam in her eye. Geez, they really are sisters.

A door...or at least, that's what it looks like appears in the middle of open air, directly across from Sara. Several dozen of those horrible little white ghouls come tumbling out, falling all over each other, clambering to get to us...and I'll have to tell Gwen I remembered that word when she comes home...clamber, to climb.

"Go!" Jamie snaps as fur explodes out of me and Kai, and Amira vanishes. Several of the little ghouls fall...missing heads, arms, and legs...some fall into two separate pieces.

"She's good," Vance says with his hand cupping his chin.

"You're not helping?" Jamie asks as Kai and I go into motion.

"We will when we're needed," he says simply and loosens his tie.

I begin tearing these little asshats apart, remembering when one bit me back in January. Kai's making short work of them too. "Crap," I groan, remembering where these things come from.

"Fulgur!" a familiar annoying voice barks, and I instinctively duck to the left...as an arc of blue lightning sails over my head. I stand up straight and glare at Bethany, standing in all her goth girl glory...but that's weird, she looks tired...maybe even sick...plus the last time I saw her was in that portal, when we went to get Jamie, Kai, Meghan, and Quincy back. Then she was wearing a dress that made her look like an upside-down top...now, she's wearing pants, black of course, and a t-shirt under a long black coat.

"Damn it!" she growls. "Why won't all my exes just die?"

"It wouldn't matter," Kai says in a mocking tone. "Because he was never your boyfriend!"

"Shut up! Shut up! Shut up!"

"What were you people doing out here?" Daphne asks, stepping out of the door next. She frowns and looks around as if taking a tally of everything going on.

"Oh, you know, mom," Jamie says. "Just wanted to stop by, say hi, maybe borrow a cup of sugar?"

"I do not like this smart-ass mouth you have lately," Daphne replies in an even voice. "Sara."

"Daphne," Sara returns with just as big a smile as always.

Out of nowhere, Amira appears next to Daphne...katana raised above her head.

"MIRI NO!" Jamie practically shrieks.

Amira stops on...I'd say a dime, but she could've stopped on a dime ten times with her speed. She glowers at Daphne, who returns her stare.

"You're lucky, you're my sister's mom!" she says, pointing at her.

"You're not lucky, you're her sister!" Daphne replies, holding her left hand under her right arm. "FULGUR!" she snaps, and a bolt of lightning covers Amira!

"MIRI!" Jamie cries again.

"What?" Amira asks, right next to her.

"Don't do that to me," Jamie breathes with her hand over her heart.

"Done!" Sara says, throwing her hands toward the sky, while still on her knees.

"FINALLY!" Tony snaps, from the spot next to Bethany with a left hand full of lightning.

"YEP!" Quincy says with a watermelon-sized fireball in his right hand, aimed at Daphne's head.

"Expugnationis!" Daphne barks, making whatever that was sound like one word. She throws her hands out to her sides and a translucent blue bubble surrounds her and Bethany. Quincy and Tony slam their respective magic attacks into it. "Fellas," Daphne says, eyes darting from Quincy to Tony. "We have to stop meeting like this!" She pushes out, and lightning flies back at Tony, throwing him off, and the flames begin to push back against Quincy.

"Why do they get to try and kill your mom, but I don't?" Amira asks, crossing her arms and pouting like a little kid.

"Because they might actually hesitate, unlike you who'd probably just lop her head off."

"Nuh-uh!" Jamie just glares at her. "Well, not her whole head."

"We should retreat for now," Daphne says.

"What? Why?" Bethany whines.

"Because they have us outnumbered by a lot…and you're running out of ghouls to throw at them." She glares at Jamie. "Besides, whatever it is they were up to…they've already done it!"

RAAAAAAAAWWWWWWWWWWWWWRRRRRRRRR! Comes out of nowhere as a huge black wolf pounces on Daphne's shield. It collides with it with so much force that it pushes them, bubble and all, back toward the door. Daphne gasps and stares at it for a moment as it does the same, doing that slow circling thing wolves do before they're about to end it. I growl and start doing the same, moving in the opposite direction.

"Who the hell are you supposed to be?" Daphne asks. The wolf just growls as a response. "Whatever." She lifts her hands and starts backing up…the bubble contracts to make it through the door.

"Next time, Daphne," Jamie says with arms crossed over her stomach.

"Count on it, baby-girl," Daphne returns, just before the door slams behind them and disappears again.

"That was not pleasant," the guy in the suit…Vance says…although, he's definitely not in a suit now…well, unless you count birthday. Jamie struggles to cover Amira's eyes as the unnaturally redheaded Latina rushes over to him, carrying his clothes.

"Wolves," I mutter as my own fur vanishes.

"I'll say," Kai says, staring at him in a way that makes me want to move away from Kai.

"Well, on the bright side," Vance says, pulling his jacket on. "Mission accomplished."

"Damn right!" Sara says with a wink.

#####

Chapter 6: Feather

Angela

"We could've run and gotten here an hour ago," I say, staring out the window of this tiny taxi. The driver steals another glance at me in the rearview. His pupils dilate briefly giving me the once over. I learned from sire-dad that that means he finds me attractive…they'd have probably stayed dilated if he knew he was in the presence of a vampire…especially in the middle of the day.

"Yeah," Natavius, sitting next to me in all his Northern African gorgeousness, starts in a whisper so low that the driver has no chance of hearing us. "And we could've gotten the kitsune to open a portal that would've brought us here straight from California."

My head whips around to him before I can tell it to do that. "People can do that?"

He nods. "Well, not people…witches…kitsune…fairies…couple other fae, some daemons." I nod. "I still really dig your haircut," he says at a normal volume, staring at me now.

"And I still don't care," I reply and go back to watching Nanbu go by, chin resting on my hand. It's surprising how big this town is, considering it's been over an hour since we left the airport. I still don't feel right about shipping my knives back to New York, but what're ya gonna do, huh? Explain to a Japanese customs agent why I need four razor sharp knives in my carry on? I shake my head as we pull up to a house surrounded by a shoulder height wall.

Natavius says something to the driver in Japanese. The driver responds in kind and motions to the meter. Natavius counts off a few colorful bills and passes them over the seat. The driver collects the money and bows his head. We climb out of the tiny car, and it pulls away swiftly.

"And since when can you speak Japanese?" I ask.

"Since Nathan spent three years here after World War II." He scowls. "He was heartbroken all over again…after they dropped the bombs." He shakes his head. "We wanted to help as much as we could, considering…" I nod…kinda want to hug him to get that look off his face. I almost do, until his eyes come back to me and that smile…that smile that feels like a slap to the face it hits so hard, flashes across his face.

"Almost had me," I say, patting his surprisingly firm, trim chest.

"May I…help you?" a young guy says. Speaking of trim physiques, he's hot in that British rock star kind of way with his short black hair in spikey tufts. He has piercing blue eyes, and a stare like angst, flirting, and sex in equal measure.

"Yes," Natavius says. "We're looking for Abe-do. Is this it?"

"It is."

"Barrel of laughs this guy is." His eyes dart to me. I shrug.

"Gavin, stop it," a cute little redheaded Japanese girl says, stepping around him. Her eyes are bright green, and she's wearing the cutest little pink hoodie. She motions to the house. "Yes, this is Abe-do. I'm Gwen, and this is my brother, Gavin."

"Gwen," I say with a point. "And you're a kitsune in Nanbu." She frowns. "You must be Alex Garner's girl."

"Wife," she says emphatically flashing the wedding ring inside of an engagement ring on her finger. She looks me up and down like she could just tear me apart with her bare hands. "How do you know my husband?"

"Easy," Natavius says at the same time as Gavin.

"She has a point," a statuesque blond-haired woman says, stepping out from behind Gavin. This girl has bright green eyes too, but she has a build like an athlete, curves like a swimsuit model, and a tan that makes me wish my default setting wasn't burning in the sun…pre-ritual, that is. "I'd like to know how she knows my cousin, too."

"Sora Garner," Natavius says to her. "Good to see you again."

"Right," Gwen purrs. "I thought you looked familiar. You were with the wolf who gave the eulogy at Rais's funeral."

Natavius nods. "I'm Natavius, and that wolf is our current Alpha, Nathan Dumont," Natavius explains. "And this is his best friend and the Vampire Chief Magistrate's number two, Angela Price."

"You're Angela?!" Sora and Gwen reply at the same time. "Meghan was so worried about you!" Gwen adds.

"You know my cousin?"

"We're best friends." I nod.

"I hate to break up…whatever this is," Gavin groans. "But we should get this over with, before we attract too much attention." Natavius nods. "We'll be journeying on foot to Emperor Tenma's…the kitsune emperor's home to make the exchange." He scowls, and his face takes on this overconfident, cocky glare. I know that stare too well. Nate wears it often. My heart sinks thinking about him all over again.

"I'm sure you can keep up," Gavin adds as the left corner of his mouth turns up.

"Like you wouldn't believe," Natavius says, probably sounding even more overconfident to them. I snicker because I know he's not overconfident, just plain, old confident.

"Fine," Gavin, who's clearly not in a mood for jokes, replies. "Let's go," he adds as his eyes glow a brighter blue, and pale blue flames appear at his shoulders. He darts off to the left. Sora and Gwen, with reddish-orange flames and brighter green eyes, follow him as the world turns electric around me…but the air around Natavius seems to catch fire… He steps, and he's already gone. I move and catch up to Gwen and Sora as Natavius does a lap around Gavin.

We run through a sullen forest with the smell of honeysuckles swirling around us. We dash up the side of a mountain, but never lose the cover of trees, approaching one of those old Japanese tiered castles…a pagoda, I think it's called. We reach the huge gold double doors at the front and stop. Well, most of us stop. Natavius takes two laps around the building before coming back to stand next to Gavin as if he never moved.

"Show off," I mutter to him. He peers at me over his shoulder and shoots me a wink.

There are two large men standing in front of each door. They're dressed in all white, including the white fox masks over their faces. Each of them holds a spear that looks razor sharp at the tip.

Gavin says something to them in Japanese. He motions to Natavius and says, "Okami Natavius" and then he holds the same hand out toward me, "Kyūketsuki Price Angela." Both of their fox masks turn to me, tilt up to see the sun, and then come back down to me.

The one on the right offers a complaint, while motioning to me.

Gavin shrugs and replies.

"They asked how you're out in the daylight as a vampire," Natavius explains. "And he said that they were told the two coming to retrieve the feather are…'special.'"

"Yep, that definitely describes you," I joke. He snickers.

The man on the right nods and pushes the door open. He signals for us to enter, and we do. Once inside, Gavin goes over to a bench and removes his shoes. Gwen and Sora do the same. I look down, and Natavius is already holding his.

"Little help," I say with a shrug. I feel a slight jostle, and he's holding mine in his right hand and his in his left.

"How does he do that?" Sora asks, staring at Gavin, who hasn't stopped glaring at Natavius since his first lap around him.

"Natavius is the fastest being on the planet," I explain.

"Impossible," Gavin snarls.

"I believe you kitsune employ 'swift paw,'" Natavius says. "…which is one of my more refined techniques," he brags without actually bragging, because I don't doubt that he's speaking facts. "But you," he continues, pointing at Sora. "…still use 'hunter's step.'" He nods. "It's definitely good for short bursts and while fighting, but when you have to travel a long distance…"

"We get it," Gavin complains, stepping up the single step and into a pair of fuzzy house shoes provided by a woman, wearing the same uniform and mask as the guys at the front door. After getting our shoes, we follow Gavin into the interior of the castle.

The most gorgeous Japanese guy I've ever seen meets us coming from the other direction. He wears a pale blue outfit under this silk jacket thing with dark blue crossing lines on a white background. His beautiful brown eyes search us over quickly. He's surrounded by six women in the white uniforms with swords at their hips and wearing the white masks.

Gavin, Gwen, and Sora kneel as he closes the distance between us.

"Should we…?" I start.

"We're not his subjects, but deep bow, hands at your sides…no sudden movements." I nod as we do what he just spelled out.

"Heika," Gavin says.

"I've told you, Gavin, call me, Tenma-sama if you must."

"Hai!" Gavin snaps back.

"And you two, must be Natavius, Alpha Mosi'son's bodyguard…and Price Angela, Magistrate Raven's personal assistant and sire." I bow my head a bit. He extends his left hand to me like he's going to shake mine, but at shoulder height. "I would love to hear the story of the beautiful day walking vampire, but my advisors have heard some disturbing rumors…" He motions back the way he came with that same open hand. "…so, shall we?"

My eyes bulge as a fox with pale white fur, standing on his…no, her hind legs, approaches us, carrying a glass case. She has two long streaks of hair on either side of her nose, and nine large fluffy tails swishing behind her, begging me to run my fingers through them. I won't, but man, do they look fluffy!

"With this," the emperor continues. "We'll conclude this exchange and open a fire gap back to New York for-" He stops talking abruptly as something seems to occur to him. I listen, but I don't hear anything.

One of the guards yells out and steps in front of the emperor as the others take up positions around him, all with one hand on their sword and the near-side hand on the weapon's sheath.

"We'll take that," a familiarly annoying voice says.

"Bethany!" I snarl, turning to her.

"In the gorgeous flesh," she says, wearing a huge bell dress with suspenders over a black t-shirt. She extends one of her fishnet-glove covered hands toward me. "Hi whore," she grumbles.

"I'll hi…"

"Fulgur!" comes from behind us, and before any of us can react… BOOM! …lightning strikes the space between Natavius and me…no, wait…he reacted. He got away from the strike and runs at Bethany. THROOM! He bounces off a shield directly in front of her. I try to shake the electric numbness moving through my body, because I didn't even feel the electricity touch me…but my ears are ringing…and bleeding, I think. Gavin, Gwen, and Sora are taking even longer to recover.

I look beyond them to spot that gorgeous model woman that Nate and I ran into in New Orleans…with Quincy. "Daphne?" I ask…I think, I still can't hear myself. She says something back while lifting her hand, revealing a square with all kinds of Latin words written in it. She says something else, and a fireball rushes toward me. "Flamma!" I snap and catch it, spin, split it in two, and throw a softball sized fireball out at Bethany and Daphne.

Bethany's fireball explodes harmlessly against the shield in front of her, and Daphne extends her other hand, with a triangle in it, and absorbs the other fireball.

Daphne shouts something that sounds like 'Meh met' to my ears, while pointing at the floor behind me. Three gross, little, slimy golf balls with arms and legs climb all over the old fox, who's face-down on the floor. They kind of remind me of that gross boar we ran across at the Blackshear's estate. One of them holds the jar above his head as the long golden feather inside shimmers with what looks like fire.

Bethany signals for the thing to come to her, and I dart at it, wishing I had a knife. A wolf made of ice jumps out in front of me, a frosty wind wafting away from its side. It howls and then runs toward me. I backflip and drive my foot into its midsection, kicking it away. I recover just in time to see a bull made of fire rush toward Gwen and Gavin. They both erupt in fox shaped flames across their entire bodies, bright red around her and pale blue covering him.

They catch the fire bull as if he were a solid creature. Gavin groans but lifts it above his head. Gwen jumps straight up and does a spin kick that decapitates…or more accurately, dissipates the bull's fiery head. I turn back to the witches as one of the little slimy things delivers the feather to Bethany.

"Oh, hell no!" I snap…and feel a warmth in my core. "Fulgur!" I snap and a bolt of lightning shoots out from my fingers and strikes her shield.

She stares at me with huge eyes. She points at me, while half-turning to Daphne. "Did she just…?"

"Let's go!" Daphne says, sauntering away. "That shield is similar to the one my daughter used against us, but it's not nearly as strong."

"Glad to hear it!" I bark. "Fulgur!" I snap my fingers. Lightning hits the shield and vanishes. "Fulgur!" I repeat with the same finger snap. Again. Again. And again. The shield cracks.

"We'll take it from here," Gavin says, moving past me in a blur of flaming blue. His fist collides with the shield, and a spiderweb-style crack moves out from his fist.

"RARGH!" Natavius barks, running at the shield full speed with his arms shielding his head. He shatters it and continues toward the witches, who stand in a glowing circle carved out of space.

"Impressive!" Bethany says.

"We'll send Ezekiel your regards, Natiel," Daphne says as the portal shrinks to a dot and disappears. Natavius spins on the ball of his foot, and his eyes are glowing. This is the closest I've ever seen him come to changing into a wolf.

"They got away," the kitsune emperor says, holding the arm of one of those slimy golf ball things. "…with my father's feather."

"Tenma-sama," Gavin says as he and Gwen drop to one knee in front of him. "We swear we will not rest until we get it back."

The emperor tosses the arm away, and it shatters like porcelain on concrete. "I fear that if you don't get it back…the world may be the one to suffer…not me." He turns his back on us and walks away as his six guards continue watching the surroundings, checking for any other threats.

"Well, that sucked," I complain.

"You okay?" Natavius asks… I gasp. …while wrapping his arms around me. I groan, because, besides Nathan and a growing tolerance to sire-dad, I've never found a wolf's scent appealing…until just now.

I almost sink into the hug but remember myself and the situation. I push him off me…gently. "We need to get back to New York." He stares into my eyes and nods, despite wearing a scolded puppy expression. "And I'm fine," I whisper a second later. "Thanks." He smirks and washes it away as the situation hits him again.

#####

Chapter 7: Consequence

Gwen

I grind my teeth. "How did they find out?"

"They've obviously got spies everywhere," Gavin says as if it were the most obvious thing.

"Actually, they've got a psychic," Angela interjects. She looks at Natavius. "We always forget about the human," she whispers.

Apparently, it wasn't the most obvious thing.

I move my neck slowly from side to side thinking about the conversation we'll be having with sofu…and probably obāsan later about this. At least Gavin is here for this. Then I completely deflate thinking about having to go before the emperor to formally apologize for losing the treasure his father bestowed upon the Tsukino Clan. I absently slide my thumb over the smooth part of my wedding ring. Bethany is such a…

I feel my phone vibrate in my pocket. The screen shows that it's Meghan calling. I wish she were here right now. I tap the button and put the phone to my ear.

"Hey, loser. How's it going?" she asks before I can say anything. A chuckle escapes me before I can stop it.

"Good news, and bad news, bestie. Your cousin, Angela, is here…," I say.

"Oh, thank goodness," Meghan cuts me off. "Tell her that she needs to check her texts! Wait, what's the bad news?"

"We lost the feather," I state.

"I really hope you mean misplaced," she returns heatedly.

"…no. Bethany, Daphne, and company showed up and stole it," I sigh.

"Ugh. That bitch!" she exclaims, and I laugh. "How did they find you?"

I shrug even though she can't see me. "As Gavin said, they've got spies everywhere," I say.

She sighs this time, and the line falls silent, which is a rarity with Meghan. She mutters something quietly on the other end of the line. Someone with a deep voice says something back. "The human?" she asks absently. "Huh," she emits next and then asks, "So, what're you gonna do?"

"First, we've got to talk to sofu and obāsan. Then after that, I'm sure we will meet with the emperor and apologize formally for this going wrong," I say.

"Yikes. Good luck with that, bestie," she says.

"Not 'loser'?" I ask.

"Not today. You feel bad enough already," she laughs.

"Thanks."

"Oh! The reason I called!" I nod again, knowing that she still can't see me. "You'll never guess who we ran into while we were checking out Central Park."

"Who?"

"Only the new Alpha Wolf, Nathan Dumont…his stupidly gorgeous wife, the Midnight Princess, Alana…and their almost as stupidly adorable baby daughter."

"Aw, that's nice."

"Not so nice. There were a bunch of dudes trying to kidnap the baby."

"WHAT?"

"Yeah, we put a beatdown on 'em. Apparently, some of her security detail got snatched up by En-everybody's-business-Quosque and tried to get them to steal their baby for a ritual or something."

"No," I breathe as my mind races over the possibilities…especially since they just stole the feather and simultaneously tried to take the…

"GWEN!"

"Huh? What?"

"I gotta go. Apparently, the Chief Magistrate for all vampires…also, stupidly gorgeous, BTW…and a natural red head…wants me and Stephen to sit in on some kind of meeting. Keep me updated, okay?"

"You got it and same," I say.

"Later, bestie," she says with a laugh.

"Later," I say ending the call.

I look around and see Sora, who is also on the phone.

"I told you she's fine," she says. "Alex," she whispers to me putting her finger over the microphone. I nod and feel a wave of longing for him.

"Okay, you too," she says ending the call. She turns to me. "He asked me three times if you were okay," she says, rolling her eyes. I hide a smile.

"Okay," she says, turning to Angela and Natavius. "Are you sticking around here?"

"No. We've got to get back to New York," Natavius says.

"Yeah, we don't even have any bags here," Angela explains. "I was promised that this would only be a day trip," she adds, glaring at Natavius. He looks away, pretending to whistle. "Oh," Angela says, turning back to us. "One thing to remember…because we've forgotten a few times ourselves. You probably don't have spies in the kitsune camp…"

"We don't go to camp!" Gavin snaps.

"You know what I mean, dick," Angela returns. He grumbles and crosses his arms. "En Quosque has a human member, who has nearly perfect future sight…" She bobs her head unevenly. "…or at least, that's how Jamie Baggett described it to me."

"Right," I moan, feeling disappointed because like her, I apparently forgot that too. Maybe, there's some kind of perception spell or glamour over him, making him forgettable.

"Okay. Gavin and I can create a fire gap to send you home," I tell them.

"Dang. No frequent flyer miles," Natavius says with a smirk.

Gavin turns to them. "New York, huh? Where specifically in New York are we sending you? A physical location, area, landmark…whatever you can tell us will help us get you closer to your destination."

Angela shrugs and makes a ball tossing motion toward Natavius.

He turns to Gavin. "U.S. New York. New York City. Manhattan. Wolfram Tower. Blackout." Gavin frowns.

"It's a special conference room in Wolfram Tower," Angela explains.

"Alright," Gavin says, moving opposite me. He stares at me and nods. I return the gesture. I lift my right hand at the same time he does. Blue flames cover his, and red flames move across mine. "Ready?" he asks. They nod.

"Ready?" he repeats, asking me the same question. I nod and focus on the fox magic flowing into my hand. We each place our hands on the floor in front of us. Red flames carve out a circle in both directions away from my hand as blue flames do the same coming from his. Gavin's magic hits mine with a jolt, but it doesn't overpower mine. It amplifies mine as they swirl together, creating purple flames. Gavin creates the sigils to spell out the appropriate words for the destination in New York, while I fill in the origin point.

When the last spark burns out the last of the fire gap, it erupts in purple flames. "Whoa," Angela gasps.

"Alright, step through," I say, while helping Gavin hold the portal open. He bobs his head and motions for them to step through. They bound over the outer ring of flames, and Angela gives me a wave.

"Don't forget to give Meghan a call!" I shout as flames rise with the increased release of our magic. Angela gives me another nod before they vanish behind the flames and just as swiftly, the portal closes.

"Wow," Sora says with a shake of her head. "Still impressive." She pecks Gavin on the cheek before I can complain.

"Alright," Gavin says with a slight smile. "Let's get out of here and get this over with. Sofu and obāsan definitely will want to know what happened."

We walk the short distance back to Abe-do. We approach the gate, and Gavin turns to Sora and me. "I'll handle this," he says before continuing to walk.

Sora raises her eyebrows and looks at me with a look of "we'll see." As we enter the house, I slide off my converse and slide into my soft pink house shoes. I look beside where my shoes had been and notice a sand-colored pair of shoes with a small "A" on the back. They've already gotten Alex a pair of house shoes. My heart swells a little, and I slide my thumb over my wedding ring. Sora now has her own shoes as well.

Sofu greets us in the hall. Gavin and I give a quick bow.

"Sofu, I…" Gavin begins.

Sofu holds up a hand. "I already know about the feather, Gavin." He lowers his hand. "We've already begun making preparations to deliver a gift of atonement to not only Tsukino Toshiro and his betrothed, but also to Emperor Tenma."

"Are you alright, Gwen?" obāsan asks, making her way over to us. Impossible to say, but she looks even more adorably, tiny grandmotherly as she shuffles toward us.

"I'm okay, obāsan," I say with a bow. "Just sad about the feather and some other news I got. "

We head down the hall and then adjourn to our bedrooms to change into more traditional clothes. I put on a kimono that is light pink up at the shoulders and moves to a dark pink color at the bottom. Light pink flowers decorate the fabrics of the skirt toward the bottom on each side. Obāsan fastens the white obi around my waist. I slide on the traditional sandals with socks. I meet Gavin in the hall, and he is dressed in some of his best. His dark kimono has deep blue flames on the bottom of both sides. He has the traditional sandals with socks on as well.

"Don't you dare make an American joke about wearing socks with sandals," Gavin growls.

"What?" I ask in surprise.

"Never mind," he says. "Let's get this over with."

We stroll the short distance back to the emperor's estate. We can see the towering pagoda that looks over his estate almost from Abe-do. I feel smaller the larger it grows as we approach. I keep reminding myself that I will see Erizabesu and maybe Etsuko…even though I let them down. I can almost hear Gavin grinding his teeth and know this isn't the time to reach out to him for reassurance…not that there have been many times I could reach out to him for reassurance. A put-down, maybe. A snide, sarcastic comment, definitely. But reassurance? Nah.

I peer over my shoulder and take in Sora's sky-blue kimono with little white clouds adorning it. I instantly know that Gavin got it for her and that she has no idea. He's such a jerk sometimes…although, he does call her 'his' sky, so I guess it makes sense.

Beyond them, I see obāsan and sofu walking behind them in full fox kitsune-mode but walking on hindlegs. They're both wearing black kimonos with matching black haoris bearing the Abe clan's seal.

We approach the doors, and the guards open them immediately without prompting. We are quickly guided to the emperor's parlor. He sits at the far end of the room with six older kitsune sitting on either side of the path leading to him. Toshiro and Erizabesu sit on the end to our left and across from them are Mr. Tsukino and Tokuhime. Etsuko dutifully stands behind her sister.

Gavin steps forward, lowers himself to his knees, then bows his head, and extends the gift that sofu prepared toward the emperor. "Great Emperor Tenma," he says in Japanese. "Please accept this humble token on behalf of the Abe Clan for our disgraceful performance in defending your great family's treasure."

The emperor merely lifts his right hand and bows his head a bit. One of the older kitsune to his right rises and claims the tiny gold box from him. He puts the treasure down directly in front of the emperor and then returns to his original place.

"And to the honored, Tsukino Clan," I pick up, turning to Toshiro and Erizabesu. I lower myself to my knees and bow my head. "We, of the Abe Clan, will not rest until this tribute you sought to return to the emperor…the Great Tenma Clan is restored to its proper place."

Toshiro pushes his glasses closer to his eyes and bows his head a bit. He looks to Erizabesu, and she nods. She rises and walks over to me as I stand. I offer her the small token that obāsan slipped into my palm as we left Abe-do. She holds it between both hands and bows. I bow, making sure to go a few inches lower than her. She rises, and I do immediately. She completely shatters tradition by smiling and taking my hands. At this point, even Toshiro smiles a little.

"We accept your token," Toshiro says as Erizabesu returns to his side. "Though we don't feel it necessary, considering all that you specifically, and the Abe Clan in general have done for our family." He nods. "We will exercise patience and faith in your abilities in the trying times ahead." He bows a bit. Gavin and I return the gesture, before turning back to the emperor to bow again.

#####

Chapter 8: Goal

Alana

I bounce Kya in my arms, trying to keep my emotions even, warm, and generally in a good place.

"Love?" Nathan calls walking into the room, which absolutely helps lighten my mood. "Why are you in here?"

"Kya likes the light here," I say, passing in front of the windows. Her light brown eyes focus on my face. My eyes phase to dark blue and as if flipping a corresponding switch, hers become deep blue as well. I smile, showing her my fangs, and she giggles. My eyes move over to silver as my fangs return to normal canines. Her eyes do as well… I gasp.

"What is it?" Nathan asks, rushing to my side. He stares at our daughter. "Is Anara okay?" She giggles and moves her arms up and down, opening and closing her hands.

"Kya," I correct. Kya's face scrounges up, and she pokes out her tongue as if she tastes something not to her liking. "Oh, fine," I groan. "Anara." She smiles, and her eyes seem to glow in silvery tones as emerald and gold streaks entreat on the silver.

"What was that a moment ago?" Nathan asks.

"For a second...for the briefest instance...her emotions began to influence mine, rather than the other way around."

"She's a prodigy, just like her mum," he says and kisses me on the temple. "Speaking of which…were you able to…?"

"Yes. I managed to get my entire security detail sorted. Although Christopher insisted that they all be reassigned." I sigh. I'll miss Jackson. He had good taste in classic movies. "I begrudgingly agreed and did a preemptive deep dive on all of the new team."

He nods. "Uncle Mosif is fine. He's all healed up and a little mad at himself for not being able to help you more."

I laugh and shake my head. "That horny old wolf will outlive us all."

He laughs. "True."

A knock comes from the glass door. We turn to Meghan, peaking in from behind it. "Hey guys," she says. She points back down the hall with her thumb. "Sorry to interrupt, but that pretty red-headed lady said that the other magistrates are here and that the fairy representatives should be arriving soon…as well as some surprise guests from Japan…oh and that she'll try to keep Stephen safe while I'm gone." She frowns. "Is she joking, or do I have to knock someone's head off?"

"No," Nathan and I return at the same time.

"Fortunately," Nathan continues. "Raven could easily kill all the other magistrates effortlessly."

"Cool," Meghan says and leads us back toward the grand conference room that Christopher had installed for meetings away from Blackout and outside of the floor populated by vampires.

"...so, yeah," Stephen says to Raven, who seems to be hanging on his every word. "...we were in Nanbu when it happened and..." He spots us, and his mouth snaps shut instantly.

"It's alright," Nathan says. "I know all about it...my bro...I mean, my father died fighting my younger brother."

"Right," Stephen purrs. "He was your dad, wasn't he...I'm sorry for your loss...but..." He tips his head to Meghan, whose eyes are glistening with tears. He hurries over to her side and takes her hand. "She um..." He motions to her. "...he kind of offered her the chance to be his next mate."

"I still can't believe he did that," Nathan rumbles.

"Nathan," I sigh, tipping my head to Meghan, while trying to keep Kya from noticing her emotions.

"Right," he breathes. He goes over to Meghan. "My br...father always had an eye for spotting that something special in others. For him to offer you even the option to be so involved in his life...must mean that he saw something utterly amazing in you."

"Thank you for that," she sighs. Stephen pulls her to the side, claiming both of her hands.

The door opens behind us. Six vampires enter the room, some I've seen before in passing with father, some are strangers, one I recognize almost immediately. "Duchess," I breathe, moving over to her.

"Hello, Renee."

"Aunt Alana. Nathan," she hums with the most infectious French accent. "So, good to see you again." She wraps one arm around me and gives me a squeeze. She bends to get a better look at the loveable bundle of joy in my arms. "Hello, Anara," she purrs in a song-like voice. "...hello, Anara...I'm your cousin, Renee. It is so very nice to finally meet you."

"Wait," Michael, the Australian Magistrate, says, staring at us. He removes his hat and points at us. "Are you saying...?"

"Michael, do you mean...what is that?" a gorgeous woman with medium brown skin says, while wearing a second-skin style dress. I can smell her rose scented perfume nearly across the room and judging by the expression on Kya's face, so does she.

"J'Sala," Raven says in a warning tone.

"That?" Nathan growls, stepping forward.

I put my free hand in front of his chest to stop him. "I have this." He nods and takes a step back. "This," I say, lifting her a bit. "Is Kya Anara Dumont. She is my and Nathan's daughter."

"Abomination," a thin blond-haired man says from somewhere near the door.

Nathan growls. I can feel his eyes moving over to honey and emerald. "Nathan," I say in a calm voice. He takes a deep breath, and I feel a bit of tranquility return to him. I come back to the blond-haired man practically cowering away from Nathan. "Have a care how you speak of our child, friend," I say.

"They may be the last words you ever say," Nathan adds, and I nod along with his assessment.

"You dare threaten a Magistrate!" he returns. "You mongrel!"

Crack! He falls to the floor, clutching his leg, and sobbing. "And you, Yon, dare insult someone in their own place as a visitor," Raven says, walking away from him.

"Savage," Stephen whispers to Meghan, prompting her to bob her head.

"You knew," a large mahogany skinned man with a bald head complains, standing next to the woman who called Kya 'that.' "You knew, didn't you, Raven?"

"Of course, she knew, darling," J'Sala replies. "Charlotte, we voted on this."

"Who's Charlotte?" Stephen asks.

"Context clues, sweetie," Meghan suggests.

"Indeed," a curvaceous woman in a very tight pencil dress says with raven-colored hair laying tight to her head. Her accent suggests some variation of a Portuguese dialect...I'd have to suppose South American. She claps her hands together, while staring at Raven. "If majority rule counts for nothing, we might as well return to the days of your father."

"What are you going to do about it, Florencia?" Raven says, staring at her, surprisingly without any malice behind it, her hands resting against her stomach. She faces all the magistrates. She extends her hands out from her midsection. "What are any of you going to do about it? The child is here now...and..." She motions to us. "...in addition to having to take on Nathan and Alana..."

"Et moi," Duchess adds, raising her hand.

Raven nods. "...to get to my niece, you'll have to go through me, the entire A'Kani tribe of wolves, who've vowed to protect their next Alpha..."

"...and us!" Meghan bellows from the side. Stephen works to get her to lower her raised hand.

The woman motions to Meghan. Raven shrugs. "And them, and that is madness…"

"Agreed," J'Sala says.

"No, I mean, that you would go through all of that to get to…" She extends her left hand, half turning to us. "…her." She walks over. "May I?" she asks, extending both hands. I nod and pass Kya to her. Kya hums and makes grabbing motions toward Raven's face. "Hello, beautiful."

"Ya-ya-ya-ya-ya," Kya returns.

Raven cradles her and shows her to the others. "How can you hate this?"

"She's just…wrong," Yon says, rising from the floor. I suppose his leg healed already.

"Although," J'Sala says, moving toward Raven. I look to Nathan. He nods. I sigh in relief, because I'm sure if he felt something…anything approaching malevolence coming from her, that I didn't sense, he'd have torn her apart by now. "I can feel the same warmth," she continues. "…that emanated from Alana as a child, coming from this child."

J'Sala stops about four feet away from Raven and Kya. Her eyes shift over to vampire's blue as she clasps her hands together. She flashes a huge smile and turns back to the man with her. "You see, Rook?" she says through a laugh, while motioning to Kya. "Remind you of anyone?"

"Alana's eyes did the same," he returns with a laugh, moving up to her side.

"And remember how hesitant the two of you were when father first introduced her?" Raven asks.

"True," Rook says, maintaining his distance, but staring at Kya.

"She's an empath," I explain. "…like me and my mother before me."

"You expect us to follow this…this thing?" Yon asks.

"The shrimp has a point, Sheila," Michael adds. "Besides the little one in his pants," he follows up while glaring at Yon.

"No," Nathan pipes up for us. "Anara…" He groans. He extends his right hand toward her. "Kya Anara is already slated to be the next Alpha of the A'Kani tribe, should I fall," he explains, and I cringe at the thought of losing him, but my dreams have only ever shown our daughter with me.

Kya begins to cry.

"Oh, no," I purr, hurrying over to her. "I'm so, so sorry, my love," I say, reclaiming her. "Mummy didn't mean to let her emotions slip." The second she's in my arms again. "Oh, it has nothing to do with me…Love, she's hungry."

"I've got you," Nathan says, running for our bag on the floor, near the head of the table. He returns with a bottle from the warmer stashed inside.

Florencia tilts her head back and sniffs. "She drinks blood?"

"Yes," I say as I place the nipple to her lips. Kya begins to feed while staring up at me. It's going to be a handful trying to put her down for her nap today. "She doesn't have very many teeth yet, and we don't believe she has fangs...but..."

"Denisoff," Duchess says, staring at the large muscular man standing behind Yon. "You've been strangely quiet since you entered."

"I have no opinion, little one," he says in a heavy Russian accent. "She is a child...there is no way of knowing what she will become." He motions between himself and her. "Look at the two of us, who would've guessed that we'd be here, given the way we met?"

"Indeed," Duchess replies, bowing her head. Her eyes glisten with tears, and Kya begins to cry instantly because even I couldn't block out that amount of sadness.

"Reiner?" Nathan asks, putting a hand on her shoulder.

"No matter how long," Duchess replies. "He's always with me." Nathan nods.

"We lost," Natavius grumbles, marching into the boardroom. "We lost the damned feather...oh," he hums, looking around the room. "I didn't realize we had company."

"Damn," my Nathan grumbles. "That makes this meeting all the more impor..." He trails off staring at the person entering behind Natavius. "...tant...Ange...?"

Angela steps through the door and gives a tiny wave. "Hey, everyone...I'm –ulp!" she barely gets out as Raven wraps her arms around her. "Hey, mom."

"Don't ever do that to me again," Raven demands.

Angela looks to me...no, beyond me, of course, at Nathan. "I'll try not to," she mutters, tapping Raven's arm.

"Hey, you," Meghan says, wrapping her arms around Raven and Angela.

"Umm, what are you doing, lass?" Raven asks.

"Raven," Angela says. "This is my cousin, Meghan...Meghan, what are you doing here? In a meeting...with the Vampire Magistrates...and the wolves' Alpha?"

"Oh, easy," Meghan says casually. She lifts Angela and Raven off the floor effortlessly. "I might've helped save Nathan and Alana's baby from being kidnapped!"

"Kidnapped!" Angela says, looking at us. "Hey, put us down! And how are you doing this?!"

"Yes," Nathan says, half-turning to look at Duchess. "Which is what actually brings us to this meeting today."

"Yes," Duchess picks up.

"Renee?" Angela says. "What are you doing here? I thought you were going back to Paris."

"Perhaps later," Duchess returns with a casual swagger. "My fellow Magistrates," she starts again, turning to face them. "...you have the dossiers I sent you on the organization known as En Quosque or the Claimed."

"Fellow Magistrates?" Angela asks Raven, who nods in return.

"And we're just supposed to believe this," Yon snarls. "That this cabal is supposed to bring back..." He scoffs. "...the boogie man."

"No," Duchess returns. "Sometimes Eden has returned as a woman. As she will this time if allowed to reach their goals...most of which, given Natavius and Angela's report...they've achieved."

"What else are they after?" Denisoff asks, moving up beside Michael. He's just as tall as Michael is, but he's muscular, like Alexander was.

"You're looking at her," Nathan says, motioning to Kya and me. "They want our daughter to be the vessel for Eden."

"Then the simplest plan is to simply kill the child," Yon says, and everyone else in the room cringes, mentally, physically, or both.

Duchess sighs. "Oh, Yon...I wish I could say that I'm going to miss you."

"What do you mean, you wish you co-ulk!"

"Duchess, what are you doing?" Raven asks, as Duchess buries a blade in Yon's stomach up to her wrist. I didn't even sense any malice or anger from her. I look at Nathan. Did he? And if he did, why didn't he stop her?

Ding. Ding. Ba-ling! Ding! Ding. Da-ding! "If you check your phones," Duchess says, still maintaining her stabbing position with Yon, who's now gripping her wrist, trying to pull the silvery blade free. "...you'll find the reason and proof of why I'm doing what I'm doing." Yon glowers at her as blood pours from the corners of his mouth. "You...are a filthy traitor," she says, staring into his eyes. She leans in closer. "I told you over a hundred years ago...it's one thing to betray me, but if you betray my family...I'll kill you."

"You...," he groans and coughs up more blood.

"Thank your second and the Fairy Queen's sisters for your demise." Yon's eyes bulge. Duchess, in a blur of motion, withdraws a step, pulls her weapon free, and then brings the blade across Yon near his neck. A splash of blood flies away...and Yon's head tumbles off. His body drops a moment later.

"Damnit, Xiao!" Michael says, looking up from his phone. "Where's that little shrimp?"

"No doubt off somewhere plotting something," Florencia says, putting her phone away.

"At the moment," Duchess says, using a handkerchief to clean off the surprisingly long single edged blade in her hand. "...he's down in Edenton, along with the Fairy Queen's betrayer."

"Interesting," seems to come from everywhere in the room at once. A finger snap sounds and then two more. A woman with platinum blond hair, red and gold armor, and translucent bee-like wings appears, surrounded by two other, younger women, also with wings, minus armor. They wear simple tunic-style dresses in pale blue and burnt orange.

"Stefana!" Meghan chimes, raising her right hand to wave.

"Meghan of the Light," the fairy in the red armor, Stefana, says, bowing her head. The other two fairies follow suit. "Angela Price. Gathered Magistrates. Natiel, it's been far, far too long." She smiles warmly at him. He nods once with a similar smirk. "Alpha Nathan Mosi'son, Midnight Princess..."

"Queen," I correct. I lift Kya a bit. "She...is the Midnight Princess now."

"Indeed," Stefana returns. "We will track down my sister..."

"The traitor Arielle," the other two fairies say in strange echoing voices that sound hauntingly sad and somehow resonate even after they're done speaking.

"...and," Stefana continues. "...the child will be protected as surely as the future Fairy King will be."

"The Children must be protected," the others say, lifting their left hands. Two snaps sound, and they vanish.

"I'll notify my adoptive sister of this threat as well." Stefana snaps her fingers and vanishes.

"The fairies are actively moving against this...En Quosque?" J'Sala asks.

"And they've...aligned with you two," Florencia adds, pointing at Meghan and Angela. "They called you both by name."

"You guys gotta get out and make more friends," Meghan says with a huge smile, and her cousin nods along with her.

#####

Chapter 9: Prey

Jamie

"This is so unfair!" Amira whines, leaning against the counter in John A. Holmes High School's main office. She's wearing a little black T-shirt with ripped and tattered jeans underneath. Much better than the cut-off, short-shorts, and barely there, *I should be working at an owl themed wings restaurant* tops that she usually wears around the house.

"Mira," dad hums, massaging his temples with his right index finger and thumb. He leans against the same ash gray counter, resting his right elbow on top as his left forearm runs parallel to the floor. "We've already gone over this…"

"No, dad, tell me how it's fair that we're enrolling me in this crappy ass school on the same day that Jamie gets to test out?"

"Because," I start, explaining for the 'I don't know how many-ith time' now. "…I've been studying and prepping to test out of the twelfth grade since last spring…whereas you, skipped your last year of high school, so technically, you should still be in the eleventh grade and not starting your senior year."

"Still," she complains. "Shouldn't we be focusing on…you know…" She looks around suspiciously before resuming with a lowered voice. "…end of the world stuff like fighting En Quosque and evil Ezekielites?"

"Yes, of course," dad replies as if he's answered this question for the 'he doesn't know how many-ith time.' "But…I'm being an optimist for once."

"For once?" I ask. "You were always the glass half full guy in the house…and then you'd fill up the other half of my juice."

"I changed a little…after your mom…after I…"

"Eh," Amira and I moan and wave him off.

"Right," he murmurs. "But as I was saying, optimistically, we have to consider that we will win the day and once the day is won…you'll need a high school diploma, Mira."

"Fine, I guess," Amira groans and turns her back to the counter.

I groan a second later because that bout of indigestion from breakfast hits me again.

"Jamie-Lynn, you okay?" dad asks.

I nod and tap my chest with the side of my fist. "Yeah, but I think your…" I make air quotes. "…'breakfast' is repeating on me again."

"Hey, those eggs were barely burned this morning," dad replies.

"Ugh," Amira groans at the same time that I do. "Don't remind me," she follows up with while covering her mouth.

"You know," I start. "...for someone with heightened senses, you'd think you would catch that sort of thing before it happened!" Amira nods while pointing at me with her thumb.

"Alright," Ms. Habersham says, walking out of the break area for Principal Stanford's office. "How can I hel...?" The last part of the word catches in her throat the second she spots dad standing on Amira's right. "James? James, is that you?"

"Hey Whitney," dad says with a casual demeanor.

"Whitney?" Amira and I say at the same time.

He sighs. "Long time no see, huh?" he asks.

"Long time?" she mutters, stumbling over to the counter. "James, I thought you were dead..."

"A lot of that going around," I mumble.

"Jamie-Lynn..." I give her a finger-wiggling wave. "...Hi!"

"Hello."

"Yes..." Her eyes dart over to dad and back to me. "...you have an appointment. You're hoping to test out of senior year."

"Yep."

"Well, you'd need a parent to sign off..." She throws two offering hands out to dad. "...which, I guess, you have..." She inhales deeply and exhales it in a "Huh."

"Do you need a second to collect yourself, Ms. Habersham?" I ask.

"No." She looks at dad. "No." She comes back to me, seeming a bit out of breath. "Maybe." She shakes her head. "Let me, help this young lady before we get started."

"Oh, this is gonna go over well," Amira jokes.

"Right?"

"Girls," dad says in a warning tone that I still remember to this day.

"Sorry, dad," Amira and I purr at the same time.

"DAD?!?!" Ms. Habersham says, sounding as if she should grab something before she falls over.

"Yes, Whitney...it's a bit of a long story..." He nods. "...can we talk? Over here?" He motions to the far end of the counter. She nods, and he walks in that direction with her.

"You think dad and her used to hook-up?" Amira asks, pointing at them with her thumb.

"I heard that," dad rumbles.

"Heard what?" Whitney asks.

"Nothing," dad says, regaining her attention instantly, and starts whispering again.

"God, I hope not," I complain. "She does seem extra clingy though."

"And extra cringe." I tilt my head to the side in concession. "Hey," she starts, sounding upbeat for the first time since we started this particular excursion. "Is that fine ass ex of yours still going to school here?"

"I heard that too," dad says. Amira waves him off without even looking.

"No," I reply. "Tony dropped out as soon as he moved in with his girlfriend...Shay."

"I'm sorry."

"For what?"

She leans closer and puts her hand on mine. "That thud in your heart when you said 'girlfriend.'" I bow my head a little. "What about that cute ass best friend of yours?" She's trying to lighten the mood again and I love her instantly, all over again for it. "What was his name...? Alex?"

"Yeah, he still goes here, but remember I told you that he and Gwen are married now." Dang it! I snap in my head because I feel like I owe Quincy another five dollars.

"Ugh," Amira groans again. "I hate it here already!" She walks out of the main office.

"I'll...show her around," I say to dad and Ms. Habersham.

"Take a pass!" she says, quickly scribbling her signature, a date, and the time on a hall pass.

I hurry over to the counter, claim it, and rush to catch up with Amira. "Mira!" I whisper, knowing that she can hear me. "Mira!" Okay, Jamie...breathe. Remember what dad told you about your hunter side. I exhale a deep breath and close my eyes.

"Seriously, you have two daughters in high school!" Ms. Habersham asks dad.

"Yes, and somehow, you never managed to get married, Whitney."

"'Somehow,'" she replies. "As if he didn't break her heart in the tenth grade."

Ugh, ignore Ms. Habersham trying to flirt with your dad, despite hearing that he has two teenaged daughters who are basically twins by two different women. Then again, dad doesn't look that much older than he did ten years ago. I wonder if all hunters age slower like that. Were those hunters who kidnapped me really around my age or were they in their twenties?

Wait, what's that shuffling noise? My feet start moving toward it, before I even get a loose notion of what the sound is. I catch the scent of something over the knock-off pine scented cleanser the custodians use here. Peanut butter? "Amira," I breathe and start running in that direction.

"Young lady, if..."

"Call me, 'young lady' one more time, and I'm gonna knock your block off, old man!" Amira says, squaring off with Principal Stanford.

"Old man? Don't you threaten me...you..."

"Mr. Stanford!" I say, hurrying over to the pair.

"Ah," he pants as if he'd been holding his breath. "Jamie-Lynn, if you would give me a moment to deal with this..."

"Um, Mr. Stanford," I say, walking over to Amira's side. I put my arm over her shoulders. "...I'd like you to meet...my slightly younger sister, Amira!"

"Your..." He points at her, me, and then her again. "...your sister...you don't have a sister." He leans forward. "Unless your mother adopted a..."

"Nope," Amira snaps.

"Turns out, I do have a sister, and here she is," I reply. I point at her. "This is her."

"Don't be a smart ass, Ms. Baggett," he snarls.

"Better than being a dumbass," we reply at the same time and look at each other with nods and matching smiles, recognizing dad's bad habits in both of us.

"Wait," Amira snaps out of nowhere. "No effin' way!"

"Amira!"

"What? I said, effin'."

"Young la-" Before Principal Stanford can finish, her right index finger juts out at him. "Jamie-Lynn, tell your sister..."

"Zip it, dude!" she snaps, pinching all four fingers and her thumb together in his face.

"I-" She cuts him off with a glare.

"What's going on, Mi-Mi?"

"Mi-mi?" I nod. "I like it. I smell vampires."

"Really?" She nods. "How would they have ...?"

"Probably broke in last night and waited until school started," she says, sounding like she's envisioning the entire thing.

"I'm sorry," Principal Stanford starts. He points at Amira with a bit of a quiver to his finger. "Did she say vampires?"

I move over to his side and put my hand on his back. "Yes, she did, sir," I say and start making a circle on his back. "But you won't remember...res minor, minor res," I say as I start moving my hand in a circle in the opposite direction. "What you'll remember is that you were heading back to your office, when you encountered my very pleasant biological sister and me."

His eyes close slowly as he nods. I move back to Amira's side. His eyes open. He flashes a huge smile. "Well, it was very nice meeting you, young lady." Amira tries to buck at him as I catch her arm, stopping her. "I'll see you ladies later." He walks away without another word.

Amira huffs and then starts walking toward the 300-hall. "Where have you been for all the messes I've encountered over the years?"

"Messes?" I ask, following her.

"Kicked a vampire through a window once…didn't realize the window led into a room full of normies eating dinner. When he got up and ran away, it raised a real stink with the higher ups."

"Why would that…?"

"He might've been on fire at the time."

"Oh." She stops next to a science class…I think, this is Mrs. Pritchard's class. "What's up?" I whisper. She puts her finger to her mouth and then taps her nose. She then holds up one finger. I frown and shake my head.

She rolls her eyes so hard that I worry that she's going to lose them for a second there. "Quiet," she whispers holding her finger in front of her mouth again. "I smell…" She taps her nose again. "…one…" She holds one finger up and then points at the door. "…in there."

"O…K," I reply making the corresponding hand sign. She glares at me, shakes it off, and reaches for the door. I catch her wrist…and I think we're both a little surprised by how fast I did it. "What are you doing?" I ask.

"I'm about to go inside and kick a vampire's teeth in," she returns.

"Do you smell blood?" I ask. She shakes her head. "Then we wait…class will be out soon, and we can go in then." She scowls at me and does a slow nod.

The bell rings a few seconds later, and I pull Amira to one side of the door as it opens. A gathering of…I'm guessing, tenth graders files out, most of the boys staring at Amira and receiving glares from her.

"Do you smell that?" Amira asks, ignoring the boy approaching her. She extends her hand to him palm first, halting him…without ever looking at him. He wanders off.

"Smell what?"

"Copper…something that smells like a penny…with water…and a sweet smell that you can't quite place," she explains slowly.

I close my eyes and take a deep breath. "Yes," I say.

"Memorize that scent," she demands. "That's their scent…if you're around enough of them, you'll begin to differentiate through multiple scents." I nod. "Let's go," she says, peering at the classroom door. I nod, and we head inside…to find Mrs. Pritchard and a girl, both being held by the neck by some random dude in a hoodie.

"You came," he says. "I thought that was you whispering outside the door. And here you are!"

"What do you want with me?" Amira growls.

"You?!" he grumbles with a snarl. "I don't even know who you are."

"H-h-help me, please!" the girl weeps.

"Shut up!" he snaps, giving her a shake.

"Try to stay strong, dear," Mrs. Pritchard says although she can't see anything with her face buried on her desk.

"Okay," I say, holding my hands out to him.

"Hands down!" he barks. "Not a word from you!"

"So, he really does know who you are?" I nod. "Shall I?" I shrug, and Amira vanishes. Crack! The vampire falls to the floor. The girl runs at me, and I wrap my arms around her.

"I was so scared," she weeps.

"I know, I know," I say, making a circle on her back. "Res minor, minor res," I repeat, and her arms fall away. "It's funny how you remembered that sad thing you saw on that show," I whisper. "…and it made you start crying in the middle of class. Luckily, no one saw you…so if you hurry to the bathroom and clean your face, you should be fine." She nods and hurries over to her desk. She collects her backpack and darts out of the room, keeping her face low.

I turn to Mrs. Pritchard, who's staring at me. "So," she moans. "You're a witch just like your mother and grandmother."

"She knows?" Amira asks with a thumb point. I shrug.

Mrs. Pritchard rolls up her sleeve and reveals a series of indentions along her left forearm. "When I was a young girl, your grandmother saved me from a wolf that looked like it had blue skin." She looks at the former wound. "When it bit me…the pain was excruciating…she pulled the poison out of me with magic…and then healed the wound as best she could." She looks at me. "She used that same spell to make me forget…but I didn't. I realized why she tried to make me forget though…knowing that there are horrible things like…that wolf…this man…"

"Vampire," Amira corrects.

"Really?" Amira nods. "Well, also knowing that there are people like your grandmother, your mother, and now you, Jamina…" She nods this time. "…makes me feel much better."

"Thank you, Mrs. Pritchard."

"I understand if you have to make me forget now," she adds.

"Can't," Amira and I reply at the same time. "That spell only works within an hour," I explain. She nods. "Besides, even if I could, I wouldn't if you've managed to keep our secret this long."

"Thank you, dear."

"Thank you," I return.

"Uh oh," Amira says, staring at the idiot on the floor. "He's healing."

"Are they like movie vampires?" Mrs. Pritchard asks, heading toward her whiteboard. "Fire, sun, wooden stakes?"

"Yes, yes, and no, silver," Amira says.

"Good," Mrs. Pritchard says, tossing the yardstick from the marker tray to Amira.

"Bad…ass," Amira says as she catches it. "The tip is made of silver!" She stabs the guy in a blur of motion. "One down," she says, standing up again.

"There are more?" Mrs. Pritchard asks.

"Yeah," I say. "And we have to find them."

#####

Chapter 10: Hometown

Alex

"There's no way," I growl, hurrying down the hall. "I can't be smelling what I think I'm smelling! I have to be going crazy, right?" I look over my shoulder at Gwen and Kai behind me.

"If you're crazy," Gwen whispers. "I'm crazy, babe."

"Babe?" Kai mocks.

"Let some of them go," I growl. He shrugs.

"Wait," Gwen snaps. "I smell blood…"

"Damn," I growl.

"No," she interrupts before I get even madder than I already am. "It's vampire blood."

"Ugh," Kai groans. "Is that what that syrupy penny smell is?"

"Yep," Gwen says and takes the lead. I follow her down the hall until we reach Mrs. Pritchard's class. "Oh no," she hums.

"Can't be helped," I say, grabbing the handle.

"You guys are so loud!" Amira says in the now open doorway. "Get in here!"

I take Gwen by the hand and pull her inside with me as Kai follows. Amira peers up and down the hall before closing the door behind us. "What…?" Gwen asks, pointing at Amira. "What are you doing here?" she snarls, wrapping both arms around mine.

"Chill," Amira says. "I already know what's up. He's your husband and blah, blah, blah."

Gwen's eyes narrow glaring at her.

"More important subject of conversation," Kai says, raising his right hand. "Why's there a dead guy on the floor, and Mrs. Pritchard isn't screaming about it?"

"Oh," Gwen says, turning to the interior of the room.

"Apparently," Jamie says making her way over to us. "She's known about supernatural beings since the days of my grandma."

Mrs. Pritchard nods. "I'll admit, I didn't know they were so…varied."

"Well," Kai starts. "Crib Notes version…" He motions to himself and then me… "…skinwalkers…" …before going to Gwen. "…kitsune…" And finally, he gestures between Jamie and Amira. "…witch and hunter!"

"It doesn't matter to me honestly," Mrs. Pritchard says. "As long as you're friends with Jamie-Lynn, I'll just assume you're good people, and that's all that really matters."

"Awww," Amira purrs. "Now that that's out of the way. We have some really bad people, walking through the school like they own the place doing really bad things."

"How are we going to stop them?" Gwen asks.

"Well, since you guys came here," Amira says. "...and Mrs. P. here has a free period, I'm gonna risk assuming that you guys can sniff out the fang heads."

"Hey, we have a friend who's a fang head," Kai grumbles. "I mean, vampire...and she's more like an acquaintance."

"She's a friend," I interrupt.

"Whatever," Amira moans. "I only have this." She holds up a bloody yardstick. "But you guys have claws and fire...and..." She looks at Gwen. "...whatever it is that you do."

"Hey!" Gwen whines.

"So, we should split up. Jamie, go with blondie here. The happy couple goes together. And I'll go alone."

"You don't know the school," Jamie says.

"Nope, but I know vamps, and I have this!" She wiggles the stick. "I'll be fine. If you run into any of them...feel free to tear their heads off, rip out their hearts, or just burn them to a crisp." She walks toward the door. "Or you could throw them outside and let the sun do all the heavy lifting."

"What about him?" I ask.

"Him who?" Amira returns.

We all point at the dead body on the floor. "Oh, him...hmmm, we usually have cleaner crews for that." She takes out her phone. "I guess I can call dad and ask him."

"Miri, where are you?" Mr. Baggett's voice comes through the phone instantly. "Is Jamie-Lynn still with you?"

"Yes, dad," she says in an annoyed voice. "You wouldn't happen to have a gun, would you?"

"What? Why?" he snaps. "Miri, we're in school...what have you done?"

"Nothing...except off a vamp...in room..." She covers the phone. "...where are we?" she stage-whispers.

"Room 321," Gwen says.

"Room 321," Amira repeats, taking her hand away from the phone.

"I heard her," he replies. "And I'm already on my way. Who is that anyway? And where's Jamie-Lynn?"

"Just get here and see for yourself. Geez, dad!" She ends the call and slips her phone into her back pocket, ignoring all the slack jawed faces staring at her. Five seconds later, there's a knock at the door. "Who is it?" Amira sings.

"You know damn well, who it is! Now, open this door!"

Kai opens it and motions for him to come in.

"Kai, Alexander…" He frowns. "…we didn't get a chance to meet at Jamie-Lynn's party, but you're Gwendolyn, right?" Gwen nods, while clinging closer to me.

"James Baggett?" Mrs. Pritchard says, sounding surprised for the first time since we got here. He nods. "I thought you were dead!"

"Yeah, that's a long story…which, I'm sure my daughter will tell you all about," he says, motioning to Jamie with a suggestive tone. He then tips his head toward Mrs. Pritchard.

"Dad," Jamie says. "She knows. Like, knew about grandma, mom, and now me…knows."

"Oh," he replies, scratching the back of his head.

Kai leans into him and points at his face. "Hunter!" he sings. Amira joins in from the other side, pointing at his face.

"Will you knock that off?" Mr. Baggett complains. "This is serious."

"No," Jamie jumps in. "What's serious is that apparently there are more vampires in the school."

"What? How? Are they daywalkers like…?"

"Daywalkers?" Amira asks.

"Long story," I say. "Doubt it. Considering how much sunscreen this guy's wearing and the heavy hoodie on his back."

"Hey," Amira says. "Good senses, cu-cu-cu…I mean, Mr. Garner…husband of Gwen."

Gwen growls as a response. "Okay," I hum. "We should get going and try to find the others. How many scents did you pick up?"

"At least, three more," Amira says.

"Here," Mrs. Pritchard says. She hands each of us, excluding Mr. Baggett, a hall pass. "Just in case."

I nod, and then Gwen and I head out. "I could just rip her head off," Gwen says, sounding the least calm I've ever heard her and that includes when I was dying right in front of her.

"No, you won't."

"Who's going to stop me? You?"

"Fox-Face," I purr.

"Whatever, let's just get this done." She rushes ahead of me, and I hurry to catch up. I take her right hand in mine and wrap my left arm around her. She pauses and inhales deeply as if I just knocked the wind out of her. "Alex," she whispers. That electric pulse that moves between us feels like a steady heartbeat at this point…I can't believe that she thinks I'd risk this…even for a second.

"You, Gwen. I could have never met you…and it would still be you. Period." I kiss the back of her head.

She puts her left hand on top of mine on her stomach. "Promise?"

"For you, anything."

She takes a deep breath and leans into me. "Uh oh," she moans.

"What?"

"Vampire…ugh, and his scent is so strong, it's actually bothering my stomach…" She retches and covers her mouth. "…a little."

"We'll get you something to drink like a ginger ale or something after we find this vampire and rip his head off." She nods and starts walking, and I follow.

Something hits me…this smell makes my stomach roll. It's like rotting meat mixed with rusted pennies and…

"Crap!" Gwen groans, covering her mouth all over again. She looks around and hurries over to the trashcan near the door. She sticks her head inside and "Blerghhhhhhhhhh!"

"Gwen," I say, pulling her hair back away from her face and out of the line of fire.

"I'm okay," she says, wiping her mouth against the back of her hand and then repeating with her forearm.

"Bae, your breath says otherwise."

"You used otherwise," she says, caressing my cheek.

"Honey," I complain, fishing a pack of gum out of my pocket. I offer her a stick. She pulls it and puts it in her mouth, pretty quickly. She blushes and turns her head away. I tap her chin. "Sorry. I didn't mean to embarrass you."

"Embarrassed flew out the window when my head went in the trashcan," she whispers.

"I still love you though."

"You always love me, according to you."

"Well, you should listen to that guy…he sounds smart."

"Oh yeah…?"

"Yeah." My phone vibrates. "Kai and I found another vampire with some weird lizard things. Didn't know he was that good a fighter…another vampire down."

I look at Gwen. "Jamie."

"We'll pick this up later," she says and gives me a quick peck on the cheek. She steps back, and her eyes are glowing. She vanishes, leaving a burst of bright red flames behind. I don't even try to follow her with my eyes. I follow her scent, kind of surprised I can even keep up with it with this rotted meat stink in the air. I arrive at the gym, where she's peeking inside the door.

"Gw-?"

Before I can finish, she turns with her finger to her lips. "This is the gym right...there are classes all day, right?" I nod with a frown. "Then why isn't anyone in here?" I turn to look inside over her head, and I don't see or hear anyone.

"Come on," I say as the fur emerges out of me.

"So cute," she purrs following me as the flaming ears pop up in her hair and four fiery tails swish around behind her. I reach for her, and she takes my hand...and a fifth tail appears. "Ugh," she groans. "The smell's getting worse," she adds, covering her mouth and nose.

"Who are you two supposed to be?" a boy with long, greasy black hair says. He steps out of the girl's locker room wearing a long black coat with black slacks and a t-shirt rounding the goth boy ensemble. "I'm supposed to be waiting on the Witch of Light..." He shrugs. "...but I guess I can warm up on a fire girl and a furry."

"I'll show you furry," I growl.

"Really?" He snaps his fingers, and the doors to the boys' and girls' locker rooms open immediately. Also, that nauseating smell increases. A groan comes from that direction, and a person appears...or it looks like a person, made out of beef jerky. No, there's two in each room...now, three...six...

"There are people with them!" Gwen says as a gasp.

"Yeah," the guy says, running his fingers through his hair. "I figured if I take a bunch kids hostage, I could get the witch to give herself up an-" His words cut out as my fist collides with the side of his face. He hits the polished floor and slides across it like a hockey puck on ice.

"Alex! He's probably a necromancer, so..." I'm already pulling the first piece of beef jerky's head off.

"Take out the people raisins and save the students, right?"

"Yes," Gwen says simply, but there's something in her voice. As more of these disgusting things come out of the locker rooms, dragging students along with them, Gwen extends both hands in front of her...right over her left, on top of it in fact. She extends her left leg in front of her, bending her knee slightly. She takes a deep breath in and when she breathes out...flames explode out of her. "We have to be fast...or they'll start..." Crack!

"Ah!" a girl cries as her arm bends up the wrong way.

"NO!" I snap as Gwen vanishes. Ten jerky bits get tossed with flames coming from their torn off arms and legs. "Right," I growl in my two-tone voice. Remember what Nate said...move like the beast, strategize like a man...okay, he didn't say that exactly, but still. Gwen went for arms, that's probably the best bet. I rush forward, remembering how easily our distant cousin threw me and Kai around the Blackshears' back patio. I do the same, but I just end up twisting their arms off…good…can't take anymore hostages without arms. Eleven…twelve…eighteen…how many of these things did this guy bring with him?

"Alex!" I stop, and my eyes follow Gwen's…to the guy standing over goth-boy…holding a girl by the throat.

"I'll be with you two in a minute," he says with a little bit of a German accent and while holding his right finger out to us. "I toldja," he growls, putting his foot against goth-boy's bruised face. "I told you these little meat puppets you brought with you wouldn't do anything against the Witch of Light. I mean, they aren't even slowing these two down."

A rumble comes from the back of my throat. "Aht-aht," he issues, holding the girl out at arm's length by the throat. Her face is starting to turn white, and her lips are turning blue. "I flick my wrist, and her neck goes snap."

"You asshole!" I growl. "You're talking about him messing up…talking about us like we're nothing, but you're so weak that you had to take a hostage?" He glares at me. "And you bring that crap to my hometown…? Why? Because you plan on killing my best friend?" That's it, jerk. Focus on me…and completely ignore…

Gwen launches a spear made of fire aimed directly at his arm. He pushes the girl forward, moving her into the path of the spear…that evaporates before it even reaches her. "HA!" he barks…until my claws dig into his arm… "How fast are you?" he gasps.

I use my momentum to pull me around his arm…I spin and rip the arm off with one hand while grabbing the girl with the other. She inhales deeply as I slide to a stop a few feet away from the one-armed vamp.

"NAAAARRRRGGGGGHHH," he screams, holding his stump. Until a sword juts out of his left arm…wait, no it came out his chest first then his left arm. He looks over his shoulder at Amira with her katana in hand. She pulls her sword out, takes a step back, and moves it outward from herself at eye-level. The vampire stops complaining about his injuries…and then his head slides off and tumbles across the floor.

"Nice work, you two," Amira says. "Dad's already calling in a favor to get a cleaning crew in here…and Jamie's asking some witch friends to come in and set everyone affected straight."

"Where did you hide that?" Gwen asks. "And why didn't you use it earlier?"

"Because I left it out in the car, and I didn't have the keys…or a driver's license that would explain me having the keys," she adds in a lower voice.

"They're fighting dirty," I rumble. I hear the beast…breathing in my ear…heart beating fast…a growl rumbling in the back of his…our throat…I want to just tear them apart for doing this…for coming to my home and hurting…

"Alex?" Gwen says, taking both of my hands. "Alex, listen to me…feel my emotions, I'm trying to calm you down…I'm trying to feel out your emotions, but all I'm getting is a swirl of violent anger…" We've heard this before…I-I've heard this before. "Alex…Alex, it's me. It's Gwen."

"Gwen?" I snarl.

I open my eyes and see two bright emeralds staring back at me. "Calm down, you're scaring me." She moves her hands up to either side of my face and starts caressing my ears. "I love you, Alexander Bryan Garner."

My hands slip over hers. "I love you too, Gwendolyn Elizabeth Frost-Garner."

"Damn, why didn't I meet him first?" Amira mutters.

"Wouldn't have mattered," Gwen says, draping her arms over my shoulders. "Even if he'd never met me…" She shrugs. "…me."

"You," I reiterate and kiss her.

#####

Chapter 11: Struggle

"Okay, mom," I say into the phone.

"I love you."

"Love you too. Bye."

"Bye."

I use my key to open the apartment door. I can't believe no one broke the exterior door the entire time I was gone. That thing usually gets busted at least once a month, and they have to replace the lock and issue new keys. I open the door. My hair tosses with a gust of wind. A gust of wind…? We're in a brownstone walk-up…where would…? I growl as I push the door open and spot Natavius sitting on mom's plush white sofa.

"Comfortable?" I ask, tossing my keys in the bowl next to the door.

"Very," he returns. "Party at the Price House!" He lifts his arms above his head and 'raises the roof.' My brow arches, and I shake my head. "No?" I shake my head again. He hops off the sofa, turns around, and starts shaking his ass. "None of this?"

"No."

He smacks his own butt. "Or this?"

"Hell no!"

He stands up, turns to face me, and nods. "Good to know."

"What are you doing here?"

"I was…" He motions out from himself. "…sent to check on you."

"Tell Nate, 'I'm fine.'"

"Not Nate," he says, tapping the tip of my nose. He crossed the room before I even realized he took a step. I frown and glare at him.

"Alana picked up on your emotions. She said you might be repressing even more than you know, because she felt like she was 'standing in front of a dam, waiting for the bloody thing to give way, but all that happened were the occasional leaks that were quickly plugged!'"

I give him a stare that suggests he might be crazy.

"Her words," he says, pointing away from himself and most likely in the exact direction of the new manor.

"Well, go back and tell my loving auntie that I'm fine," I say, walking past him, heading to my bedroom. My things won't make it back from California until tomorrow probably. I can't wait to try out those knives that…

"Are you?" he asks, his voice feeling like a wet blanket toss over my head. It drags me down…until the tips of my fingers tingle, feeling as though they're covered in… Click. I jerk before I can stop myself. Click. Click. Click.

…I try to get my breathing under control as my left hand grabs my right…trying to stop it from pulling the trigger.

"I'm fine," I snap and shiver. "The monster's just fine."

"You are not a monster!"

"Aren't I?" I snap turning to face him. "I kill people…people," I repeat nodding at him. "People don't kill people…monsters kill people," I reiterate the lesson mom…sire-mom taught me, and that Nate reinforced. "That's me," I mutter, tapping my heart. "I…kill…people!"

"NO, YOU DON'T!" he snaps, clutching my shoulders. Damn his speed. "You are not a monster!" he whispers, sounding as if he's even more despondent than me.

"Get off me," I snap, shoving his hands away from me.

He stares at me as if I just tried to stab him. He holds praying hands up to his mouth…those perfect lips rub against his thumbs. He points those hands at me. "Monsters," he starts with this aridity to his voice that kind of breaks my heart a little. "…don't call themselves monsters with that much pain in their voice."

"If I had my knives, I'd stab you."

"You couldn't stab me if you had all four knives, and I was asleep," he brags. I throw a punch at him as fast as I can…as my arm fully extends, I literally feel the slight touch of his lips against my skin like a warm, little nope against my knuckle. I pull my arm back slowly, and he comes back to his regular standing position. He smirks.

I throw another punch. This one he does me the courtesy of at least ducking under. "Fight me," I snap. He shakes his head. I throw a one-two combo, followed with a roundhouse kick, and then a spinning heel kick…and he's literally holding one finger against the sole of my shoe. "I hate you," I grumble as I lower my foot.

"You know I'm in love with you, right?"

I swallow a lump and take a step back. "Shut up, you can't be in love with me…who would ever love…"

"Don't you do it," he warns with the most serious voice I've ever heard him use. "Don't."

I press my lips into a line and stare at the floor. "You know the last person to tell me he loved me…" I look at him. "…I shot him in the stomach three times…" He frowns. "…and then I shot him in the face until the gun emptied." Click. Jerk. Click. Jerk. Click. Je- He grabs my arms. I inhale…at some point, I forgot to do that. He reaches up and caresses my left cheek…no, he's wiping a tear away.

"Monsters don't cry over their 'victims.' No matter who it was." I swallow a lump and stare into those gorgeous eyes of his. Ba-bump. What's that sound? Ba-bump. Ba-bump. It's getting louder and faster. Ba-bump. Ba-bump. Ba-bump. I stare at him. His heart…his heart is racing…it's literally never done that before. I reach up and caress his cheek. Ba-bump. Ba-bump. Ba-da-bump… Did it just skip a beat?

I lean forward, and he reciprocates. I leap at him and kiss him. I hold his face in my hands as his rest at the small of my back. He holds me in a way that I've never been held. Like he not only wants to hold me close, but that he's…I don't know…afraid he'll have to let me go at some point. I throw my arms out and slip my jacket off. I put my hands on his chest as we come together again, and his tongue meets mine.

I move my hands out and start pushing his jacket down. He takes his arms away from my back and lets it fall. I cup his face again and start pulling him toward me. He moves with me over to the couch, and I recline with my head against the armrest. He lays on top of me and continues kissing me, moving across my lips…over my left cheek…at my neck…and I sigh, because his lips are like warm silk, and his tongue is a thing of magic. His thumbs brush against my hips, feeling like hot, eager attraction, before they move under my shirt.

I position my thighs on either side of his waist while pulling at his belt. His hands slide up my back, and I feel like my bra should've just jumped off just because. I get his belt undone and start on his button.

"Wait, wait, wait," he says, sitting back. He stares at me like he could eat me up…and my mind plays with both meanings, and my body seems down for whatever. His left hand sweeps across his mouth. "This is…amazing, but…I gotta be honest with you…"

"Now?" I ask because I'm a big ball of turned on…ness. That was awkward. I shake my head to clear that dumb ass thought away.

"Yeah, now," he returns, still staring at me hungrily. "Look, if the only reason you're making out with me…doing this…or anything else, is because you're trying to feel something…anything…or worse yet, prove that you don't feel anything, then stop it." I frown and sit up.

"Because if that's the reason," he continues. "…it's not fair. It's not fair to me, and it's definitely not fair to you!"

I scoff and move my legs from around him and get up from the couch. I readjust my shirt as I walk away from him. I glare at him over my shoulder, standing up. "Dude…are you seriously passing on a chance to hook up with me, because you're trying to spare *my* feelings?"

He sighs and fastens his belt. "I guess so." He scoops up his jacket and heads for the door.

I scoff and cross my arms. I shake my head…wondering what the female equivalent of blue balls is. "Fine. Whatever."

Natavius stops at the door and glares at me. He tosses his jacket on the floor and marches over to me. "Stop doing that!" he growls, and his eyes change to amber for a second…but I still don't feel like I'm in any danger…in fact, I feel like I should be ashamed of myself, for the way I'm treating him. I mean, he's obviously into me and look at him. He's gorgeous, he's funny, and he's the sweetest guy…but I'm a-

"You care," he interrupts my thought as if he could hear it. "…you care about so much. Okay? That's why you ran away! That's why you paused…you paused when I told you how I felt before you left. That's why you called your sire-sister to help you, and that's why you called your biological mother every…single…day, so that she wouldn't worry about you." I shake my head. "Don't lie to me. I was here. Visiting her, talking to her, about you…telling her how I felt about you."

His jaw clenches, and he shakes his head again. "I don't know why you're trying to force yourself to believe that…that…"

"That what?" I snap, feeling my shame waffle between embarrassment and anger.

He raises his hands as if he's going to choke the air and shivers. He grabs my face and…pulls me in for a kiss. He tugs at my lower lip…not forcefully, not hungrily, or even playfully…there's something to this kiss. My body feels lighter, like I just…put something…down…what? I sink into the kiss. I feel his hands move to the small of my back, and it feels as if they're the only things holding me up but somehow his lips are lifting me…I feel dizzy and…turned-on, but in a different way than before. This is…

We part. He holds his hands up as if I'm mugging him this time. "Sorry. I shouldn't have…I mean, it's just that…I…I mean…we…" He stares at me, and his eyes are pleading with me to feel what he was trying to say with that kiss.

And here I am…my goofy ass, trying not to…I had a crush on him at sixteen, before I'd even seen him. All I knew about him was that he was my friend Kyra's older brother, who took care of her and Tybalt, worse name ever, when their parents died. I remember thinking that someone like that…yeah, he's the kind of guy you should fall in l… I stare at him as my eyes swell.

"Ange?" he says after he apparently continued talking, and I was in my own little sixteen-year-old, pining away for my best friend's brother world. "Ange, are you…?"

"Shut up," I gasp. "Just…shut up…okay…I need to see something." He nods. I step into him, hands on his chest…and then slide them over his shoulders. I kiss him…and it all comes back again…the dizziness, the heavy-lightness…the something stirring in me that I can't place. I lean back, and he holds me up, kissing me more passionately…not sexually, but with more emotion…it's like I can almost reach out and touch his feelings toward me…and I think he might've uncovered mine toward him…at least, a little.

We stand up straight and separate…my eyes remain closed for a few seconds, my lips still in kissing position. I wobble because the dizziness did not let up. "Whoa," I breathe in a heavy exhale.

Natavius smiles, and it's not playful…he's happy. "I know, right?" he says, still holding me.

I frown and swallow a lump. "Okay…but now I'm scared."

Natavius bobs his head as his smile comes down to a bit of a smirk. "I know…me too. I've never been scent-bonded to anyone before."

"And you are…aren't you?"

"Everything in me tells me I should be with you, Ange," he says just before his tongue sweeps across his lower lip. I nibble mine, still staring into those gorgeous eyes of his. Is this what Raven meant about sire-dad…when she said it's a little overwhelming being the object of a scent bond…that it's as if something in you welcomes that feeling…that emotion…reciprocates it. Like it's natural, the way it should be. "And you," he picks up. "…feel something, right?"

I nod.

"For me?"

I nod again. "Oh yeah," I sigh. "…but I don't know what happens now."

"We get you some help." I frown. "I know post-traumatic stress when I see it." I bow my head a bit. "It's nothing to be ashamed of Ange."

"I know."

"But I'm here, okay…whatever you need. I'm here."

"Thanks, but what do we do…right now though?"

The corners of his mouth turn down. "Well, one idea…I mean, we could…we could kiss again."

I smirk. "Yeah, you have really good ideas and stuff," I murmur, before he leans in and kisses me again.

#####

Chapter 12: Training

Gwen

I look across the table at Gavin. He's come over to have breakfast at the Taylor's house often. He's been sulkier and broodier than normal since Sora has been away. He shovels a forkful of eggs into his mouth with a sigh.

"I'm fine, Gwen," he says as he clears his mouth without even looking up. Then he raises just his eyes to glower at me. He emits a low growl. I feel his aura out, and he's being playful. I start to laugh, and so does he.

Then I hear a crackling sound behind me. Gavin heard it too, and we both jump from our seats. Sparks fly from the edges of the opening, but they don't burn the linoleum or the vinyl cabinets. Obāsan steps through the newly opened fire gap, and we both breathe a sigh of relief.

"Obāsan!" I move forward to hug her, but she stops me.

"I've come concerning the defeat you recently experienced at the emperor's palace."

"Oh," I groan. Gavin says nothing but bows his head as his mood plummets.

"Yes. Oh." She turns back to the fire gap. "Come along," she says simply in Japanese.

"Can we finish breakfast first?" Gavin asks.

Obāsan turns back to us, taking on all the trappings of a kindly grandmother, complete with a warm, comforting smile. "No." She motions back to the fire gap as all the warmth she displayed only a moment ago evaporates. Her expression takes on a hard edge as her true youthful visage emerges. I glance at Gavin over my shoulder while typing out a text to Dr. Taylor, explaining my and my brother's absence.

We step into the fire gap and immediately emerge from it into Abe-do's courtyard. "Gwen-picchan," sofu says, wrapping his arms around me. "How's that new grandson of mine?" he adds, showing more affection than I thought him possible of displaying. "Is he still as amazing as I remember him to be?"

"I hope so," I reply awkwardly. "Since it's only been a few weeks since the last time you saw him!" He laughs and gives me another squeeze.

"Sora's doing well too, sofu," Gavin supplies while motioning to himself.

"Yeah? Well, you should marry her, so that she can be my grandchild too," sofu grumbles, still holding me, proving that Gavin got his attitude from sofu all along.

Obāsan quietly clears her throat, and sofu releases me. His attitude grows sterner. "Right!" he declares. "We have things to do."

Gavin and I change our shoes and then follow them to the dojo. Obāsan and sofu stand in front of us. "We may not be able to join you in this fight, so we need you to be prepared," obāsan says.

"This fight is much bigger than what you realize," sofu says.

I can almost feel Gavin rolling his eyes. I glance at him; his expression surprises me. His face hardens, and his jaw sets. Given his aura, not only is he frustrated by this summoning, but he is also embarrassed that they have had to bring us here.

I turn my attention back to sofu and obāsan. "There are still things that we have left to teach you," he nods to obāsan.

She creates a spark in her right hand, then brings her hands together. Her eyes focus intently as she rounds her hands into fists. She pulls one upward while pulling the other down. As she pulls her hands apart, a shaft of flame appears. She pulls one end straight down, while the other she pulls into a point.

"Your flame spear," I breathe, half in awe and half in with the realization that she's about to teach me this difficult skill.

"You are ready," she says with a satisfied smile.

"And you, Gavin, we will work on this," sofu says with a smile that looks almost menacing. He falls into a crouch that looks like a haka, with his feet set wide apart, a slight bend to his knees, and a bit of a tilt forward at the waist. His upturned, clawed hands remain at his hips as his fox fire roars and flares outward around him. The pale-yellow flames concentrate around his two hands. Before long, flames overshadow his hands in the shapes of two large fox paws. Sofu swats at Gavin with the fan-sized, fiery appendage, causing my brother's clothing to ruffle from the ensuing draft he created.

"Whoa," is all Gavin manages as a response.

"Gwen, you try first," sofu says, half-requesting, half-commanding. He looks at me and nods. Obāsan nods at me once to prompt me.

I create a spark with my right hand and bring them together just as I saw obāsan do. My hands round like I'm holding a pole between them. I start to pull my hands apart but struggle to maintain its shape. I try to pull harder and faster, but the more intensity I use to pull, the less control I have. I don't want to show my struggle, but I know obāsan can feel it. I finally look up to find a bemused expression on her face.

"This is not done with brute strength," she says without moving from her spot. "This is accomplished like forming clay into a bowl. Try it again, but not as forcefully."

The three of them look on as I try again. This time I gently, but intentionally pull my hands apart as I saw her do. It's more like brittle, but moldable kinetic sand made of fire magic than clay, but I understand her analogy. My fox wedding ring catches my eye, sparking red in the fire spear's glow. When I have a finished spear, I look up to see the approval I already feel. She nods in affirmation. Gavin even feels a little impressed though he doesn't show it.

I try to hold onto that feeling as the flame spear dissipates in my hand. "I thought I had it," I complain.

"Did you think you would be able to accomplish what took me years in the span of one lesson?" obāsan asks, sounding insulted.

"Maybe," I admit under scrutiny. She chuckles, hopefully, getting that I'm trying to lighten the mood.

Gavin's mood shifts, and he rubs his hands together in anticipation. Sofu gives him a nod this time. Gavin crouches as he saw sofu do. He extends his arms, and the fox magic flames flow around him.

"Focus it in," Sofu says, lifting his fists to promote his point.

Gavin concentrates on focusing the power to his hands, but I can feel that he's struggling to project the hands. Gavin's lips press into a line, and he falters. He isn't used to failure and doesn't take it well.

"Kuso!" Gavin spits, while turning away from us.

"You need to focus!" sofu snaps at him.

"I DID!" Gavin snaps back, surprising not only me, but sofu and obāsan too. "I mean…," he starts again, humbling himself. "…I did, sofu."

"Mago," sofu says stepping closer to Gavin. "For as long as you have been in my care, you have never ceased to amaze me…you will get this…because you are amazing…" He steps back. "…not to mention, you're my grandson," he adds with an enthusiastic thumbs up.

Gavin smirks at sofu's attempt at humor. He nods once more, shoring himself up. He takes that same haka stance as blue flames explode out of him. That same stream of fire, seems to mute itself, coming to burning just on the surface of his skin…slowly, fiery waves move down his arms toward his hands. He spreads his fingers wide as flames seem to make them extend…into long sharp claws. He gasps as his flames douse themselves, and he pants as if he'd been holding his breath.

"You're getting it now, mago," sofu encourages. "You're getting it now."

"As always," a charming familiar voice calls from behind obāsan. We turn to find Toshiro, flanked by Erizabesu and Etsuko, with his father trailing dutifully behind him. "…the Abe Clan is hard at work training."

Erizabesu covers her mouth with her free hand…the one not held in Toshiro's and blushes. "Technically," she hums in a light-hearted voice. "…Gwen-chan is Tenma Clan."

"You're right as always, dear," Toshiro replies, glancing at her face as a bit of crimson fills his cheeks as well. They are so adorable together!

"You're trying to pass on your techniques?" Tsukino-san grumbles from the back of their numbers. "Do you think these to half-gaijin could ever…?"

"HAVE A CARE HOW YOU TALK ABOUT OUR FRIENDS!" Etsuko explodes at Tsukino-san in a way that tells me this isn't the first time this has happened. "Because whatever you say negatively about Gwen, you're also saying about your soon-to-be daughter!"

Toshiro raises his free hand with his palm facing us. Etsuko bows her head and takes a step back. "She's not wrong, father," is all he adds, which prompts his father to bow his head as well.

I throw a quick elbow into Gavin's stomach. He coughs, while asking, "Why?"

"Because you were about to laugh," I grumble softly between clenched teeth.

"You…are not…wrong," he complains, while trying to reclaim his breath.

"I-I," Tsukino-san starts again in a much softer tone. "…I was merely suggesting that perhaps they would benefit more from a demonstration than mere words."

"He might have a point, dear," sofu says, slightly mocking Toshiro's response to Erizabesu.

"Are you up for it?" obāsan taunts.

"Always." With that, Gavin and I swiftly move away from sofu as obāsan moves to the spot opposite him. They stare at each other, and all the love and admiration they usually exude leeches away. Their expressions suggest that they're about to do battle with their fiercest enemy. Sofu shifts back into his full kitsune form, obāsan merely sprouts her nine foxfire tails. She drops into a stance as sofu crouches in his haka. He growls as bright yellowish-white flames stream through and then off his fur. White flames enclose both of her hands as she brings them together. They separate, and her normal flame spear looks more like a flaming staff. Sofu's hands expand into two large, white foxfire paws. He smirks, and so does obāsan…before they both vanish.

They come together in the middle of the dojo. His right paw meets her staff…and I would swear lightning strikes at the point of contact. Sofu swipes at her in a blur of motion, which seems to be easily deflected or avoided altogether by obāsan.

"You're getting rusty, Tomo-kun," Tsukino hums as he comes to a rest in front of Toshiro. He claps his hands together as flames move across his shoulders. "You'll never beat Mina-chan like that." Suddenly, two more flames ignite on either side of him. I gasp…it's the same technique I've been working on…but where my clones only appear to be manifestation of flame illusions, his are as corporeal as obāsan's staff or sofu's paws. Tsukino-san's eyes snap open, and his two clones rush forward joining the fray, making it three-on-one against obāsan.

"Now, it's getting interesting," she murmurs, sounding more excited than concerned.

"I'll show you interesting, Mina-chan!" Tsukino says, before darting forward making it four-on-one.

"Can she…?" Etsuko starts, taking a step forward.

Gavin extends his hand toward her to halt her. "In all the years we've lived with obāsan and sofu…"

"…he has never once beaten her," I finish, staring on in amazement as obāsan demonstrates just how powerful and skilled she really is.

"You seem to be getting tired, Saito-kun," obāsan says.

"Ha," he pants. "Speak…" Heavy breath. "…for yourself."

"Fine," obāsan snarls. "…but the kids aren't learning anything like this."

"Uh oh," Gavin says as I think it.

"What?" Erizabesu asks, trying to focus on the melee in front of her.

"Obāsan's decided to get serious," I say…right before obāsan cuts one of Tsukino's clones in half, causing it to explode in flames. She kicks another, and its head goes flying before turning into a fireball and fading in mid-air. She then brings a knee up, into real Tsukino's stomach, causing him to gasp just before he's sent flying. She then blocks a punch thrown by sofu. She steps into him, dropping her flaming staff, and delivers an innumerable number of rabbit punches to sofu's body. He stumbles back as if responding to each blow in a delayed reaction.

"Gah," he spits right before he falls over backward. Obāsan stares at him for a moment, keeping her guard up before her eyes dart over to a very unconscious Tsukino.

From the corner of my eye, I see Gavin's hand go up. "Can we trade teachers?" he asks, staring at obāsan with admiration. I'm beyond admiring her, because she actually believes that one day I'll be as good, if not better, than she is.

#####

Chapter 13: Protection

Alana

"Clear!" Richard snaps, gun extended out in front of him.

"Hey, vamp-guy!" Kyra, the newest and least vampire-friendly member of my Nathan's pack, says. "Between all of our heightened senses, the princ- I mean, Alana's ability to feel emotions, and our Alpha's senses, if someone or something were trying to get us, we'd already know!"

"Kyra," Nathan says in less of a warning voice and more of a gentle reminder voice. "Remember, the vampires are our allies now, my wife's name is Alana, and you're a part of my pack now…call me, Nathan or Nate."

I internally cringe because I have never been fond of the shortened version of his name. Kya's response is much more outward, though that may be more because of my emotions, rather than her personal feelings on the matter.

"Also," he continues. "Given how wide reaching and clandestine our enemies are…you can never be too cautious."

"Sorry, my Alpha." Nathan glowers at her. "I mean…Nate. And I know," she says, sounding more relaxed, if only by degrees. "I mean, Ange and Tiff convinced me to go out with them…" She shrugs. "…and I won't lie…it was kinda like old times…complete with Tiff recently being dumped by a new boyfriend."

"The infamous 'Tiff,'" Nathan says with bit of a laugh. "Angela suggested setting me up with her…"

"SHE WHAT?" Kyra and I ask at the same time.

Nathan laughs all over again. "It was back when she was human and had a boyfriend all her own."

"Who turned out to be the vampire, who nearly killed her," Richard grumbles.

"This can't be the place," Kimiko complains walking in behind us. Mimiko examines the abandoned office space her sister is currently deriding.

Kimiko holds her katana's hilt with her right hand while giving her left arm a shake.

"How's your arm?" Richard asks, walking over to the two of them.

Mimiko tries to wave him off with bulging eyes behind her sister's back, but it's too late. "I'm fine," Kimiko grumbles, while rubbing her left forearm. "It healed and…" Mimiko cuts her off by gently tugging on her left sleeve. Kimiko sighs. "Still a little numb, but it's been getting better week to week."

"I'm glad," Richard says.

Kya moans and starts reaching for a random corner just past the counter that I can only assume served as a receptionist's desk at one point. "What is it, my Love?"

She continues reaching and adds a chant of "yah, yah, yah, yah," as if trying to answer my question. A tiny pyre erupts from the carpet just where Kya's focus remains. It spreads outward in two directions before both of those flames, spread in two directions, until there's a burned-out circle with several Japanese markings in the carpet there. A flame roars out of the circle, nearly reaching the ceiling and then returns to about ankle height instantly.

"WHAT?" a young girl says, rising from the flames. She looks around with large eyes, sending her long, brunette ponytail flying. She wears a katana at her side similar to the twins, but she has a leather jacket with a Union Jack on the back.

"I told you," the man wearing a long dark trench coat says, standing beside her. He has a firearm at his side, and I can smell several pieces of silver weaponry on him from here.

"Nathan," I start, gently tapping his arm while shifting Kya's full weight to one arm. "Should we...?"

He steps away, approaching the pair. The girl spots him, and her hand moves to her katana so fast I didn't even register the motion. The man with her extends his hand out in front of her.

"James," Nathan says.

"Nathan," 'James' replies.

"I didn't think the Order would be sending you as their representative." Vampire Hunters...of course, I keep to myself.

"Well, Marko is engaged elsewhere, and I wouldn't trust anyone else to come along with this one...," he says, tipping his head toward the girl. "By the way, this is my..." He clears his throat. "...other daughter, Amira." He half-turns to the girl. "Miri, this is Nathan Dumont...formerly Francois." She nods. "And I can only assume that that's the vampire princess..."

"Queen," Richard and Kimiko correct.

"I was speaking of that adorable bundle in her arms," James says, giving Kya a wave. She claps her hand and continues, making 'yah' noises in his direction.

"No, freakin' way," Amira says, never relinquishing her grip on her sword. "He smells like a wolf...and..." Her finger moves over to me. "...and she...smells like a vamp...and something..." She trembles. "...but the baby..."

"Allow me," Nathan says simply and makes introductions for the rest of us as well as giving a brief history of Kya's biological history.

"So, she really is...?" Amira asks and breaks off, while maintaining her distance.

James is not so standoffish. He makes his way over to us and offers Kya his finger. "You are just too cute," he says as she claims his extended digit. "Yes, you are...yes, you are."

"You're still such a softie, James," Nathan says with a shake of his head.

"Comes with fatherhood, Nate," he returns as he allows Kya to move his finger around. "I can already tell it's having an effect on you..." He gasps as Nathan growls. "...Nate?"

"Kimiko...Mimiko...don't," Nathan growls, and I feel it a moment later.

"Why not?" Kimiko rumbles. "They nearly cost me my arm." Mimiko nods along with her.

"Not them," I return. "They had nothing to do with the assault on the manor." The pair hedge forward as if preparing to attack. "Think about what the Eye of Ezekiel almost cost me. If I can separate them from the organization that they were a part of...so can you."

"We're not even a part of the Eye of Ezekiel anymore," James says. "My daughter and her mother are a part of the Order." He holds his hand over his heart. "I'm not even a part of either. I'm only here to support my friends, like Nate...and my daughters."

"Please stay your hand, vampires and hunters a like," a voice says.

"Yah, yah, yah, yah," Kya says, staring into open-air as her eyes flash silver. Her eyes dart to the left and then the right.

"The child can see us? How can she see us?"

"She can sense you," I clarify as my eyes change to silver. "And so can I...now."

A snap resonates and then two more, and three women appear before us. The one in the center wears red armor with golden accents and an intricate gold necklace around her neck. She holds a sword at her side with her left hand as she bows. "Nathan, Alpha of the A'Kani Tribe of Wolves."

"Stefana, Seventh Fairy of Devi," he returns with a nod.

"Midnight Queen...Midnight Princess," she follows. "Amira, sister of my adoptive sister, Jamina." She smirks and nods. "James."

"Stefana," he returns.

"Allow me to introduce my sisters, Titania, First Fairy of Devi," she says of the muscular redhead standing next to her. "And Selene, Eighty-second Fairy of Devi," she adds motioning to the dower looking raven-haired girl in all black next to her. Nathan introduces the others in-kind.

"Is this all of your number?" Selene asks, motioning to us.

"I believe so," I return while patting Kya's back.

"Hold," Stefana says, extending her hand out in front of Selene. "Will you keep a civil demeanor?" she asks the twins. "We will not present you to our Queen unless you promise to do so…"

"…furthermore, one hundred fairies will gladly strike you dead, if you don't," Titania suggests. Stefana nods a confirmation.

"Kimiko, Mimiko," I say and give Kya another gentle jostle.

Kimiko looks to her sister, who nods. "We'll keep it together," she says, coming back to us. "This is too important."

Stefana half-turns to Selene and gives one stern nod.

Selene returns the gesture and steps away from Stefana. She extends her right hand and begins moving her arm around in a circle as if wiping a window, only nothing is there…until slowly…there is something there. The world begins to ripple beneath each swipe of her arm as if pushing water around. Her arm starts to make larger swings, until a portal forms in open air.

"After you," Selene says, motioning to the portal.

Stefana pauses on the far side of the portal as Titania steps through. Nathan moves forward as James and Amira follow Titania. The twins move with me as Richard and Kyra bring up the rear.

On the other side of the portal, we seem to step into a forest…only not…the floor appears to be marble, but trees line the walls if those are actually walls…this space is…

"Disorienting," Richard says in my place.

"Yeah," Amira growls, falling into a crouch…hand on her katana.

"Miri?" James asks.

"I feel like I'm getting pinged from all sides, dad," she grumbles. "Like all five of my senses are being tapped at the same exact time. I even taste cinnamon at the tip of my tongue."

"She's not wrong," Nathan growls, clutching his forehead.

"Kya seems to have adapted," I admit, watching her face light up as she watches fireflies glow and then fade away. Her silver eyes move over everything all at once, but somehow picking out tiny details, very much like her father does.

"Apologies," a voice like a song says. At the top of a small set of stairs, proving that this is more indoors than out, is an ebon-haired beauty wearing a shimmery blue dress that seems to glow softly. "The realm of faeries can be often…mystifying to non-fae."

"Queen Twelana," Stefana pants as she, Selene, and Titania drop to one knee.

"Rise, sister," Twelana says.

"I know you," Nathan says, stepping forward.

"You should Alpha Nathan…James Baggett."

"You know me?" James asks.

"She was in Chicago," Nathan clarifies. "…back then."

"Oh," James says in a somber voice.

"Sister Amira."

"So, you're Twee," Amira says. "My sister talks about you almost as much as she talks about Quincy and Alex."

"I feel honored to be in such beloved company," she says.

"Aaaahhhh-ah-aaaaaaaahhhh," a small child says, toddling over to Twee. She huffs a laugh and collects the cherub-cheeked angel.

"Your son?" I ask.

"My husband," she returns. My jaw drops along with most of our party. "When he comes of age," she adds, staring at him as he stares at her…as if no one else is in the room.

"No child should have the level of focus that that one has," Kyra gasps.

"This is Tibal…he is the 108th fairy and only biological child of Devi…the previous Fairy Queen." She looks to me. "In the years to come, he will be a great ally to the next Alpha of the A'Kani tribe…or Midnight Princess…whichever route she takes."

"You know?" I ask.

"My adoptive sister keeps me well informed." She heaves a heavy sigh. "I would love to offer protection for your daughter…but I cannot…not the protection you hope for at least."

"But, your majesty," I begin. She lifts her free hand to me.

"I would love to protect your daughter…truly, but I cannot risk the safety of Tibal, for the protection of another."

"Now isn't this interesting," a voice says. Titania and Stefana draw their swords at the same time that Twelana wraps her arms around Tibal and takes a step back. A snap echoes, and a woman wearing a brown dress appears out of nowhere.

"Arielle!" Twelana snarls. "You have a lot of nerve coming here!"

"I have nerve, little sister?" she barks in return. "I'd been serving that old crone for more than three centuries before you were even born, and she chose YOU over ME?"

"And I served Devi since my mother, Sharon, fell following Eden…," Titania declares. She steps forward, and mist flows away from her sword. "…just as you will, traitor!"

"I didn't come to fight."

"Sounds like you came to die," Nathan growls. He bolts forward with impossible speed. He and Amira, with her katana drawn, cross as another snap reverberates. The woman vanished somewhere between their attacks meant to gut her and decapitate her respectively.

"I actually came to give you one more chance," Arielle says with her voice seeming to come at us from all sides. "Abdicate your throne. Name me your successor. Join En Quosque, and you may be granted some degree of safety."

Twelana bows her head a bit, and her frost blue eyes glow like the moon reflected on the surface of the ocean. She lifts her head swiftly, and a sharp whistle cuts through the air.

"AGH!" Arielle snarls as she falls out of nothing. She lifts her head and a trickle of blood moves over her shoulder. She glowers at Twelana. "You'll pay for that bitch!" She pulls a leaf from her hip and slams it on the ground! A burst of fire rises around her…surrounding her…encompassing her. It subsides and…in her place…there's a large monster that looks like…

"A troll?" Twelana says, covering Tibal's head, taking another step back.

"Three trolls," Nathan says as two more rise from the fading flames. "Kimiko, Kyra, protect Alana! Stefana, Selene, get the Fairy Queen and Tibal out of here! Titania, James, the troll on my far left! Amira, Richard, the one on my far right! Mimiko, with me…we're taking the one in the middle!"

"It's a good plan," Twelana says. "Follow him!"

"Agreed," James adds, pulling a gun from his hip.

"Come on," Kyra says, pulling gently on my shoulders.

Before Kimiko can even get into position to cover us, Amira has already removed the right hand of the troll she was assigned as Richard puts two bullets into its chest. Titania stabs her troll in the leg as James shoots out one of its eyes. Mimiko slices into the leg of her troll as Nathan tears into its back, making his way to its head.

Amira slices into her troll's throat as Titania stabs out their troll's other eye…and possibly into its brain. Nathan buries his claws into his troll's chin with his left hand as his right hand tugs on the top of his head. He pulls with both hands. A loud crunch fills the space and then his troll falls with a thud…followed by Amira and Richard's…and then by Titania and James's.

"Is everyone alright?" I call and get a chorus of yeses.

"This can work," Twelana says, stepping forward. "We can work together. I cannot give you twenty-four-hour protection, but I will give you what assistance I can…and when the time comes to strike at En Quosque…we will be ready!"

"AAAAAAAAAAAAAAAAAHHHHHHHHH!" Tibal calls out, raising his tiny fist at the same time that Kya says, "Yah, yah, yaaaaaaaaahhhhhh!"

"Well said," Richard says, peering from Kya to Tibal and back.

#####

Chapter 14: Council

Jamie

The pyre dies out around us, and we look around. I can't believe Gwen was able to show me how to create fire gaps. "This is London?" Quincy says over my shoulder, taking in what we're all taking in. A lot of fog and a dreary, ash gray sky over head. The air is so saturated with moisture and the scent of fresh rain that it might as well be pouring.

"Yeah," Tony groans, putting his arm around Shay. She bundles up tighter after a shiver. I shiver too, but it has nothing to do with the chill in the air.

I look at Quincy. "Sorry," I mouth.

"Don't worry about it," he murmurs and gives me a kiss on the cheek.

"Where should we get started?" Vance says, walking over to us with that stupidly gorgeous, dark-haired wolf, who came to Rais's funeral with Nathan and who Angela's apparently just started dating…much to Amira's chagrin (yeah, I'm using chagrin), close on his heels.

"If I remember right," Tony says. "The witches council or global coven is right around the corner."

"Okay," I say, taking in Tony and Shay…who if I didn't still have a twinge of feelings for Tony, I'd swear were the cutest couple ever besides Quincy and me, of course. Stephen sans Meghan steps up beside them. Okay, second cutest couple. Ugh…forgot about Alex and Gwen…definitely third cutest…but it's close.

"Can we go?" Tracy says. "Before this stupid humidity makes my hair all frizzy?"

"Mine too!" Natavius says, drawing a nod out of Tracy.

"Same," Stephen jokes, running his hand over his low Caesar.

Vance Purdue, the wolves' resident cleric in the video game/RPG kind of way, stifles a laugh. Tracy doesn't even bother stifling. She lets out a big belly laugh.

We make our way around the block stepping out onto the street. The building's surrounded by a large, gray stone wall. I've only ever seen pictures of this place, never visited. Even if mom had ever taken me anywhere except vacations in Florida and Georgia, she might've brought me here…if she didn't hate the Witches' Council and everything they stand for. Well, not everything, but definitely the controlling, conniving, power-hungry parts.

We approach a break in the wall, covered by a metal gate. It opens to a drive that takes you up to the front of a large building that looks like a castle, you know if God put his hand on top of the castle and kept pushing down until it was about the size of a huge mansion.

Quincy presses the button on the little, metal call box on the right.

"Allo," a voice comes through.

"Yes, umm…Jamina Baggett, Witch of Light from America…"

"The States," Tony corrects.

"…here to address the Witches' Council," Quincy finishes.

"Comb in," the voice replies. A buzz rings out, and the gates swing in.

We make our way up to the front of the building, being stared at by an inordinately large number of young Witches of Light…all practicing around the yard…creating tiny fireballs…orbs of water…swirling some leaves around. They all wear navy blue school uniforms, the girls in pleated skirts, and the boys wear slacks with sharp creases.

"Wolves," one of the girls tries to whisper to another. Damn, super hearing is something else.

"What are those two?" another girl asks a friend, trying not to stare at Quincy and Tony.

"Don't stare, dear," an older witch says, ushering some of the younger girls away from us.

"Awfully witchy out here," Quincy says.

"I've never seen so many witches in one place," I add, looking around.

"You're glowing!" a little girl says, running up to me. She's an adorably chubby cheeked little girl with medium brown skin and two black pigtails on either side of her face in her little navy-blue jumper…and not the British 'jumper.'

"Am I?" I ask, giving myself a once over. She nods staring up at me, a mix of awe and curiosity in her eyes.

"So bright," another girl, about the same age, adds walking over to me.

"Nora, Elizabeth," an older woman says, hurrying over to us. "Come along girls. Please don't bother the young woman. Oh, my," she breathes finally looking at me. "They're right. It's like staring at the sun."

"Hey, that's my line," Quincy says, putting an arm around me. I laugh.

"Well, Nora, Elizabeth," I say, leaning over with my hands on my knees to bring my vantage point closer to theirs. "My name is Jamina…and it was really nice to meet you."

"Oh," Nora purrs, putting an arm around Elizabeth and pulling her closer to the woman. "Her nek'ace," she says, staring at my Crescent Moon Pendant and its Philosopher Stone core. "Pain…it hurts…"

"I'm sorry, sweetie," I say, tucking it into my shirt. She moves back over to the woman and pulls Elizabeth along with her.

I sigh, and Quincy rubs my shoulders. "Let's go," I say as we walk toward the front door. Two young women…and by young, I mean in their twenties, stand on either side of a pair of thick mahogany doors.

"Jamina Baggett," I start.

"We know who you are," the one on the right says, giving me a little bit of attitude. Her eyes scan the group with me. "We can't let all of them inside."

"Maybe, half?" the other woman says.

I look over my shoulder. "I'll wait outside," Tracy says.

"Where've you been?" I ask, forgetting that she even came along with us.

"Perimeter sweep," she says as if I should've known that. She looks around and then points her thumb at Natavius. "He came with me! He's REALLY fast!" I nod. She lowers her hand as her mood drops. "I wanna do another one. Something's not sitting right with me here."

"I'll join you," Tony says.

"Same," Shay adds.

Vance tips his head to Natavius. "Fine," he groans with a shrug and appears standing with Tony, Shay, and Tracy as if he'd always been there.

"Alright," the first girl says, pushing the door open. "That'll do." I nod and step inside with Quincy, Vance, and Stephen with me.

The door closes behind us as we walk into a dimly lit vestibule…kind of like at the Blackshears' estate. It's wood-paneling everywhere, floor, walls, and ceiling with its iron chandelier with candle-like bulbs above us.

Beyond the entryway, there are two square pillars, one on the left, one on the right, with a matching pair on the other side. The four of them frame this open larger room. Just beyond the pillars are two other women wearing long black dresses like Pilgrims, one on each side of us, blocking off the two hallways behind them. As if performing a choreographed dance, they both motion for us to keep moving forward. We do, moving through all the varying woodwork into a hallway with a bit more light.

"Okay," Quincy says, leaning over my shoulder. "….is anyone else getting creepy vibes?"

"I'm glad it's not just me," Stephen says, sticking close to Vance.

"Every single one of them seems tense is what it is," Vance says, looking around. "With the possible exception of the children outside, everyone here is on edge, nervous…afraid…" He cups his chin…I didn't think people actually did that in real life. "…but for the life of me, I can't discern why they're on edge."

"So," I start. "…it's not because they're being visited by a vampire hunter, a powerful Witch of Light, two question marks like the Blackshear Brothers…"

"Hey," Quincy whines.

"No offense, babe. …a being descended from a fae bloodline, a relatively unknown human, and two wolves?"

"No," Vance returns, making the word seem like a period. Not a word, just a period. "That tension is a little different than this. It's there, sure, but it's not as prevalent as whatever it is boiling beneath the surface."

"I definitely see why Nate sent you with us on this excursion," I say. "Thank you."

"No," he returns, bowing a little as we walk. "...thank you for everything you've done for not only my clan, but for my pack and my Alpha." I wave him off, and he smiles.

At the end of this funhouse hallway, with its cream-colored walls above the continued wood paneling starting at the midway point to the floor. We reach a pair of mahogany double doors. "Here goes nothing," I say, as I raise my hand to knock, trying to ignore the almost overpowering scent of wood oil.

Before I even connect, the door swings in, and we enter... into one of the most clichéd scenes I have ever seen. There's a bright white light shining down from the ceiling in the center of the room. Across from the door, there's a dais with six women sitting behind it. On the dais above them, there are nine women seated, and in the center, sits Anna Grace...current reigning Witch of Light and leader of the Witches' Guidance Council.

Not only do I recognize her from her pictures, the visual of her coming to visit me and mom when I was five is burned into my mind. She wasn't the leader of the council then...Siobhan Higginbotham was calling the shots then, and she was one of her two attendants...attendants, more like future Council Heads in training. She was so smug then, all of them were in fact and that was without the awkward lighting effect.

Anna tosses her long dark brown hair, and those dark brown eyes seem so dark that I could fall into them. A couple of the younger girls on the first row make googly eyes at Quincy. I steal a glance over my shoulder, and he has that weirded out left eyebrow raised.

Anna scoffs, prompting me to scowl. She raises an offering hand, held out to me. "Reigning McCabe Witch of...," she begins.

"Baggett Witch," I, Quincy, and Stephen amend.

She covers her mouth with her fist and faux clears her throat. The women on the front dais all peer at her over their shoulders. The women on the seating level with her look to her. She emits a groan before taking her fist away from her mouth. "...Baggett Witch of Light," she corrects. "To what do we owe the honor of this visit?"

"I believe you know why we're here...now," I reply. "I was told you received intelligence from the information broker, Duchess, that En Quosque, a clandestine organization, is determined to bring their fallen leader, Eden, back to life, and that that being threatens all of reality. "

A snicker comes from most of the room. "An overestimation of the situation," Anna dismisses.

"A what?" Stephen snaps.

"Stephen," Vance whispers, pulling him back a step.

"You doubt her information…even knowing what's been going on in and around Edenton, my hometown," I say. "A hometown that my family…" I aim my right thumb at Quincy. "…and my boyfriend and his brother have been defending for the last two hundred years, getting ready for this very occurrence. You have to hel-"

"HAVE TO?" Anna snarls. She bolts out of her seat with both hands on the dais. She points down at me. "You McCabe Witches…," she starts, making my mom's family name sound like a curse.

"Baggett Witch!" I snap. The right hand of every witch on the first row comes up, aimed at me with their palms facing me. Quincy tries to step forward, and I stop him. "Don't make it worse…" He looks at me and nods. "…and that goes double for you, Stephen," I say, looking over my shoulder at him, being held back by Vance.

"Let me at 'em!" Stephen snarls, kicking at them.

"Your request is denied," Anna says, returning to her seat. "Go back to the States and find someone else to sell your nonsense to-"

Before she finishes, a sharp whistle cuts through the air. It hits with so much force that it feels like it shakes the entire room and even rattles in our bones. The chandelier-style light beaming down on us jangles and sways slightly.

"What was that?" one of the younger witches asks.

"Shay?" I say to Quincy. He nods. "Go! We'll catch up!" He vanishes.

"Stay put!" Vance says pointing at Stephen. "I mean it. My granddaughter would be very upset if I let something happen to you…especially since you're so very breakable, being a non-magical human!"

"No argument there," he returns.

"No, Vance…you should stay and protect the Council and Stephen, just in case," I say. He ponders for a moment before giving one solemn nod.

I follow Quincy out the door. He's already moved away from the front door by the time I reach it. "The wall!" he snaps, pointing to my left. I turn and follow him.

"Children, hurry…hurry!" one of the older witches says, ushering the children away from the destroyed part of the wall with a lot of smoke rising from the wreckage.

"Aaaaahhhhh," a kid yells from…I don't know because all I see are a couple of downed trees and rubble from and broken parts of the former outer wall.

"Keep going," Quincy says. "I'll find the girl." He darts off in the direction that we heard the yell.

"Does anybody need any help?" I ask, taking in the huge hole in the fence…well…I guess it's not a hole since the top part of the wall is gone…hell, you could practically drive a bus through that gap!

"Jamie!" Natavius says, appearing next to me. He has a silver straight blade in his left hand and grabs mine with his right. He pulls me closer and then moves his hand to the base of my neck just below my skull. "Brace yourself…"

"Wha-?" I start while doing what he asked. He bolts forward before I can finish, and we're on the other side of the wall and… "OH MY GOD!!! SHAY?!?!" I kneel next to Tony, kneeling over her…cradling her bleeding head…there's so much blood! "What happened?"

"She saved my life," Tracy says, clutching her dangling left arm with blood moving away from her forehead and left eye too.

"That fairy was here," Tony rumbles. "The one who was hiding in the study at the manor." I've never seen him so tense before…then again, considering…

"I couldn't cut her," Tracy says. "She was too small. Shay hit her with a sharp note…and right when she was about to blow her away…," she breaks off in a shiver and motions out from her.

"She said she was planning to save the spell she used for the New Fairy Queen," Tony snarls.

"We'll figure out what crazy-pants' plans are later," I say, extending both hands to Shay. "After we heal her up…"

Natavius's mouth falls open. "Jamie, she…"

"LET HER TRY!" Tracy barks.

"Tetigerat Deus Creator omnium," I begin. "Angeli lacrymas fudit, ipsi largiri nobis. Corde. Anima. Spiritus. Corpus. Mentis. Omnes, sicut unum. Vive!" I feel the magic leave my core…travel down my arms…and…it doesn't connect to anything. "It…it didn't work?"

Tony trembles and holds Shay closer.

"No!" I snap. "I'm gonna try again!" I wrap my left hand around the Crescent Moon Pendant and Philosopher's Stone. I hold my right hand out to Shay again. "Tetigerat Deus…" Tracy puts her hand on top of mine. "Trace, what are you…?"

"Her heart stopped as soon as she got hit with that spell, Jamie," Tracy says, trying to keep her voice even. "I wanted to see if there was still time… if you could bring her back, but…"

"No," I weep and tremble. "Tony, I'm sorry…I'm so sorry…I should've…" Before I can finish, Tony roars, clutching Shay's head against his chest.

Tracy wraps her arms around me as Natavius falls to his knees.

"Damn it," Stephen snaps, standing just behind us.

"I'm gonna kill them," Tony snarls. "I'm gonna kill them all…I swear it! I swear, my little songbird," he whispers to Shay.

#####

Chapter 15: Allegiance

"Why?" Kai complains as Sora takes a swipe at me. I lean back and watch her claws go sailing over my head. I dart back, hopping away from her to get some separation. She uses Hunter's Step and appears behind me. She's still better at control than I am... She swings at me again. ...but lucky for me, I fought our cousin, Nathan, who's stronger and faster than all three of us together. I catch her wrist, and her other hand comes at me right behind it. I block that wrist.

"Good," she growls. "I still can't get over how much stronger you've gotten, Alex."

"Thanks," I rumble back, because the beast is telling me to go on the attack, while the human in me sees three different places I can attack her. I'll have to thank Nate again the next time I see him. "I know you held back, because you didn't wanna scratch me...mess up my clothes...get blood all over this nice marble floor."

"True," she says as her black on white fur recedes into her tan skin. Her long hair turns back blond. "I'm feeling a little antsy though, so thanks for sparring with me." She groans and clutches her stomach.

"You okay?" I ask.

"Nervous stomach, I guess," she says, rubbing her forehead next. "I think the weight of everything is starting to hit me."

"Like what?" I ask sarcastically.

"End of the world?" Kai joins in.

"Fighting intense, insane bad guys?"

"Meeting with people who nearly killed me like a few months ago?" Kai says with a shrug.

"Taking over the leadership of our entire clan?"

"Yes," she returns, lowering her hand.

Kai and I look at each other and turn back to her instantly. "You got this!" we say at the same time with four big thumbs up.

Sora smiles and then starts laughing. "Thanks," she says, walking over to us. She puts her arms around each of us and even I feel Kai go rigid in her arm. "I don't think I could do this without you two knuckleheads backing me." I put my arm around her, and Kai does the same. She separates from us a little. "And if you tell anyone I said that, I'll call you both liars to your faces."

"That's the sister I know and...have been verbally and physically abused by growing up." She lets us go and then punches Kai on the shoulder. "Ow! Exactly," he says, rubbing his shoulder. "That's more like it!"

"Sorry, t'e keep ya waitin'," the stupidly gorgeous redhead Chief Magistrate says with her just as gorgeous blond-haired sire-daughter beside her. "But t'e ot'ers've only just arrived."

"Thank you, Chief Magistrate," Sora says with a bow. "But you didn't have to come and tell us yourself."

"One leader ta anot'er," Raven replies, hand over her heart and then hand out to Sora. "...it only stands ta reason." She turns. "T'is way." We follow her and...starts with an M...Maggie to the elevator. We step inside and head up. We step off and follow them through the winding hallways until we reach a meeting room with two guys in full police riot gear on either side. They pull the doors open for us. "T'ank ya," Raven says and steps inside.

"Alex?" Mitchell says on the far end of the table with another muscular black guy standing next to him.

"Mitchell," I reply, hurrying around the table to meet him. I give him a handshake, and he pulls me in for a one-armed hug with it. "What are you doing here, man?"

"I'm reppin' team Jamie while she's in England with Shay and Tony talking to the Witches' Council." I nod. "Oh, let me introduce you to my new best friend..."

"We are not friends," the guy who smells a little like Nate complains. "...we're allies at best." He turns to me and offers his hand. "Hello, Alex...Sora and Kai...I'm your cousin's cousin on his father's side, Christopher Dumont."

"You're the one who took care of him?" Kai asks.

"Yeah, next to his brother...I mean, his dad...you're the person he respects most."

"Ahem," he says, straightening his tie. "Thank you for that." A bit of blush fills his cheeks as he looks away.

"Alexander, Sora, and Kai?" Dr. Taylor says, walking in with two super dangerous looking women. The tan woman with the long ponytail wears a long trench coat with several visible weapons. The other woman...a black woman with a muscular build has more of a relaxed outfit but doesn't appear to be any less deadly.

"Dr. Taylor...I..."

He lifts a halting hand to us. "I knew there would be a delegation from the Wernier Clan here, but I wasn't sure it'd be the three of you." He motions to his left first. "...this is Sera 'Marko' Markovich, Head of Training for the Order..."

"And Amira's mom," I add.

"You know my daughter?"

I nod. "I'm Jamie's best friend, Alex."

"Right," Dr. Taylor continues and then motions to his right. "...and Jessica 'Jess' Beales, former member of the Order."

"Former?" Sora asks.

"Retired," Jess says with a confident bob of her head.

"I wasn't aware people retired from the Order," Christopher says with a deep scowl.

"They made an exception." Christopher emits a positive noise with an impressed expression.

"Are ya aut'orized ta negotiate on behalf of t'e Order?"

"I've been authorized to negotiate and come to an agreement within certain parameters," Taylor returns.

"Oh, go back to your books, librarian!" Marko grumbles while shoving him aside. "We are willing to join this alliance of vampire, wolves, and whatever else...as long as certain considerations are made for my daughter, who is the future of the Order as well as having any defectors from the Ezekielites turned over to us."

"That's a fairly big ask," Christopher states taking a step back. "...and risk."

"Especially when we're talking about people who are trying to kill us," Sora adds.

"People who have killed members of my coven," Raven adds in a stern tone and with a British accent now.

"Most of the Chief Magistrate's coven," Christopher emphasizes. Raven gives him a conciliatory nod. I wish Gwen was here to confirm I used that one right.

"We realize that there has been fault..."

"Fault?" Christopher barks. "You've been used...bred and led about by the nose in fact..."

"Good one," Raven says.

"Thank you. ...to be the personal army of En Quosque. Half of your number are still under their control, and you want to cite fault."

"I..."

"He's got ya there," Jess says, drawing a huff from Marko and a smirk from Taylor.

"This is why I am here," Christopher says. "I have been negotiating business deals for more than a hundred years...and I know a bad deal when I see one, and what I see with what you're proposing is a bad deal."

"I don't see how..."

"If we submit to your request, you stand to gain because your former co-fellows are much less likely to hurt the lot of you, whereas they will kill any of us that En Quosque deems as enemies. To put it bluntly, we'll be slaughtered trying to save your people."

"Damn," Sera groans.

"I told you that they wouldn't go for it, Marko," Taylor says.

"We've got two goals from what I understand," I say, surprising even me. "We have to protect Nate and Alana's daughter…because she's who they've picked to be Eden's new vessel."

"And because she's a baby," Kai jokes. "Apparently, they can't defend themselves." He shrugs. Sora whacks him across the arm.

"And to stop them from carrying out this crazy ass ritual."

"From what Tony told us," Mitchell jumps in. "They can resurrect Eden without the baby…they'd just prefer to use her."

"And if they carry out their goal," Raven says with her hands on her hips. "Things won't be good for any of us…not you, humans…not us vampires, wolves, or any other supernatural beings."

"This isn't the time to negotiate, is what I think they're trying to say," Jess says. "Look…I want out of this fight for good. I do. But even I recognize that this isn't just their fight. It's all our fight. Campbell was willing to kill me rather than have me go back to 'the Order,' when it turns out he was worried about how the split shook the Ezekielites' faith."

"The assault on the Chief Magistrate's manor cost us…," Marko complains. She goes over to the table and takes a seat. We stare at her for a moment before Sora takes the seat opposite her. The rest of us follow suit, sitting around the table with her. Marko heaves a heavy, gut-wrenching sigh. Her eyes dart around the table. "…this does not leave this room. Swear to me…every single one of you."

"I swear," I snap. The room does too.

She nods and pinches the bridge of her nose. "Campbell took your departure as a sign, Jessica," Marko says. "I…assumed that the lack of empathy toward your mother's passing was the reason, but he and…Samuels refused to believe it."

"Alpha?" Taylor says.

"Alpha?" Mitchell asks, leaning forward.

"Our leader…," Marko says. "…my daughter was ranked number one of the field agents, but even above them were the Calls…at the top of the chain."

"The Call of Ezekiel," Jess says. "They've gone by a lot of different names…my mom said they went through a name change during her time…went from using Latin names to call signs." She huffs a laugh. "She said they felt like it fits since they were the Call."

"Were being the emphasis," Marko mutters. She lifts her eyes. "Alpha, being the most devout follower of Ezekiel…killed the other Calls one by one if they raised a question. Anything that was seen as disobedience, was a death sentence."

"What the f-?" Jess trails off.

"He decimated our leadership," Marko says, playing with her fingers. She shivers. "He demanded absolute obedience…made those that remained swear an oath of allegiance to him and by extension En Quosque. If we don't get those numbers back…if this goes sideways…Ezekielites or Order…we're finished." Her eyes meet Christopher's with a glisten of tears. "I have lost so many people that I considered friends…if my daughter wasn't as good as she is and if James wasn't with his other daughter, I would be terrified for them every single minute of every single day. I am begging you to help me save humanity's shield…" She shakes her head. "…no, help me save what I've devoted most of my life to…one of the few things I believe in."

"Now we're being honest," Christopher says, clasping his hands. He glances at Raven. "And I didn't even need Vance's training to see that."

Raven smirks and nods.

"Wolves were asked to be the protectors of men," Christopher says. "…from vampires. I'm sure I speak for our Alpha when I say, we'll try to save as many of your people as we can."

"Agreed," Raven adds. "Even if we're usually on the threat side of humanity."

"We're half human," Sora says. "We'll try as well." I nod, and Kai does too.

"Besides you guys, I'm probably the most human person in the room," Mitchell bellows. "You know I'm down."

"Thank you…all of you, thank you," Marko says.

A buzz moves through the room. Then another and another. My phone starts to vibrate in my pocket too.

"Alex?" Sora asks as I pull it out.

"WHAT?" Mitchell snaps with his phone up to his ear. "You're lyin'…you-you're lyin'…" He falls back into his chair and begins to weep. "…you're lyin'…"

"Hello?" I ask…I think with my phone up to my ear.

"Alex," Jamie cries through the phone.

"Jamie…? Are you…?"

"Shay's dead," she sobs before I can even ask how she's doing.

"I understand," Christopher says with a clenched jaw. "We'll make arrangements…" He sighs. "…does she have any…"

"Yeah," Mitchell groans. He stands and wipes his eyes. "…me. I'm her family." He stalks around the table, heading toward the door. "You get her back here. Do you hear me?" he demands whoever he's talking to just before he steps out.

"Alex?" Jamie asks.

"Yeah…yeah, sorry…just…" I scoff. "…I'm worried about Gwen…and you and…"

"I know," she returns. "I was always thinking that we'd all make it through this and look back on this and…and now, Shay's…she helped me get ready for Prom, and Quincy and Tony's… Oh my God…Tony…he rushed off and…"

"Go find him, Jamie. We'll get back to Edenton and…" I sigh. "…we're going to get through this Jamie. We're going to save the world, and we're going to make them pay for what they've done…for Shay."

"Hello?" Raven says, answering her phone. "You were what? By whom?"

"Raven?" Christopher says, stepping closer to her.

"Nathan and Alana were attacked during their meeting…they are fine, but…" She puts the phone closer to her ear. "…you have to get back here…something's happened. We've lost…someone."

#####

Chapter 16: Powers

Angela

"I am so glad that this is all happening along the East Coast," Meghan says, as we make our way up the stoop leading to mom's apartment building. "Because if I were traveling across multiple time zones, fire gaps, or airplanes, I'd be so jetlagged and ready to physically fight you right now."

I take out my keys, preparing to unlock the heavy metal door. "You are still such a priss," I say back to her as I put the key in the lock.

"Did you not hear the part about physically fighting you and…why, thank you," she says, holding her hand over her heart, like a proper southern belle. I laugh, because she absolutely did not take that as the insult that I thought she might. Honestly, I'm pretty sure she knew exactly how I meant it and decided to take it as a compliment.

I open the door, and we walk inside. "Trust me," I start again, as we make our way upstairs. "You get used to it. Sadly." She heaves a heavy sigh as we reach mom's door. She goes to knock as I put my key into the lock.

"Do you still have a key for your mom's place?" she asks with both of her perfect eyebrows arching toward the center of her perfect little forehead. "Even though, you don't live here?"

"Well, according to moms, both bio and sire, apparently, my home is wherever they are."

The door swings in on its own, and mom is standing in the doorway. "And don't you forget it," she adds to my last statement as she puts one arm around me.

I put both around her. "Hey mom." She pats my back and then breaks the hug.

"Hey Aunt Maria," Meghan says just before she hugs her and gives her a kiss on the cheek.

"So good to see you, Meghan," mom returns. "It's been far too long." She steps back and opens her arm. "Let me get a look at you," she adds as Meghan does a magazine cover or runway twirl, sending her tiny dress and her gorgeous blonde hair flying only to have both come back and settle into place as if they never moved. I roll my eyes, even though I tried not to. My mind instantly goes back to all the instances where my mother and uncle tried to bring our families together, only for Meghan to be the center of attention no matter what.

"Honey," mom says, caressing my cheek. "Don't do that. You know enough about this stuff to know that your cousin has a glamour around her that makes people react this way to her." She shakes her head. "It's bad enough that I have to focus not to pay more attention to her." She half-turns to Meghan. "No offense."

"None taken. In fact, I've been trying to figure out ways to rein it in." She leans closer to me. "After a pretty bad break up with my boyfriend, who it turns out is resistant to my glamour, thank God, I've been trying to figure out how to make it not affect people so much."

"So, I wasn't just being paranoid when we were kids...? People really were paying more attention to her than me, even on my birthday?"

"Sorry, sweetie." Mom shakes her head. "It wasn't just you. And your uncle and I knew about it. We just didn't know what to do about it. We put up our defenses as best we could, but we couldn't shield everybody."

"Sorry," Meghan says putting an arm around me. "I only found out last year, thanks to some friends down in Edenton."

"I have friends down in Edenton," I admit. Meghan nods.

"Okay," mom says, clapping her hands together. "On to less depressing things... I asked the two of you to join me here, because I wanted to teach you some of the things that our family knows. Basically, I'm going to officially induct you into the Powers Family of witches." Mom turns and goes over to the coffee table where there is a folded leather jacket sitting on top. Wait, that's not a jacket. It's a book, a really thick, old, leather-bound book. She sits down on the couch and then pats the spots next to her. I sit on her right, and Meghan sits on her left.

She cracks the book open, and I nearly gag from the mildew, and God only knows what other smells come off it. "Sorry," mom says. "I keep forgetting that you're a vampire so you can smell everything way better than we can."

"Oh, no worries," Meghan says, holding her right index finger under her nose. "I smell it just fine with my normal human-ish nose."

"Show some respect, both of you," mom says glaring at me, then at Meghan. "This is a Powers grimoire...this book has been in our family..." She pauses to look at me again. "...since we first came to the States."

She bobs her head unevenly. "At least, that's how my grandma put it." She flips to the sixth page from the front. There's a drawing of a five-sided star on this page with Latin words written at each point, Latin words between each of the furthest points, running along each of the lines constructing the star, and along each of the interior lines, as well as a large word in the center.

"Now," she says, pressing her hand against the star. "Meghan, if anything, you're probably like your father and are a water sign, meaning that you're probably strongest with water magic and healing spells."

"Yeah," Meghan says with a nod. "A healing spell was the first spell I ever used." She looks at me. "Mrs. Turnipseed showed me how to heal Stephen. She said we probably saved his life."

"Marissa Turnipseed?"

"Yeah, she's the former mayor of Edenton's vampire wife…" She makes a sad face. "…or widow."

I nod. "She's also my niece…" My eyes dart to mom. "…sire."

"Huh?" Meghan emits. She leans forward to get a better look at the grimoire. "It's like it's all connected."

"That's what I said," I say, while taking up a similar posture to hers.

"Well, like I was saying," mom continues. "Meghan, you're a water affinity, and sweetie, because you can't generate your own fire, but you can control it, you're probably a fire affinity."

"You can use magic?" Meghan asks.

"Yeah," I return, while bobbing my head unevenly. "It was all a part of the daywalking ritual. I mean, I only had to fight a daemon, one-on-one in a deathmatch that nearly killed me. Then I had to drain his blood. Sure. But, end result, not only can I walk in the daylight, but I can use magic that self-replenishes just like any other magic users." I look at mom. "I recently used a lightning spell."

"You did?" I purse my lips and nod again. "Then that probably means that you're actually a lightning affinity…and that because you killed…" I flinch. "…survived," mom redirects. "…a deathmatch with a fire type daemon, you have a special connection to fire through his blood." Mom nibbles her bottom lip while humming.

"What?"

She turns to me and looks me in the eye. "Do this…," she says while lifting her right hand, palm facing the ceiling. "Fulgur!" she snaps, and tiny sparks of electricity dance across her palm. "Incendia," she murmurs as she brings her fingers together around the sparks with the tips aimed at the ceiling now. A tiny candle-sized flame appears at the top of her joined fingers that look like a beak. Her eyes come back to me. "Don't focus on creating a flame, so much as on using the electricity in the air to ignite it."

I nod and open my right hand. "Fulgur," I whisper, replicating what she did. I take a deep breath and hold it as if I could accidently blow out the fire if I can make it. I finally add, "Incendia!" while closing my fingers around the sparks, just like mom did. A tiny pale blue flame appears at the tips of my fingers. "Wow," I breathe, eyes darting from it to mom and back. "It doesn't even feel heavy, like it normally does."

"How can fire feel heavy?" Meghan asks. Mom tries to shush her with a finger in front of her mouth and takes it away as soon as she sees me watching her.

"What?" I ask.

"Nothing," she replies, going back to the book.

"Mom?"

Mom takes a deep breath. "He told me you've been struggling," she says, eyes still on the book.

"He? He who?"

"Natavius," she replies. "Who else?"

"Oh, who's Natavius?" Meghan asks. "Is he your boyfriend?"

"No. Yes. Shut up!" I come back to mom. "What did he tell you?"

She takes another deep breath. She leans into me. "I'm glad you agreed to go to therapy," she whispers. "How's that been going?"

I huff, because I'm a little mad at my brand-new boyfriend telling my business, but at the same exact time...I know he means well and that I should've told mom myself. "It helps to get some of it off my chest," I admit. "It helps even more knowing that because she's a witch, I can tell her everything."

"Oh, good, I was worried," mom says, slipping her hand between both of mine. She holds down my twitchy right index finger.

I lean until my head's resting on her shoulder. "Thanks, mom."

"Of course, baby." She lifts her head a little and reaches over to take Meghan's hand. "Powers witches have a long and storied history...we've suffered, we've lost, but we've endured." She tilts her head forward to see me before turning to see Meghan. "That is the legacy you'll both continue...as our newest water mage and fire mage." She gives us both a gentle shake. "That being said, I think we could all use some fresh air." Mom collects the book and heads for the door. We follow...in fact, we follow her all the way up to the roof.

She moves out toward the center of the roof access area with the book in her right hand and her left hand raised toward the sky. She moves her fingers as if daintily unscrewing the cap on a jar. "Operite nos in velamine mendacii," she says. My eyes move over to witch-vamp eyes, and we're surround by a pale blue dome.

"Is this a glamour spell?" Meghan asks.

"Yes," mom says. "You've encountered a glamour spell before?"

"Yeah," Meghan admits, with her right hand on her cheek. "Besides the natural one that covers me and mom, this super creepy guy who used to stalk me had one cast over his entire life." She gasps and then covers her mouth. "Don't tell Stephen I said that."

"Stephen?"

"Her boyfriend," mom says. "They stayed with me a few days just before you came back."

"Stayed with you! You wouldn't even let me have boys come over when you were here, but her boyfriend gets to stay here for a few days with her?" I complain.

Mom shrugs. "She's not my daughter."

"Whatever. And why can't we tell…Stephen?"

"Rich…used to be Stephen and Alex's best friend…before he went crazy and tried to kill all of us with this shadowy, sludgy familiar." She bows her head. "He used to just be this nerdy guy, who hung out with the emo kid, who's married to my best friend now, and the guy I had a crush on. Then one night…he came over to me when I was sitting with some 'friends,' and he told me how much he'd thought about me…and how long he'd had a crush on me…and that someday we'd be married. Then he asked me if I wanted to go out sometime." I can't help noticing that her entire mood sank and that she put air quotes around "friends."

"Then what happened?" I ask.

Meghan heaves a heavy sigh, and I don't know, it feels like the air inside this glamour got heavier. "He always gave me a bad vibe…and I was still so into Stephen, even back then. So, when he said those things, I told him…I-I called him a pathetic, skeevy loser and that he was a blip of a nothing." She lifts tear-filled eyes to me and for the second time since I've known her, Meghan's in real, actual pain. "And that he could disappear tomorrow, and no one would notice…" She swallows a lump. "…not even Stephen."

"Meghan," mom purrs. "No, you didn't."

She draws her lips into her mouth and nods. "Stephen never talks about it…but sometimes when he falls asleep on my shoulder, he calls out to him, trying to stop him. And sometimes, when he's not really thinking about anything in particular…I can tell he still thinks about him."

"Why? Where's Rich now?" I ask.

"Mrs. Turnipseed…Marisa killed him for using that shadow familiar to kill her husband."

"Oh," I groan.

"Maybe, Angela's not the only one who needs to talk to someone," mom says. She claims Meghan's hand. "Back in my day, my mom…your grandmother," she adds, eyes moving from Meghan to me. "…she used to tell us all the time that life and death always hung in the balance when it came to dealing with supernatural beings." She shakes her head. "Still never felt like it was as simple as she said. I mean, you'd have to be some kind of sociopath to deal with this much death and not have it affect you."

"So, how do you deal, auntie?"

Mom's head dips to the left a bit. "I try to focus on the important things…my daughter…my niece…how even though I've lost my husband and my brother…there are still so many people who still need me to keep moving forward."

"Because that's what Powers women do," I say with a confident smirk.

Meghan laughs while wiping her eyes. "Yeah, it is. Just like how we're gonna help Gwen and Jamie…"

"…and Alana and Nate," I add.

"…and Alana and Nate," she says with a slightly bowed head. "…save the world!"

"Damn right!" I shout, throwing my fist in the air.

"Language!" mom snaps.

"Sorry. Wait!" She erupts in laughter and wraps her arms around us both.

"Are you ladies ready to get this lesson started?"

"Lesson?" I ask.

"Or lessons?" Meghan continues.

"That one," mom says, pointing at Meghan. "Lesson number one, as a magic user, your reality is your belief…therefore, if you believe that a fireball has weight, because of the personal guilt you feel toward acquiring that power…" I slow nod and bow my head, because she's literally saying what Terry told me in our first session…after she stopped marveling at me being a magic-wielding, daywalking vampire. Jamie was right; I am badass.

"Are you even listening?" mom asks.

"What?"

"You missed all of lesson two," Meghan says. "I can tell by your blank expression." I poke out my tongue at her, and she does the same. We start laughing all over again.

#####

Chapter 17: Backup

Gwen

"So, you think the fight is coming here?" Stephen asks, looking across his four-seat wooden kitchen table at us. Alex sits on one side of him, and Tracy is on the other side. I've never been inside Stephen's house before, but we felt like this would be one of the safest places to meet.

"Like, we're sure it's gonna be a final boss fight here in Edenton?" he asks.

Tracy looks at me, and I nod. "If their aim is to resurrect Eden…then this is the place."

"So, what do we do? We can't just leave everyone here defenseless," Alex says with exasperation.

"We're gonna have our hands full trying to take these guys down," Tracy says.

"But what about our parents, Trace? They didn't sign up for this! They don't even know anything about this," Stephen says.

"And the Hamishes and the Taylors…," Alex trails off with an expression that looks like nausea.

"What do we tell them? I don't know that even Hugh Taylor knows everything that's going on," Tracy says.

We sit in silence for a moment trying to figure out how to tell adults about things they won't understand.

"We're just gonna have to be as honest as we can without revealing everything. I think people will listen to Dr. Taylor, and I think he's wise enough to determine what people can handle," Alex says.

Stephen nods in assent, and Tracy shrugs. "What do you think, Gwen?"

I nod after a moment. "I agree. Let's go to his office and see if he will help us."

"Okay," Tracy agrees and grabs her bag. "I'll drive."

The ride to his office is short, which is nice since the atmosphere in the car is anxious and tense.

We walk across Elizabeth City State University's campus to his office, and I timidly knock on the door. "It's not office hours, but come in. The door's unlocked," the voice inside calls.

I press the handle down and push the door in. Dr. Taylor's office here is very similar to his study at home, filled with books and charts but with a print of *Starry Night* on the wall here. He looks up as we enter and stands.

"Gwendolyn," he looks past me to the group outside the door, "…and Alex, Stephen, and Tracy. Come in, but you'll have to forgive me for not having enough chairs. To what do I owe the surprise?"

I scuff the toe of my shoe on the cracked checkered linoleum of his office. Despite the car ride, I still don't really know what to say.

"Dr. Taylor, we need your help with something," Tracy begins.

"I assumed that much," he says with a smile. He takes a seat behind his desk. "How can I help you?"

"Dr. Taylor...we think the people of Edenton are in danger," I say.

His face becomes serious, and he adjusts in his chair. "Shut the door, please, Alex," he says.

Alex obliges. "Now, I know you're not one to be over-dramatic, Gwen," he says once the door is closed. "I'm sure this has something to do with En Quosque looking for the pieces of a spell."

We all nod, Alex elbowing me in an "I told you so" kind of way.

"So, what can I help you with other than speculation of what will happen?" he asks.

"We have reason to believe they will perform the spell here, well...in Edenton," Tracy says.

Dr. Taylor's eyebrows peak with interest. "How sure are you of this, Gwen?"

"Sure enough that Jamie Baggett and the Blackshear Brothers have come up with a contingency plan involving finding twenty-five-hundred-year-old blood," I say. "Sure enough to come and tell you all about it."

"So, I can guess what their plan is...considering, but what is your plan?" he asks.

"Well obviously we're going to fight," I say with more certainty than I feel. Alex and Tracy nod. "But we were hoping you could help us come up with a plan to evacuate the normal people...the people without supernatural powers."

"We can handle this, and we really don't want to have to evacuate everyone," Tracy says. "But even if Jamie's plan works, they WILL kill any non-supernaturals still."

Dr. Taylor sits back in his chair and puts his fingertips together. "Do any of the other human members of the town even have a hint of what's going on?" he asks.

I look at Alex, who shrugs, and then Tracy. "I don't think so," she says. "At least, I don't think anyone knows the full story."

"I think some of them might know about one or two supernatural residents," I say, thinking about the Hamishes and their friendship with Marissa Turnipseed, Emily at Jelly Bean Coffee, and Mrs. Pritchard, who has apparently known about supernaturals since the days of Jamie's grandmother. "But I doubt anyone, other than you, knows about En Quosque."

Dr. Taylor nods. "Okay. Let me make a few calls, and we will see who shows up at the square tonight for a town meeting.

~~~~~

Tracy pulls up to the town square, where Dr. Taylor has invited everyone, including the mayor. I see Tracy and Stephen's parents, Mrs. Taylor, The Hamishes, Emily, and Jennifer. I even see a few of our teachers, including Mrs. Pritchard.

My thoughts drift back to the night at Jelly Bean, when I found out that Emily knew about the supernatural world. Emily told me her account after it happened. Emily and I were cleaning up after closing for the night. Emily went to the back to get another microfiber towel to wipe down the shiny surfaces. She came back out but heard something coming from the back. She thought something might have fallen, but instead she found Stefana, Seventh Fairy of Queen Devi or…as she knew her, her girlfriend.

"Whoa, girl, you look amazing!" she said to Stefana dressed in a ridiculously lavish and ornate red and gold dress with several intersecting gold necklaces around her neck. "Where have you been?"

Stefana groaned, and her hand slipped from her shoulder, revealing a gash where Emily could see to the bone beneath.

Emily steeled herself from gagging. "Stef! Oh my God, what happened to you?"

Stefana swayed on her feet, and Emily caught her just before she hit the floor. Blood poured from the wound and pooled beneath her. Emily tried to hold her microfiber towel to the wound, but the rag quickly became soaked.

Stefana struggled to remove the rag. "Don't…don't bother…," she managed.

"But…," Emily countered before she held up one hand.

"Emily, I need you to listen carefully," Stefana struggled in one breath.

Emily nodded. "I need you to bring me the kitsune," she said, panting from the exertion.

Emily looked at her, confused. "The what?" she asked.

"The kitsune…Gwendolyn…," she trailed off.

Emily stared at her. "Gwen? What? Why? Shouldn't I be calling an ambulance?" Emily turned to leave, but Stefana grabbed her arm.

"No. Human doctors can't do anything for me," she growled.

"Human?" Emily asked, eyeing her questioningly.

"Get. Gwendolyn," she panted again.

Emily ran out to me, breathless and wide-eyed, "Gwen, I need help!"

"What happened, Em? Are you okay?" I asked, putting down the chair I was about to place on its corresponding table.

"Just come help me," Emily said, disappearing into the back again.

THE CLAIMED COVENANT | 125
~~~~~

I followed quickly and then stopped at the scene in the back room. The beautiful girl arrayed in ballroom finery was sprawled on the floor in a pool of blood.

"Emily…I," I began. "I don't know this person."

"Please help, Gwen. She asked for you specifically," Emily begged. I started to back up. "She knows you, Gwen. I don't know how. She called you a…a…a kitsune!" she said, sparking with recognition at the last word.

I felt my face contort, and my eyes swelled. How could she know that?

"Call 9-1-1, Emily," I said. "I'll wait outside for them."

Stefana struggled to push herself up onto her non-wounded arm. "I am Stefana…Seventh daughter of Devi, the Fairy Queen…descendant of Queen Sharon of Holli Lake. I make a formal request to the House of Abe to assist another fae-kind."

I froze and spun on my heel. "Why did you have to say it like that?" I asked, grinding my teeth. I pulled out my phone and quickly searched for his number.

"We have always been friends of the fae, back to Abbie and Edie of the Ashcroft Forest," she said.

I wave my hand at her. "I know, I know," I say waiting while the phone rings.

"Gwen? Stef? What's going on?" Emily demanded.

"I got this…hang on," I said as the phone was answered. "Hello, Gavin? I need you at the Bean." I paused. "No. There's an emergency. A fairy is here, and she made a formal request of aid."

I looked at Stefana, who had lain down on the floor.

"Yeah…she invoked sofu's clan name…okay. See you soon," I said, ending the call.

I kneeled next to her. "You must've been really desperate to come here and…" I paused and looked over at Emily. "…and say things."

Her face scrunched up, "I didn't know whom I could trust among my sisters," she said sadly before contorting into a mask of rage. "The traitorous sow will pay."

Her words were cut off as she began to cough up blood, causing Emily to move to her side and kneel next to her. "Babe?" Emily whispered, clutching her wound-free hand.

"You're not scared?" Stefana asked.

Emily swallowed a huge lump and shook her head. "No," she murmured, before leaning down a bit so that she could kiss that hand. "I'm only scared of losing you…" She shook her head as tears rolled down her face. "It took way too long to find you, and I'm not losing you now. You can tell me the rest…all this craziness that you and Gwen were going on about later…just…don't die."

"I can't die," Stefana groaned. "I've got too much to do…get revenge for this injury…see my biological sister be coronated as our new Queen…go to your graduation…marry you…all kinds of stuff!"

I remembered feeling so out of place, mostly because I'd never seen Emily be so vulnerable, and for her and her significant other to be so open. I felt strange…as if I should've been getting more emotion from the two of them. As it stood, I could only just feel a portion of all the pain Stefana was experiencing. I never would've guessed what obāsan had done to me.

"Okay," Gavin grumbled walking into the back area. "What's going on? And do you guys know that you have like three people waiting to be served out front?" he added, pointing his thumb in that direction.

"I'll get them," Emily snapped. "Just…" She stood up and motioned toward Stefana. "…if you can, do something to help her! Please!"

"That's what I'm here for…apparently," Gavin said as his eyes glowed in pale blue. Emily gasped but wiped it away quickly. She hurried out to the front to help the people who clearly ignored the chairs upside down on the tables or the hours sign on the front door.

"This her?" Gavin asked.

"Yes," I replied. Gavin stared at me for a moment, before kneeling over Stefana.

"I-I-I, Stef-f-fana…Seventh daughter…"

"Yeah, yeah, yeah," Gavin said making a wrap it up motion with his hand. "It's like I'm a freakin' fae-band-aid," he complained while lifting his left hand covered in pale blue flames. He poured his healing fires over Stefana. Of course, her not knowing what he was doing, she cringed and shut her eyes tight. Soon, the injury to her shoulder closed, and she began to breathe a bit easier.

"Whew," Gavin emitted as the flames died out. "That was a lot more work than I thought it'd be."

Stefana pushed herself up to her feet and examined her shoulder as best she could. I took a shiny serving tray from the shelf to her right and used it to give her a better look.

"Remarkable," she breathed. "But, next time, maybe consider giving the person you're helping a warning." This, of course, was met by a smirk from Gavin.

"Stef!" Emily panted moving past the two of us in a blur. She threw her arms over Stefana's shoulders and held onto her for dear life.

"I love you too, Em," Stefana whispered.

"You never said that before," Emily replied, taking a step back.

"I never meant it as much before," she returned. "My long life flashed before my eyes when Titania struck out at me…and most of what I saw was of you…" She shrugged, and her head canted to the left. "…and my little sister, Twelana."

"Don't you have like one hundred six sisters," Gavin poked.

"Only one biological," she returned. She nodded as her eyes moved from me to Gavin and back again. "Thank you, descendants of the Abe Clan. I will not forget this and once my sister is coronated, I'll be sure that she offers your clan a boon."

"That won't be necessary," I said.

"Says you!" Gavin snapped.

"Now," Emily cut in. "Maybe, you guys can tell me what the hell is going on?" she posed, but never let go of Stefana.

"Well…," I started awkwardly and explained as much as I could including as few people…and supernatural races as I could.

My thoughts come back to the present. I wonder how Dr. Taylor would even begin to try to convince everyone to leave town. The mayor takes the podium after a moment, and everyone falls silent.

"Good evening, everyone," she says. "I want to keep this brief, but it has come to my attention that the people of our town are in danger." A murmur runs through the crowd, but quiets when the mayor waves her hands. "It seems that there has been a mine collapse in Winfall. Everyone has been evacuated and is safe, but it has left the tunnel that runs close to Edenton weakened and at risk of a potential toxic gas build up."

The whispers spread through the crowd again. "Don't fret," she says, flashing her campaign-winning smile. "Although the risk to us is relatively low, we are recommending residents leave the city for a few days. We've already made some arrangements with local hotels in Elizabeth City to give some deep discounts, and school and all municipal activities will be closed next week."

I look over at Alex, who bears an impressed look on his face. "Wonder how he pulled that off," he whispers.

"It's a plausible lie," Gavin says, stepping closer.

"Gavin?!?!" I snap.

"Hey sis," he says casually. "We just got back to town," he adds motioning between Sora and himself.

"It's smart," Sora agrees. "There really was a cave in over in Winfall, so it's easy enough to verify that and a gas-leak is pretty standard for that sort of thing."

"I guess, he's used to lying," I admit sullenly, thinking about my loving foster parent. I look at Sora and Gavin, before coming back to Alex. "I mean, he never told his wife anything about the Order." All three nod in agreement, which doesn't make me feel any better.

#####

Chapter 18: Taken

Alana

"So, the fairies are as good as their word," Angela says, feeling out their numbers surrounding the apartment, us, and the baby.

"Yes," I reply. "Nathan said that even if fairies were a bit untrustworthy throughout history, he trusts Jamie, and she trusts the new fairy queen."

"Please don't hold our standoffish nature against us," says a little blue light, floating close to my left ear. "Our previous queen, Devi, held close to her mother's belief of keeping the fairies safe by keeping us separated, but watchful of other supernatural beings, as well as the human world." The blue light flies closer to Angela. "We meant no harm, even if we didn't help."

"Well, you're helping now," I say, patting Kya's back. "And for your help, I cannot thank you enough." The blue light bobs up and down and given the emotion I feel from her, she's happy. The light fades as she flies up toward the ceiling.

My eyes come back down as Angela swiftly looks away. A wave of guilt washes over me...but I can't even begin to fathom what's the cause. "Would you like to hold her?" I ask, offering my daughter to her godmother.

"No thanks," Angela returns quickly.

"Alright," I reply and cradle my daughter anew. More guilt. "What's bothering you?" I ask.

"Damnit!" Angela returns. "I should've known I wasn't keeping it in check as much as I thought I was."

"A monumental feat to manage around me and this one," I say bouncing Kya a bit higher.

"I'm sorry," she breathes.

"No worries," I reply, sounding like my Nathan...or our Nathan. "If you have something on your mind..."

"No," she interrupts. She lets out an exasperated sigh. "Could you guys give us like five minutes?" she asks, staring up at the ceiling. Suddenly, the ceiling becomes a night sky of tiny red, yellow, blue, and bright green lights. The lights slowly begin to part, moving toward windows, doors, and the hallway moving into the bedrooms.

Angela comes back down to me. "I'm sorry," she starts again. I open my big, British mouth to respond, and she extends a halting hand. "I should've been here." I shake my head. "No," she continues. "Let me finish." She stands and paces away from the sofa, her right hand clasped in her left. She looks down at them as if realizing something, pulls them apart and then crosses her arms. She then looks at her arms, sighs heavily, shrugs, and lets them fall to her sides.

She turns back to her former seat. "When that witch…Bethany," Angela spits her name out as if it were something not only unpleasant on the tongue, but hot, burning even. "…took…" She looks at me, and a fresh wave of guilt flows from her. "…my feelings for Nate away…I…" She sighs and throws her head back. "…this was so much easier on Terry's couch."

"Terry?"

"My shrink…psychiatrist…Dr. Theresa 'Terry' Hamrick." I nod and make an offering motion. "…yeah," she huffs. "…I kinda wanted to…un-alive myself."

I gasp.

"I know it shouldn't have had that big an effect on me. I mean, he was your fiancé, he was my friend, and it was just some stupid emotion, you know…but it was mine, and it was real, and it kept me centered." She stares at me with tears filling her eyes. "And without it, I felt lost…and I didn't know what to do. I called Duchess, but the truth is she was already calling me and inviting herself to come out and 'hang with me.'" She sits and nods a few times. "Apparently, Raven called her in a panic, and Duchess has had some lessons in psychology.

"I needed her more than I thought I did. Like how she started making me realize that you guys probably needed me in a similar way…and I wasn't here…and that sucked, and it was selfish and…"

Before she finishes, I place Kya in her arms. She inhales deeply and stares at her goddaughter and sire-cousin. Kya inhales deeply as well only for her…

"She's scent-bonding," I explain. I huff a laugh. "She's only done that that quickly with Nathan and I before now."

"Wow," she breathes, staring at her.

"And to your point, Angela," I continue. "Like the fairies, you did what was right for you at the time. It doesn't matter that you weren't here then…it only matters that you're here now."

She smiles and holds Kya closer. "Thank you, Alana."

"Always," I reply.

"Okay, I don't even know how to hold one of these things," she says, while awkwardly passing Kya back to me. I laugh as I reclaim my daughter.

"I don't know how to explain it," the tiny blue light says floating down to us. "But something dangerous is coming…there are a lot of smaller, less dangerous somethings coming with it, but something big and dangerous is headed towards us now."

"Thank you for the warning," I say, rising to my feet and cradling Kya against my heart.

"How much time do we have?" Angela asks, springing to her feet, while drawing the twin blades from behind her back.

"None," the light returns just before an explosion rings out near the front of the apartment. "Sisters, this is Gemma, Eightieth Fairy of Devi. Hear me! Those of you who can fight, prepare for battle! Those of you who cannot, flee and tell the others that they are needed!" A snap sounds a moment later, and a tall, slender fairy appears wearing pale blue armor. Her long strawberry blonde hair hangs over her right shoulder in one long braid. She pulls what appears to be a mace from her left hip and holds it high above her head. "To the death," she snarls, as she takes a defensive position in front of us.

"Secure every room," Anaras says in his stern tone without any form of urgency or demand. Angela tightens her grip on her weapons as tension fills and flows off her. "Find the child," he continues. "Kill anyone who gets in your way, be they vampire, wolf, fae creature, or anything else."

"Sir," I believe six distinct voices reply.

Footsteps move through the apartment swiftly though meant to conceal their movements. Such steps approach the door to the study. Someone kicks it in a second later. An Ezekielite, in full combat gear, enters the room. "I found them!" he cries back into the hallway.

"You found death!" Gemma barks while rushing toward him. She smashes the side of his face with her mace, but he maintains his footing. He raises his gun, and she bats it away. Before he could recover, she hits him again with the mace. He falls this time. The gentle rise of his chest suggests that he may live… Unless, of course, we don't stop her from bringing her mace down upon him again.

"Stop!" She freezes…the weapon's head hovering only an inch or two above his head. "We promised the members of the Order that we would try to save as many members of the Ezekielites as we could."

She sighs. "Only because my life isn't in danger, will I concede."

"How considerate of you," Anaras says as he saunters into the room, trailed by two additional Ezekielites. As usual, he wears a pristinely white suit with matching tie and shirt and keeps his arms neatly folded behind his back.

"You!" Angela says, glaring at him. I can only imagine how bad their interaction went in Edenton to elicit this sort of response. "I'm not letting you take my goddaughter, ass-munch."

"Oh," he begins with a hint of mirth in his voice. "You won't have to *let* me do anything. I am fully capable of taking her by force if necessary." His eyes lazily move over to Gemma still towering over the Ezekielite near the door. She seems frozen in his presence. "Or," Anaras continues. "I could compel others to assist me in this task," he adds, filling his eyes with silver.

"No!" I snap as her eyes close languidly. I manage to give everyone a surface level resistance to our silver eyes, so that they can't be stalled mid-combat…but it only takes a few seconds, a held glance to defeat that depth of protection. Unfortunately, I have not been able to replicate the success I had with Angela.

Gemma stands up straight and lowers her mace. "Be a dear," Anaras says casually and extends his open hand to us. "…and distract my granddaughter long enough for these men to take the child, while I beat my brother's murderer to death with my bare hands." He glowers at Angela.

"Bite me, grandpa!" Angela snarls, readying her weapons. "Your lying ass 'brother' toyed with me, manipulated me, and then tried to kill me." She gives one firm nod. "He deserved what he got and so will you!" Her voice remained strong and even, but her emotions have been all over the place since Anaras called her a murderer. Anaras smirks because he felt her emotions as surely as I did. "Screw you!" she returns, taking in his expression.

"Well said," Gemma says, raising her mace.

"Wha-?" Anaras begins, but before he finishes, Gemma smashes him in the face with her mace. He's knocked back out into the hall and goes through the opposite wall, knocking over the Ezekielites in the process.

"Damn," Gemma complains, staring at the remains of her mace. The weapon's head exploded against Anaras's diamond-like skin.

"How?" Angela asks, staring at the clearly not brainwashed fairy.

"There was a reason Our Queen chose me as the leader of your protection detail," she explains, while throwing her mace handle to the side. She draws a short sword from behind her back. "Unfortunately, in terms of fighters, I barely scratch the top ten though."

"That's fine," Angela says. "It's not like- LOOK OUT!"

Before Gemma can even pretend to respond, Anaras punches her in the small of her back. "Ulk!" is all she manages before her eyes roll back in her head. He stands up straight as she drops to her knees.

"One down," he declares, before he back hands her, sending her careening through the wall into the next room. She did not yell out in pain as he struck her. Could she be…?

"You're gonna pay for that!" Angela says, appearing behind him. She strikes him across the back of his neck and Raven's blade shatters. She gasps as he spins to strike her. She manages to evade him, by leaning back, but she tries to cut him with her remaining weapon. This blade breaks against his left arm, only managing to tear a bit of his jacket away. It doesn't prevent him from reaching for her and taking her by the throat. She gasps as he lifts her effortlessly. She kicks him repeatedly as he draws back to punch her.

I step forward and kick him as hard as I can in the back, while maintaining my hold on Kya. He stumbles forward which gives Angela just enough leverage to get her legs up, wrap them around his arm, and use her momentum and his disturbed balance to hurl him over her. He flies through the doorway again, taking the door with him this time.

"We have…to get…out of here," Angela says in a gasp, while holding her bruised, but healing throat.

"Come on," I say, making my way toward the hole in the wall that Gemma left behind. I stop in the guest bedroom, when I see her lying in an awkward position on the floor, not moving.

"LATER!" Angela snaps. "They're not after her! They're after…" Before she can finish, Anaras punches her in the face. There's a snap as he knocks her through the wall…or he would've if that wasn't an exterior wall. As it stands, she seems stuck in the drywall, possibly having cracked the stonework behind it.

"ANGELA!" I shriek, taking in only the whites of her eyes and the blood seeping out of her agape mouth.

"Two down," Anaras says, glowering at me.

I take a deep breath. Kya cries, but whether it is because of my anxiety or her own, I can't honestly say. "You will not have her," I declare.

"There's not a being on this planet who could stop me."

"I will," I growl. He gives me a beckoning hand. I lay Kya down gently on the bed. "I love you very much, Angel-face." Kya reaches for my face, and I kiss her hands.

I turn back to Anaras, who's already rushing toward me. He throws a punch that I parry, but he moves his arm out, which knocks me out of my stance. He punches me in the stomach and then kicks me in the chest. The blow drives me into the wall, and he's already there driving his elbow into the side of my face. I probably would've screamed out for all three assaults, but they happened so swiftly nothing could escape me. I stumble, trying to get my feet under me. He catches me by the chin.

I try to raise my arms, but they refuse to move. "Don't…take…her…"

"That's three." With a snap, everything fades to black, and I hear Kya crying as I lose consciousness.

#####

Chapter 19: Grimoire

Jamie

"School is stupid!" Amira says, throwing her bag down by the door.

"Don't you have homework or something?" I ask as dad walks in behind her.

"I did it in the car, because again…school," she growls, walking toward the stairs. "…stupid. Especially school conducted in a warehouse, two towns over, and in the face of us gearing up for a fight to save the world."

"What's that you've got there?" dad asks, spying the church bible-sized book on the coffee table.

"This is…"

"WAIT!" Amira barks, jumping back to the landing. She sniffs the air…should've figured she'd catch on before dad did. "WHERE IS SHE?" she snarls, looking around frantically. "I can tell she walked all around the living room just to throw me off…and probably used some of that neutralizing canister spray to cover herself afterward."

I start to lift my finger to point toward the kitchen…and a blur comes from that direction. THWAP! Sounds out as Amira, using her left forearm to block and her right hand to support it, prevents her mom's snap kick, aimed at her head, from landing. Amira grabs that same leg and uses it to throw her toward the living room. Sera twists in mid-air, gets her feet down, backflips over me and the couch…and twists, landing on the edge of the coffee table opposite me, somehow without tipping it over.

"SERA!" Amira growls. "What are you doing here?"

"Ser?" dad says, and I cringe at how he calls her name, even the shortened version of it. "What…?"

She steps off the table backward and settles on her feet. She looks down at her landing spot and wipes at a little mark there, making sure it's not permanent. Geez, my dad definitely has a type. She stands up straight. "You asked me for this," she says with an accent, while pointing at the book.

"Is that the translation?" dad says, making his way around the couch.

"Yes. Taylor just finished the last three pages yesterday."

"Dr. Taylor was working on this?" I ask, while pointing at dad.

"He did," she submits. "He still does some freelance for the Order, but since the split, he definitely leans our side." Her head cants. "As did a group of younger recruits after a run in with you."

"Don't remind me," I grumble.

"Yeah," Amira says, plopping down on the couch next to me. "Because if I had been there, I would've kicked their asses!"

"Language, young lady!" Sera snaps with an instructor's finger pointing at the ceiling. "James, have you been letting her swear around you...again?" she growls.

"Hey, she hasn't been cussing anymore around me than she normally does around you," he says, missing a lot of bass from his normal speaking voice. "Plus, you know she's just as stubborn as you are."

"No excuse!" she snaps. She points at him. "You're her father. You are the adult. It's your responsibility to bring her to task!"

"Bring me to task?" Amira asks, leaning forward. "What am I? Your daughter or your underling?"

"You're my responsibility," Sera says, glaring at Amira. "And I take the responsibility of your upbringing VERY seriously." Amira and I lean back at the same time and probably for the same reason. I've never heard the word 'very' sound like a weapon before. "Now," she says, crossing her arms. "How was your day at school...really?"

"You know, most moms ask that before the without warning, out of nowhere snap kick to the head, Sera!"

"And if you know anything about me, you know I'm not most moms. Now, report..."

I cover my mouth with my fist and clear my throat.

Sera sighs and lets her arms fall to her sides. "I mean..." She looks to the ceiling as if fighting the urge to roll her eyes. "...tell me about your day. Please." She walks over to the chair to Amira's left and sits.

Amira frowns and looks at me, before coming back to Sera. "We...might've talked, while you were at school and dad was out," I admit. "I showed her some of my pictures of mom from the cloud after I showed her all the pics you and I took." Amira nods. "She wonders if me being a prodigy when I was raised on hugs and admiration might've worked with you, even though you were raised on expectations and practice."

"No," Amira snaps, glowering at her mom. "Jamie had the right mom for her...and I had the right...parental figure for me." Her eyes dart to dad. "And we both kinda settled for him..."

"Hey!"

Amira slides closer to her mom and makes a hand motion toward her that suggests choking to me. "The fact is m-Sera...during my time away..."

"Escape? Dereliction of duty? Abandonment?"

"...po-tay-toe, po-tah-toe," Amira says, waving her off. "...I realized something. Being The Eye of Ezekiel Order's Chosen One, kind of left me with a huge ego...and a lack of respect for others and their feelings..."

Sera sits back. "Three months...three months on your own and you've made this much emotional progress?"

"I saw how other people do the day-to-day thing." Her eyes go distant. "I met vampires who I didn't kill instantly, ran into a kitsune in love with a skinwalker, and the wolves' Alpha of all people…"

"Former Alpha," I remind her.

"Right. That sucks, he seemed like a really nice guy…little obsessed with his younger brother and his younger brother's new wife, but nice." She looks at me. "And hoooooottttttttt!" I cover my mouth and laugh, because with Nate as an indication of his dad's looks, I don't doubt it.

"Girls," dad says in a warning tone. "Alpha Quinton was well over four hundred years old…way too old for either of you."

"Speaking of too old," Amira starts again. I frown. "…Jamie, your boyfriend just pulled up out front." I look at the door instantly with my heart feeling like it's about to jump out of my chest. Amira grabs my hands. "Look at me." I do. "Totally adorable…" She bobs her head unevenly. "…and understandable considering how hot he is…" Dad groans. "…that you still get this excited just from seeing him…" She holds her left index finger up in my face. "…but you are way too cool and gorgeous yourself to be spazzing out like this every time." I frown. She presses her lips into a line.

"It's not gonna stop, is it?" she asks as I say, "Yeah, it's probably not gonna stop." We both laugh, getting how similar our senses of humor are. "What?" she asks, staring at dad.

"It's just…since I learned about you Mira, I've dreamt of the two of you…just like this."

"Girl," we both call him and start laughing all over again.

"That's sexist," dad says.

"You would know," we reply, which triggers another bout of laughter.

"Wow," dad groans and heads for the kitchen.

The doorbell rings. "How do I look?"

"Hot as ever," she says. "Go get 'em!"

"Um, hello," Quincy says…from the open door…that Sera answered. "I…umm…" He checks the house again like he did with Amira. "Yeah…" He points at her. "…you're…?"

I hurry over to the door. "Hey," he says, flashing a smile…and oh, there goes the heart.

"Quincy, this is my pain-in-the-ass younger sister's almost as much of a pain-in-the-ass mom, Sera."

"Language!"

"You're her mom, not mine!" I say, pointing my thumb at Amira.

"LANGUAGE!" dad shouts from the kitchen, prompting me and Amira to roll our eyes.

"Come in," I say, reaching past Sera to take Quincy's hand. "Come on, we can hang out in my room…"

"NO, YOU CAN'T!" dad yells from the kitchen.

"No, we can't," I say, pulling him back toward the living room. "Backyard?" I ask. He shrugs.

"Don't forget this," Amira says, dangling the book over the back of the sofa.

I take it from her, thinking it should feel so much heavier than it does. "Are you gonna be, okay?"

"She's my mom," she says with a shrug.

I look at Sera, removing her gloves. "Should I repeat the question?" Amira laughs. I head toward the backdoor.

"It's good that you and your sister are getting along," Sera says.

"Yes, my sister…who I'm going to live with, at least, until I'm done with this last year of high school…," she replies as we reach the kitchen.

"James," Quincy says.

"I'd prefer my daughter's boyfriends call me, Mr. Baggett," dad replies.

I freeze. "Get a lot of those?" He opens his mouth. "Because by my count, even with all the smack Amira talks…two…you've met a total of two of your daughters' boyfriends."

"I hate that my daughters are such smart asses," he grumbles.

"Better than being dumb asses," I and Amira, from the living room, say. I grab Quincy's hand and hurry outside before dad can reply.

"What's going on between you two?"

"Huh?" I complain, walking over to the railing.

"You know. You, your dad…what's going on?"

"I don't know," I complain. I half-turn to look at the house. "It's just…I'm just getting used to Amira…and her mom shows up and…" I scratch my forehead. "…she's so much my mom…she's a paler, accented Daphne with ninja training." He laughs. "It's just…it sucks, and I'm pissed at him still, but I kinda get it…which pisses me off even more."

"That you're actually starting to see your dad as a person?"

"Yeah."

"Subject change," he says, slipping his hands into the pockets of his jacket. "What's that?"

"This," I start, opening it. "…is none other than Madea's grimoire!"

"Really?" I purse my lips and nod, while flipping through the pages. "Find anything good?" he asks, wrapping his arms around me, pulling me back into him so that my head rests against that firm chest of his.

"Well, yes and no," I admit. I tear myself way from the best head rest in the world to look down at the book. I flip to the next page. "So far, I've discovered that everything Madea figured out, I've learned to do naturally."

"Oh," he says, leaning down to read the page over my shoulder. I reach up and caress his face with my free hand. He feels as if he's purring against my skin.

"But," I continue, lifting one finger. "If this translation is right, and thankfully Dr. Taylor included photocopies of the original pages, because they did miss some of her lighter marks, she figured out more efficient, less costly ways of casting the same spells...not to mention, stuff I hadn't even thought of...like..." I flip all the way back to nearly the very end. "...here. She figured out how to dismantle spells before they were even fully cast."

"You mean, like disruption magic?" I frown and look at him. "You do know that I actually pay attention when you and my little brother talk about stuff like this, right?"

"Yeah, the brother who excels at gym." He smirks because he knows exactly who told me that line. "But no," I say, patting down on the book. "This spell actually allows you to negate a spell as it's being cast, not after. You literally stop the caster before the magic is even formed."

"That's insane!"

"I know, but..." I bob my head unevenly. "...you have to actually be able to see the spell to do it."

"How can you see a spell that's not cast?"

"Well, Madea had this sight that allowed her to see magic as it formed. She said that it basically looks like runes, but it starts around a caster's wrist or wrists depending on the spell. Flamma," I breathe and produce a candle-sized flame in my palm. "According to her, in the fractions of a second it took me to think of this spell, channel the magic, and utter the word..." I look at him. "Although she insists saying the word isn't necessary, it just helps the mage focus on the magic. ...there would've been a rune that formed around my wrist...only composed of semi-invisible magic."

"That'd be helpful," he says, reading the page over my shoulder. "How'd she get this sight?"

"She died," I whisper. "I mean, she didn't stay dead...but according to her...yeah, she pretty much died after an angry group of witches attacked her...and she managed to come back from the brink. When she encountered that same group of witches again...she destroyed them because she knew every spell they cast, before they casted it."

"That's...insane...," he whispers, still staring at the book. I know because I'm still staring at him. This amazing man, who loves me so much that he wants to spend the rest of...well, my life with me.

The guy who's always been so supportive and understanding. The guy who was ready to settle for being my best friend, despite his own feelings toward me...because he wanted me to be happy no matter what...the guy who's sat back and listened to me ramble on about magical theories that I've been learning about since I learned to talk, even though he doesn't understand or even care about the subject. The guy who every time he looks at me, my heart skips a beat, and I lose a little bit of my breath. The guy who's...all those things and still agreed to wait on me...no matter how long I take to answer his...

"Yes," I say.

"I know," he adds, still staring at the book.

"No," I say, shaking my head slightly. "That's my answer...yes." He steps to my right but continues staring at me. "Yes, Quincy Blackshear, if we come out of this whole mess alive, I'll marry you."

"YOU WILL?"

"I will."

"It's 'I do' when we get in front of the wedding officiant, just so you know." I purse my lips to avoid laughing at his dumb joke. I smack him across his arm that still feels like steel. He lifts his right hand, revealing an open ring box with a gorgeous princess-cut diamond ring with a platinum band. I gasp. "I take that to mean that you like it?"

"You just had that with you?"

"I been carrying it since the day I asked you..." His head bobs. "...actually, I asked you the morning after, so the day before I..." I perch on my toes, while pulling him down toward me and kiss him. He puts his left arm around my waist and kisses me passionately...and if we weren't in my backyard...or the heightened senses family Robinson weren't inside...I'd tear every stitch of clothing off him right now and...

"Ugh," he groans and breaks the kiss.

"What?" He pulls his sleeve up revealing his lust seal that's glowing like a light house. He does the same with the sloth seal...and I unbutton his shirt, not for the reason I wanted to, and reveal his envy seal and all three are glowing. "Are they affecting you?"

"No," he murmurs. "Other than the pain a second ago, I don't feel any different."

"They must be activating the seal!"

"Jamie-Lynn!" dad calls from the back door. He frowns seeing me, still holding Quincy's shirt open...that must really be freaking him out if he didn't even mention the ring. I half turn my fiancé to see him and reveal the glowing, now pulsating seals. Dad sighs. "That explains why Nathan and another daywalking vampire are on our doorstep."

"Alana's here?" He nods. "Does she have the baby with her?"

He shakes his head and points. "That'd explain why she won't stop crying...and kinda made Sera, Amira, and me start."

I look up at Quincy. "They have Anara...they're starting the ritual..." I grab the translated grimoire. "...call Tony, I'll call Alex," I say walking toward the house.

Dad stops me at the door. "Is that...a ring in his hand?"

"Not now, dad!" Unfortunately, not now...

#####

Chapter 20: Voracity

Alex

"The town looks so weird empty like this," I say. "And the fact that we had to come from school a town over just to meet Jamie is just…"

"I know what you mean," Gwen says, running through town next to me. The slightest tiny red embers burst every time she kicks off.

"This is what you guys wanted though, right?" Meghan says, hopping along beside us. The fact that she can keep up with us and carry on a conversation while jumping like that is insane. "I mean, you wanted all the normal people taken care of, right? Out of town…away from the seal and away from the fight…where they'd be safe." She lands and springs off again. "That's why Stephen couldn't come with us," she adds with a noticeable drop in her voice.

"Yeah," I say, pushing off again. I feel a buzz in my pocket and pull my phone out. Gwen looks at me. "It's Jamie! She said to head for the vacant lot across from the grocery store behind Mr. Hamish's!" I groan. "I still can't believe Mr. H didn't give me my job back."

"Not everyone's as nice as Gwen's boss," Kai says, finishing his second corn dog.

"But he gave you yours back!" I snap.

"He likes me better than you."

"I've known him since I was a little kid!"

Kai shrugs. "I said what I said." He frowns. "Who are all those people?"

We come to a stop next to a crowd gathered around Jamie, including… "Nate?" I ask. He half turns to me with this huge fricking Japanese anime-style sword strapped to his back.

"Alex. Kai. Good to see you again," he says in a growl, and his eyes are green and gold with black replacing the whites.

Gwen takes a step back. "You remember my cousin?" I ask. She nods, but still trembles.

"Sorry," Nate says, lowering his eyes. "I haven't been able to get my eyes under control since…"

"Since those heartless monsters took our daughter," the most beautiful woman I've ever seen says, stepping out from behind Nate. Her skin is pale, and her long black hair hangs over her left shoulder in one long braid. Her eyes are the color of silver…wow…she has a sword attached to her hip.

Nathan half-turns and motions to her with his left hand while putting his right arm around her. "Alexander, Kai, Gwen…this is my wife, the Midnight Queen of all vampires, Alana Gregory-Dumont." She nods, and the tears pouring from her silver eyes shimmer.

"Whoa," Kai moans.

"I'm so sorry," Meghan says, wrapping her arms around Alana, who surprisingly reciprocates. They separate, and she stares into Alana's eyes. "We're going to get her back. I promise you that." Alana nods, and it feels as if they're both convincing each other.

"Alex!" Jamie says basically jumping into my arms. I catch her and hold her up as she puts her arms around my neck. "Did they tell you?"

"Yeah," I mutter, while lowering her to the ground. "I still can't believe your mom is mixed up in all this…even after we fought her. I mean, I still remember how she used to watch us when we'd play in the sandbox."

"It always comes back to that day at the park," she says, bowing her head a bit.

"Alpha Nathan," that long, dark-haired wolf, who came with him to Rais's funeral, calls standing next to him.

Nate looks at him and nods. "You don't have to do that, Natavius."

"Yeah, I do," he says with a voice so heavy it thuds in my chest. "We have soldiers from Midnight positioned all around the town border along with members of the Order to keep any looky-loos out. So far, no issues, but some of the hunters on the outskirts have reported feeling a little sick. So far none have died, or even have had to leave their post, but…"

"Good," is all Nate says back. He nods twice then turns and inhales deeply. "Tell Midnight to pull out another hundred yards or so and have them ask the hunters nicely to pull back with them." Natavius nods and puts his phone to his ear.

"Speaking of which," Jamie says, staring at her sister…still having a hard time with that one. "…how are you feeling?" Amira throws up an okay sign, but the woman next to her looks a little under the weather.

"I just wish more vampires could be here," Angela says, stepping up beside them.

"Downside of a daylight raid," Natavius says, ending his call.

She nods. "Hey Alex, Kai, good to see you guys again. Just wish it was under better circumstances." That's probably why Amira and that hunter woman are keeping their distance.

"I know," I reply.

"Good to see you two again," Gwen says with a bow.

"Gwen, right?" Angela says.

"Nope," Meghan says, stepping over to Angela. "This is Gwen, the bestest bestie a girl could ever have in addition to being the cutest kitsune ever!"

"Bestest isn't a word," Angela says, wrapping her arm around Meghan. "Meghan, you know my…" She inhales deeply as if just looking at him turns her on. I can't lie, even I can admit that the dude's a little guy pretty. "…boyfriend, Natavius, right? Babe, this is Meghan."

"Nice pull, cuz," Meghan says, shaking Natavius's hand. He laughs in response, and Angela punches him on the shoulder.

"Abusive," he complains.

"What the hell?" Amira growls and grabs her katana like she's about to take a vampire's head off.

Suddenly, about two dozen snaps sound out all at once, and two dozen fairies appear a second later, seemingly out of nowhere. There's this gorgeous raven-haired fairy standing in front, wearing a sky blue, shimmery dress with no sleeves that goes all the way down to the ground. She looks so familiar though.

"Twee," Jamie says as the woman opens frost blue eyes that match Alana's in terms of otherworldly gorgeousness…thank you for that phrase, Gwen…because it definitely fits here.

"Sister," she replies, and her voice sounds like a song that echoes all around us. They hug. "Unfortunately, I cannot join the fight myself, but you will have my strongest at your command."

"Why's Twee talking like that?" Kai asks.

"Twee?" I pose.

"Yes, Twelana Fairchild," Gwen picks up. "She transferred into our school halfway through last year and then disappeared just before summer."

"Right," I reply, remembering that Jamie also told me about the girl, Twee Fairchild, who was really the fairy, Twelana the 107th, who told her about her destiny to fight her mom. I can't even put into words how much I hate that she was right about that.

"…also," Twee continues some conversation that I missed most of. She steps aside and swings her right arm out as if presenting some kind of prize. "The Season Sisters have been practically buzzing since yesterday."

Four girls step forward wearing long, flowing gowns. The one on the left has light brown hair and wears a bright green dress with light brown eyes. The one next to her has golden blond hair and wears a bright yellow dress with deep blue eyes. Next, is a redhead with a burnt orange dress, who has dark brown eyes. The last sister has frost blue eyes, platinum blond hair, and wears a staunch white dress.

Twee holds her hand out to the one on the far left. "Zephyr, Summer, Autumn, Winter…," she says, motioning to each very fitting name as she goes…except Zephyr.

"Zephyr is another name for spring winds," Gwen whispers, leaning into me.

I smirk because she really knows me. "Thanks."

Twee continues as they step forward. "…please tell them what you told me."

"The eve of Eden's return is nigh," all four of them say at once. It's weird their voices echo in a way that's different from Twee's. Her voice felt like a song, like someone holding a single note. Theirs feels more like a steady whisper…only louder and each voice folding into the one that spoke a fraction of a second before. "…once again, the Heavens have decreed that the Celestials must rise to stop the Garden Tender's return, led by the newest First Witch of Light," they say, turning to face Jamie. "She has her own members of the great races as her acolytes. Human…" Amira frowns, but she still hasn't taken her hand off her sword yet.

The Season Sisters hold their hands out to Nathan and Alana. "…wolf and Aldien…" Then move onto Angela. "…vampire…" They turn to me, and Gwen. "…fae and daemon…" I growl, and Gwen holds my arm tighter. They look at Meghan. "…Witch of Light…" And then they turn to Sara's coven of witches. "…and Witch of Shadows."

Sara puts her finger to her lips. "Up, up, up," she mutters. "Now that's telling."

Jamie frowns and stares at Sara's group…if she's anything like me, she's probably trying to figure out which one of them is the Witch of Shadow. None of them seem anything like Bethany though.

"As you venture forth," the Season Sisters continue. "…know that many of you will face trials…both personal and physical…many of you will be faced with what appears to be a choice…" They all shake their heads as their eyes drift closed. "…but the choice is an illusion. The Claimed Covenant is designed to take everyone to exactly where they need to go."

"What's that supposed to mean?" Gavin asks, stepping out of bright yellow flames with Sora, obāsan, sofu, and obāsan's brother…or the guy who was almost my…granddad?

"You'll see," they say at once.

"Obāsan!" Gwen says appearing next to her grandmother from a burst of flames. She wraps her arms around her. "I thought you said, you wouldn't be able to participate in this fight!"

"Gwendolyn-piichan," she says, wrapping her arms around her. "Great Emperor Tenma suggested that perhaps now is not the time to…how'd he say it…?"

"Sit on the sidelines," Gavin supplies.

"Yes," obāsan continues. "In fact, we would've brought more, but the other guardians have decided to stay near the emperor."

"I understand, Mrs. - I mean, obāsan," I say, walking over to them.

"Alex-piichan," she says wrapping an arm around me.

"The hour is nigh," the Season Sisters add, turning to the empty parking lot behind us.

"That's our cue," Sara says. "Are you ready girls?" Her coven looks at her and smiles.

"Not necessary," a woman with a French accent says.

"Another day walking vamp?" Amira asks.

"Two more," her mom adds as a gorgeous woman with dark hair and eyes, dressed in an outfit that looks like something out of one of Meghan's fashion magazines, approaches us. She's tailed by a tall, leggy redhead with pale skin and green eyes…wait, that's the Chief Magistrate lady…Raven. Behind her are a white guy with dark hair in a really nice suit, and a bald black guy who looks like he's about to do a magic show.

"Three," a youthful voice says, calling from the back of the group. "You missed one," a tiny blond who rivals Angela and Meghan for blond-bombshellness says from the back of the group.

Angela steps away and appears next to her. She gives her a hug. "Hey Maggie," she purrs as they hug. "How's Kimiko? I haven't seen much of her since…"

"She's fine. Da had to remove and then managed to reattach her arm. Luckily, she didn't even suffer any permanent nerve damage." They both look at the tall guy in the dark suit talking to Nate now. "He's the best!"

"He really is." Angela inhales deeply. "I'm changing my major to medicine because of him."

"Doctor Angela," Maggie replies. "I like it." They laugh.

"Whatever do you mean, it's not necessary, darlin'?" Sara asks as the French vampire approaches her.

"Just what I said," she replies, staring at the empty space ahead. "And you may call me, Duchess."

"That's pretentious," the really pale member of Sara's coven says.

"Oui," Duchess replies. "But I like it." She goes back to staring into space. "Where does this…glamour start?"

Sara extends her hand. "Here," she says as the space around her fingertips begins to ripple like the surface of a lake.

"Bedlam," Duchess says, holding her hand out to the bald, black magician guy. He slips a pendant with a gold chain out of his interior pocket and passes it to her. It looks like an eagle with its wings up above its head surrounding a round ruby.

Duchess extends the pendant until it is right next to Sara's hand. The glamour begins to ripple around it as well…and then stops…and cracks…like the air is cracking around the pendant. It moves out from it in a spider web pattern…going out and up as far as I can see…and then with a sound like a car accident and shattering glass, the sky detonates, revealing a huge building that reaches toward the sky behind it.

"Voila," Duchess says, turning to Sara. She examines the pendant that now looks like a melted piece of plastic. "I should've known it was one use only." She tosses it away.

"Everyone," Jamie says approaching the building. "We all know what's at stake here...a lot of things..."

"Eloquent as always, babe," Quincy Blackshear says, standing on her right. Tony's standing on her left, but he looks angry...angrier than usual even.

Jamie extends her hand to Tony. He looks at it and then takes it. She gives his hand a subtle shake before they let go, and she comes back to us.

"What's at stake is the life of a very precious child," Jamie adds looking at Nathan and Alana. "It's about century old rivalries," she continues, looking at Meghan and Gwen. "It's about putting right what once went wrong..." Her eyes move to Twee and her fairies. "It's about keeping promises..." She looks at Gavin, sofu, and obāsan. "...it's about family..." She looks at Amira, Sera, and her dad, who's joining them. "...it's about friends..." She looks at me and smiles. "...who become family." She looks to her left and then her right. "It's about fighting for everything that we love. We can't fail...we have to stop Eden's resurrection...no...matter...what."

"No matter what," we reply all at the same time.

"Let's go!" she shouts, turning to the door. She places her finger on the center and then starts making circles...and locks start unlocking...a lot of locks...like a whole lot of locks!

"I love this part," Sara says with a smirk. Jamie finishes, and the door swings in on its own. She steps forward, but the Blackshear brothers bolt through the door before she can.

"YEAH!" that long haired wolf Natavius shouts before vanishing. Gwen grabs my hand and pulls me toward the door as we all rush into and enter...

"...an empty office space," Gavin says the thought in my head.

"Don't be fooled," Duchess says, looking around.

"Each door is a hell gate," Jamie explains. "We'll have to figure out..."

"Remember what the Season Sisters said," Gwen shouts with a surprising amount of force for her. "The choice is an illusion."

Jamie nods. "Spread out!" Nate says. "Everyone group up and take a door...and no matter what happens...watch each other's backs."

Gwen grabs Meghan and pulls her and me to the right, and we're joined by the brunette from Sara's coven. Nate and Alana go for a door straight ahead, and Sara joins them...patting Nate on the back. Jamie, Quincy, Tony, and Amira take a door. Angela, Natavius, the suit wolf, and the tall red head and the redheaded member of Sara's coven take another. Sera, Jamie's dad, Maggie, and another of Sara's coven…the librarian looking woman take another door. Duchess, the magician guy, Gavin, Sora, and Kai take another. Obāsan, sofu, my almost grandad, and the pale, chesty member of Sara's coven take a door. Stefana steps to the center of the room and swings her sword outward. The fairies gathered, minus Twee and the Season Sisters, pair up and hurry to a door.

"Good luck," Alana says, drawing a nod from everyone. Nathan turns their nob. Quincy turns theirs. The leggy redhead, Duchess, and Sera open theirs.

"Here we go," I say, turning to Gwen.

"Together," she whispers, intertwining our fingers. I nod and turn the door handle…to a white, dry, hot space behind the door. It's weird, but it feels like we're being swallowed u-

#####

Chapter 21: Potential

Angela

"...in the f...?" I trail off as Natavius takes his arms from around me. "What was that?" I ask.

He shrugs and stands up... Why were we crouched? ...and then pulls me to my feet. He looks around with a confused expression on his face. He rubs up and down my arms while taking in our surroundings. I join in on looking around, and the first thing that jumps out at me...

"Where is everybody?" I ask, coming back to him. "Where are we? Is it just me and you?"

"I think so," he growls as his eyes glow amber.

"What's wrong?"

A rumble comes from his chest as he keeps looking around. "Well, to answer one of your questions, I believe we're inside an Aztec pyramid near Mexico City."

"What?" I snap as my head darts around, taking in the dank graying walls, the small deposits of sand covering the floor, and the odd greenish brown... Is that moss? Is it fungus? ...growing along most of the walls and the ceiling. "How did we get to Mexico City?"

"Hellgates," he returns, finally letting me go as he steps away.

"Why here though?"

"That's easy," a weathered, old croak of a voice says from behind us. "Like the spot in Edenton, this is one of the locations where a previous version of Eden was dispatched."

I turn and find an unassuming old man wearing large, dark sunglasses, a tweed jacket, and a fedora, of all things, approaching us.

"Zeke," Natavius says, with a bit more of a rumble to his voice.

"Little brother," the old man returns. "I saw that you got your memories back...I was hoping I was wrong as to what would happen after that."

"If you thought for one second I would ever turn my back on Nate and Alana, I don't think you really ever knew me at all, big brother."

"Brother?" I ask as my eyes metronome between the two of them.

"Yeah," Natavius replies. He extends his right hand to the older man....which is funny as I remember that my boyfriend is over 2500 years old. "Angela, this is Ezekiel, the human member of the Claimed."

"I thought that was you," Ezekiel says with a noticeable rise to his expression, but a shiver to his voice. "The last scion of my direct line." I turn around and look behind me, but no, those big sunglasses are focused on me. "I knew that if I got close enough to you, I actually would be able to see you…see your future…and that's why I stayed away from you, that's why I stayed away from all of you. I was sad when I saw your father's passing."

"Who the hell are you talking to?" I snarl, taking a step forward, only stopped from taking a second step by Natavius grabbing my arm.

He just laughs as a response, which pisses me off that much more. "I see my wife's fire still remains with our descendants."

"Descendants?" Natavius asks, as his eyes slowly move to me. "Angela? The Price Family…they were your children?"

Ezekiel just responds with a nod. "After I tossed away my family name, I gave them that one…for obvious reasons."

"Would one of you please tell me what the hell you're talking about?"

"Well," Natavius starts, taking my left hand and then grabbing my right, so that we're facing each other. I stare into those big, gorgeous puppy dog eyes of his. "When each of us became a member of the Claimed, we gave something up to gain something. I gave up my ability to transform into a wolf…I thought it was an even trade, considering I'd have a family again." I nod, because that's all I can do in reaction to the sadness I hear in his voice.

He looks at the old man, Ezekiel, and his entire expression seems to drop…as if cannonballs were chained onto him weighing his face down. "Zeke, he gave up his family, if that's not irony, considering one of the things I felt I got in the exchange.

"That's how I ended up as fast as I am…because I gave up my ability to transform. It's how Zeke got perfect sight…perfect future sight, because he gave up his family and agreed never to see them again."

"That's not exactly how it happened, pup," Ezekiel says. "I just can't see their futures like I could see everyone else's." He bobs his head unevenly. "Sure, with some of them I could surmise what was going to happen to them by the gaps that they left in my visions. Others I have no idea." He scoffs. "My wife died, and I couldn't even see it." On that last line, his voice took on a timber that I've only heard from Nate when talking about Rosalind.

"But I see it now," he starts again, while pointing at me. "It's just like I thought. It's not that I can't see them. It's that I couldn't get close to them without seeing them…and seeing it all." He huffs a humorless laugh. "That would've been torture, watching my entire line come and go."

I frown and look at Natavius, who seems just as sad as Ezekiel.

"You though…Angela, I see you, and I must say of you, my granddaughter to the I'm unsure anymore degree, you are beautiful. You are everything I hoped our lineage could be. Powerful, brave, fearless even, ready to fight to the end for what you believe in. You do your father's memory proud." He sighs while removing his fedora. He drops it. "Which makes it unfortunate that fate has brought you to me now…" He undoes his little, green bow tie and pulls it off with a fabric zip, before tossing it aside. "…because I am bound by my pledge to Eden…" He undoes the top button of his shirt, while sliding his jacket off with his other hand. "…as a member of the Claimed…" He drops his jacket, and I realize instantly…what his big, droopy tweed jacket was really doing. "…to kill you both, here and now." He flexes his stupidly muscular frame, and those biceps look like they're gonna tear through his shirt.

"Zeke, you been juicin'?" Natavius poses to break the tension.

Ezekiel smirks as he removes his sunglasses. He tosses them aside and comes back to us with white-on-white eyes.

"Is-is he blind?" I blurt out before I can stop myself.

"Yeah," Natavius replies, slipping his jacket off. Wait, Natavius…is taking his jacket off…against a blind guy? I steal a glance at Ezekiel. "He 'sees,'" Natavius continues. "…by using his perfect future sight…which wouldn't be a problem for me, except…" He drops his jacket, but has a silver blade in each hand, that hook upward moving toward the tip. "…he's almost as fast as I am, but he knows everything I'm going to do before I do it."

"What does that mean?" I freeze…the whole world feels like electricity around me…like it's bouncing off every wall, running along the ceiling, skipping across the floor, and igniting random spots in the air between. KLANG! My eyes swell to twice their normal size. I look around and see random sparks like metal hitting metal. A clang sounds out a second later. On my left… on my right… in front of me… behind me… It's the same effect as a bullet…movies always tell you that you hear the bang then the bullet hits you. Completely wrong. As I've learned during my time as a vamp, if you wait to hear the bang, the bullet has already hit you. A sound like something heavy rolling over gravel sounds out, and Natavius slides to a stop in front of me with his blades crossed in front of him.

He lowers them to his sides as he stands up straight. My eyes dart to the weapons…that looked shiny and brand new a second ago…but now, they're covered in nicks, dings, and dents. Natavius throws them away and sighs.

"Silver versus steel, pup," Ezekiel says, holding a long straight dual-edged blade out to his right side. "Also, you've gotten even faster…you actually almost got me a time or two." Natavius glowers at him.

"Babe," I mutter. He looks at me with just his eyes. I scratch my hip, aiming my thumb at my back…and the two adamant blades that that hunter Sera gave me.

Ezekiel appears on my right as Natavius does on my left. They each pull one of the knives free and vanish again. The noisy light display resumes only louder and with a lot more sparks around the room. Thunk. I look down at my feet…at the top of Ezekiel's sword, minus the rest of the weapon. I hear a groan, and something wet hits me in the face. My hands start wiping it away before I even think about it. It's "…blood?" A quick sniff tells me… "…Natavius?" My chest hurts for a second, because…he's fighting alone…

I take a deep breath and feel my eyes phase over to deep blue. I focus on my ability and see the trails they're leaving behind…I see every move they make, up to the point of impact then they separate and come together again…and again…and again… I extend my right hand. I see them…it feels like I'm missing a step or two, but I see them…but even more than that, I see the friction they're creating…how they're building up a steady charge of "…electricity," I mutter.

It swirls around me, building up more and more… "Fire when ready," Natavius whispers in my ear.

I smirk. "Levit-" The air rushes out of me all at once…I go flying… "GAH!" I snap as I hit, a wall…I guess. "Ugh," I complain when I hit the ground. I hear a rumble like thunder.

"ANGE!" Natavius yells, next to me. He puts his hand on my back.

"I'm…m…kay," I gurgle with a mouth full of blood. I open my mouth a little as it dribbles out of the corners. The pain from my back and head are already fading…I must be almost healed already.

"He hit you with a nasty elbow, before you could finish your spell," Natavius explains, pulling me to my feet.

"So, no big magic," I grumble, wiping my mouth on my sleeve.

"I can admit, things will get harder from here," Ezekiel says as he examines… Is that even the right word? …the adamant blade he stole from me. "…but it's nothing I can't handle," he adds.

I look at Natavius and gasp. He's covered in tiny cuts that are healing slowly, but even scarier than that…he's out of breath. He flips his adamant blade around and takes a stance that suggests attack.

"No," I snap as more of the fog lifts. I hold a hand in front of his chest. "Breathe. Heal." The rest of his wounds heal. "It's not much but…"

"Thanks."

"We fight him together from here on out."

"You're not fast enough," he growls.

"I'll manage."

"If anything happens to you…"

I pull his face to mine and kiss him. "…how do you think I'd feel if anything happened to you while I just stood here like a goon?"

"Like you do every day?" I laugh, and he does too. "Ange, I lo-"

"Tell me when we get out of here," I interrupt, while putting a finger to his lips. I pull out the throwing knives Raven got for me as back-up weapons…since I broke her knife…and the one I had made to look like hers on Anaras. "And I promise I'll say it right back...as long as you're alive to hear it."

"Bet," he barks, leaning forward. Ezekiel extends his free hand and makes a 'come on' motion.

"Go," I snap as that feeling of electricity whips up around me all over again...only this time, I feel it at the tips of my fingers, moving across my skin, and through my chest. I dart forward...I'm a good three steps behind Natavius. My knives cross as Ezekiel blocks Natavius's first hit. I stab at him...those white-on-white eyes move to me as if he's actually seeing me. He withdraws from Natavius and cuts the knife in my right hand in half...I suck in air as I try to stop my forward movement. He brings the knife back, going for my other knife. It meets its twin as Natavius dives to protect me...I spark with realization; I don't stop my momentum but roll instead.

"UGH!" Ezekiel groans as I slash his non-knife wielding forearm...that's still holding what's left of his sword. He smirks at the surprise on my face. His arm juts forward... I scream. ...and what's left of the sword's blade goes into my stomach. Focus, Ange. Focus. Focus. Focus.

"ANGE!" Natavius snaps, reaching for me...he ducks as Ezekiel's other arm swings out at him, causing him to lean back to avoid losing his head, or at least, a part of it.

I drop my knife and grab the sword and Ezekiel's wrist. He gasps as those eyes move back to me. "Didn't see this coming, did ya? Fulgur!" I feel all that electricity in the air move around me again...and then through me...and into him.

"ARGGGGGGGHHHHHHH!" he roars as I release him, and he releases the sword. I fall to my knees as he stumbles back.

"HA!" Natavius snaps, driving his knife towards Ezekiel's head.

"NOW, YOU'RE MAKING ME ANGRY, PUP!" Ezekiel rumbles as he parries the attack. He then drives his fist into Natavius's stomach, sending him flying. I try to move, but my abdomen's still screaming at me. Ezekiel walks toward me raising the blade above his head in a stabbing motion. "All of that...barely for a few drops of blood..." I look up at him and grimace. "...pity."

I raise my knife as he starts bringing his down...and he stops. He gasps and looks to his left. Wait...where's Natavius?

"Im-im-impossible," Ezekiel gasps.

A streak of actual lightning comes through the temple a second later...and is followed by a sound like a cannon going off mixed with a trainwreck and thunder.

"Uh," I moan as more blood splashes across my face.

"Damnit," Ezekiel moans as sound starts returning to the world. "Ya-ya...got me...pup..." I look to my left and find Ezekiel embedded in the wall.

"AAAAAAARRRRRRRRGGGGGGGGGHHHHHH," Natavius shrieks, while... I gasp this time. ...holding his left forearm...or where his left forearm used to be. Blood pours from what's left of his arm.

"Natavius," I pant, forcing myself to pull the sword out of my stomach. I drop it and hurry to his side on unstable, wobbly legs. I take off my belt and wrap it around his arm. I take the sheath from Raven's destroyed blades and slip it into the belt. I start turning it, tightening the tourniquet until the blood flow slows. "Babe," I say, cupping his face in my hands. "Where's your other...?" He frantically shakes his head. "Are you...?"

"I'll...live," he whispers as tears move down his face. "Are you...?"

"Let's worry about the guy with one arm first, okay?" He swallows a lump before nodding.

Thud. My head snaps around to look at Ezekiel, who fell out of the wall. He groans and forces himself to roll over. "An...gel...a...," he says.

"He's dying," Natavius says, his voice tense with excruciating pain. I come back to him. "He doesn't heal as fast as we do. Go to him."

"Are you...?" He nods. I give him a quick kiss and then wipe the blood away from his lip. I push myself up to my feet, glad my stomach healed.

I stagger over to Ezekiel and kneel beside him. "My line is in good hands," he says, raising his left hand.

"Sorry to tell you, but I'm a vampire...your line ends with me."

He smirks. "You'll need an advantage for what comes next." I scowl. "Take...my blood..." He turns his hand so that his wrist is closer to my face. "...won't be perfect future sight...but it will help..."

"If you think I'm gonna..."

"Zeke's a lot of things," Natavius says, staggering over to me. "...but he's not a liar."

I look down at the old man, and his skin appears gray, his eyes are less glassy, and his breathing is shallow. I take a deep breath, bare my fangs, and bite into his wrist... I could not have dreamt up a better taste than what sweeps over my tongue...it's like Johnny's Pizza, Junior's Cheesecake, and mom's chocolate mousse pie all rolled into one...in a good way.

"Delicious," I breathe as the arm in my hand grows colder than my skin. My tongue sweeps around my mouth savoring and clearing the last remnants of the blood. I heave a heavy sigh. I gasp as a vision passes over my eyes. I see Natavius kiss me...and then he does. He stops suddenly and sits back. "What? Why'd you...?"

He caresses my face with his right hand. "You feel warm."

I frown while leaning into his hand. "You don't." We look at Ezekiel, whose heart has already stopped, with a smile on his face.

"I love you," Natavius whispers.

I huff a content laugh. "I love you, too," I say, wrapping my arms around him. I hope the others make it out of this…

#####

Chapter 22: Feud

Gwen

"Huh?" Meghan complains, next to me.

I open my eyes to a darkened forest. I look up, expecting to see a leafy canopy, but no, like back in Edenton, the trees are nearly bare. I know this isn't Edenton though. The scent of this place is completely wrong. There's no saltwater kiss that comes from its proximity to the ocean.

"Where are we?" Meghan finally asks the question, swimming around my head. "And where's Alex? Wasn't he with us? And that woman from Sara's coven?"

"Yeah," I complain, trying not to because even though he was just with me one second ago, I miss my husband already.

"To answer your questions," an annoyingly familiar and nasally voice says, approaching from behind us. We turn to Bethany wearing yet another billowy black dress, complete with black and white striped, opera-style fingerless gloves. "First, we're currently standing in the Pokaini Forest near Dobele, Latvia."

"L-Latvia! We're in Latvia!" Meghan exclaims.

"Don't worry. Now that I know where we are, I can get us back." She inhales deeply and nods once.

"Second, I don't know, but hopefully somewhere being torn apart by something."

"Bitch!" I snarl, before I can stop myself.

She smirks into a little giggle. "Third," she continues, holding up that many fingers. "I'm sure he was...he is such a whipped little thing, isn't it?"

"How would you know?" Meghan returns, matching Bethany's snarky tone. "I mean, do we even have to rehash the whole, 'you were never his girlfriend' thing?" This time, I giggle, and Bethany stomps her foot.

"None of this matters!" Bethany roars. "Soon, you two will be dead, Eden will be resurrected, and we'll rule the world!"

"Cliché much?" Meghan snickers.

"As insufferable as your ancestor much?"

"Well," Meghan counters. "Like my great-great-great-great-great-great...and I mean, she seemed pretty great...grandmother did, I'm gonna kick your ass, too!"

"We'll see," Bethany says with a strange new confidence to her voice. She pulls a large, tear-shaped purple crystal out of her pocket.

"Her dress has pockets? She managed to get pockets sewn into that thing?" Meghan asks. "Oh, that's just another reason to hate her right there!"

"Yep," I agree. "But get ready, because she's probably going to use that crystal to summon something."

"You wish," she declares and then slams the crystal into her chest. She groans as the crystal begins to glow and then moves into her body as if being absorbed.

"What's she doing?" Meghan asks.

"I don't know."

"Should we stop her?"

"Probably!" I say as my shoulders erupt in fire. I use swift paw a second later as Meghan leaps toward her. I try to grab Bethany, but she catches my hand. I gasp, because she caught…my hand.

"Uh-uh, you have to let a girl finish putting on her make-up!" Bethany decrees and then throws me at Meghan. We collide in mid-air and then tumble to a stop a few feet away.

"Meghan, are you…?"

"Fine!" she grumbles. "WHAT THE HELL WAS THAT?"

"I'm guessing that's what that crystal was for."

"Oh yes," Bethany hisses taking on a demented glare. The last vestiges of the crystal disappear beneath her skin. "I hid this crystal in this forest nearly five hundred years ago…I suppose it's a weird, poetic justice that I use it now to murder you both."

"Or we could just murder you!" Meghan says, but something stirs in me. I'm seething, and I can't quite get a grip on why…nor do I think I should. I was holding back a minute ago because despite being a witch, and evil…she was still basically human and very breakable. Now, I kind of want to break her though. I steal a glance at Meghan as she steps forward, there's a bit of blood coming from a small gash on her forehead and some slight bruising on her cheek. I extend my hand out in front of her.

"I can handle it, Meghan," I say, trying to let the anger build. I step forward to protect her.

"No way I'm letting you take on this bitch alone," Meghan says, blocking my advance. "Plus, this is more than just what she did to you and Alex. I have my family's honor to protect. We've been fighting her for centuries."

"Enough of the chit chat," Bethany taunts, while examining the nails on her right hand. "I'm ready to kick both of your asses now."

"Alright. On your left," I say stepping behind Meghan's left side and feeling my entire body ignite with fox magic. All the hatred and anger I've felt toward Bethany spark into physical flames on my arms.

Meghan doesn't waste any time. She emits a shriek and jumps at Bethany with a kick aimed right for her core. She didn't arc, hoping to come at her from above, this time…nope, she's attacking head on. Bethany stops her foot with both hands, rotates her hands, twisting Meghan's foot in the process, and shoves Meghan to the side with a grunt. Bethany tosses her long black locks over her shoulder and huffs a laugh when Meghan hits the ground.

I don't wait to check on Meghan, knowing her anger will get her back up. I run at Bethany, flames streaking off me. I jump in swift paw, and I'm behind her in an instant, singeing the edges of her skirt as it whips around her. She turns just in time to receive a heel to the chin.

Bethany coughs and stumbles, and her hands fly instinctively toward her face. Her fists ball with rage, and she screams in fury as she rounds on us. Meghan pushes up off the ground gingerly, feels the open wound across the top of her left arm just below the shoulder, and is already back on her feet. She falls into a prepared stance, ready for Bethany's attack.

Bethany snarls as she looks at us, then feints toward Meghan before running at me. I take a deep breath and feel the fox magic blossom inside me like a fiery flower. I jump and feel everything go in slow motion as I sail over Bethany's head and the dumbstruck expression on her stupid face. I land on one knee with my fist to the ground in what Gavin would call a hero's pose.

I stand, still holding on to my fox magic. Meghan takes the opportunity to come face to face with Bethany. I cringe slightly as Meghan punches her hard with her left fist. "That was for my mom," she says as she shakes that fist. Then she cuts across with her right fist. "And that was for my bestie," she yells, huffing from the effort.

She shakes the second fist before coming across with her left fist again, but Bethany grabs her wrist and twists it downward and behind her. "Who? That loser?" she says, jerking her thumb at me with her free hand.

I see the anger explode like fire behind Meghan's eyes. "No one calls her a loser except me!" she barks with emphasis on the last word. Meghan kicks back and hits Bethany on the side of the knee, collapsing her to the ground.

I come behind Meghan and touch the gash on her arm, feeling the skin knit back together under my hand. She flinches slightly and glances over, but her attention stays focused on Bethany.

"Get her!" Meghan demands.

I nod and clap my hands as everything obāsan taught me as well as everything I taught myself comes rushing back to me. I separate my hands with a tiny spark of a fire between them. I pull them apart, and the flames spread along with them. Give the fire form…think of it as a solid thing, I hear obāsan in my head. "And now," I breathe. "…to throw in a little pinch of me." I focus and suddenly, the spear takes the shape of a girl…not just any girl though…it's a second me.

"Holy crap!" Meghan declares, while Bethany just stares at the double vision with large eyes. I smirk, causing my clone to do the same and then we rush forward. I punch Bethany on the side of the head before she can react or more likely, she's still in shock. My clone kicks her in the side opposite me. Bethany twists awkwardly and groans. I snap kick her in the face as my clone hits her in the small of the back. We repeat this pattern, using swift paw so fast that she can't react, with Meghan throwing the occasionally pulled punch every other hit. That is, until Meghan stops pulling her punches and hits her full out. Bethany goes flying and collides with a tree. She hits the ground like a sack of potatoes…and no, that's not a reference to how that dress makes her look…although, it could be.

We approach her as the last of my clone's fox magic dies out, and she fades away.

"Get up!" Meghan demands, kicking at the hem of her dress.

Bethany groans and stumbles to her feet in that ridiculous voluminous frock. She almost trips over the hem. Who wears red carpet style dresses to a fight? She seems to be thinking the same thing because she tugs at the waistline and rips the skirt off to reveal skin-tight black leggings.

"Well, that's a relief!" Meghan exclaims.

I snort a laugh. "Definitely not what I was expecting," I chuckle despite the situation.

Bethany sneers. Surprisingly, despite the pummeling she just took, her face is unspoiled and free of cuts or swelling. There's some light bruising, but far less than one would think. She stands and tosses away a moss-covered stone. The second the stone hits the ground, the moss blackens and falls away from the rock.

She lunges toward Meghan, but I use swift paw to intercept her and plow into her like a freight train at top speed. She drops to the ground again with a thud and rolls to the side.

Bethany smirks through the pain. She balls her hands into fists, then she releases them in a flinging motion. Hundreds of little black creatures skitter around like kittens just finding their feet. They sound like a hundred metal spiders with their tiny claws trying to find a foothold to attack.

I feel the fire flow to my hands and form fireballs to throw at them. I look over at Meghan, who has picked up a branch and is using it like a baseball bat. This scatters some of the critters, sending them flying. Quickly, the creatures catch on and grab on to the stick as she swings it. A few hang on and begin to gnaw on the branch. I continue throwing fireballs to some success, turning my efforts closer to Meghan.

I glance over at Bethany who seems to be temporarily gloating at the chaos. Meghan notices too, and she spins and makes a low spinning kick that clears a large swath of the tiny monsters and knocks those behind them over like tiny bowling pins. They disappear in tiny puffs of smoke. Bethany roars in anger.

Meghan throws the stick she's been using to take out the minions just before they reach her hands. This hits another large group of them, and they waft away.

I remember obāsan's fire spear. I muster as much calm and patience as I can. I gently, but intentionally, pull my hands apart to form the shaft of the spear. I fashion the tip of the spear and then use it to skewer several of the minions.

"Woah," Meghan says as the minions I stabbed burst into puffs of smoke when the spear touches them.

"I know!" I say proudly and twirl the spear

Meghan and I make quick work of the rest of them, all while Bethany seethes with anger. As the last of them disappears, I'm thrown to the ground by what feels like a sonic blast. As I recover myself, I look over and see Meghan lying on the ground as well. She shakes her blonde mane and rubs beside her ears, meaning hers are ringing like mine.

Bethany pulls a twisted knife from her side and rushes at us. Meghan rises, glowers at Bethany, then steals a quick glance at me. She steps to her right, putting herself between Bethany and me. She strikes Bethany with her left hand while pulling me around her with her right. I spin out from behind her, pivot, and push off with swift paw, rushing at Bethany again.

I knock her to the ground and then land a solid punch to the jaw before she gets up. Bethany coughs blood, but then I realize she's laughing. Not giggling, but maniacally laughing. Then I notice that her hands are empty, save the blood covering her left hand. She looks in the direction that Meghan moved.

I crane my neck and scan for Meghan, who looks solid for a moment, but then crumples to the ground. I rush to her side and see the hilt of Bethany's blade sticking out of her abdomen. Thick black blood trickles down her crisp floral yellow sundress.

"Meghan?" I barely whisper, trying to find my voice. I glance at Bethany, now on her feet, who wears a grin usually associated with creatures that eat feces.

"Meghan!" I scream and fall to my knees. My trembling fingers brush her hair back from her face and feel for a pulse I already know isn't there. I can't regulate my breath. The world blurs around me, but I'm frozen in time looking down at Meghan's body.

I hear Bethany gasp. I may be imagining it, but I swear I hear her whisper, "Eva..." I glance at her, and her face is pale, like she's seen a ghost. It's far from the exultant face I expected.

I force myself to take a deep breath. It doesn't suppress the rage building...bursting out of me. I take another deep breath and continue seething with wrath as I look down at Meghan's lifeless body. This can't be real...

I lift my head and look at Bethany. The fury builds faster than I can stop it. The fox magic explodes from me in a torrent I've never felt before. It washes over the forest floor like a flood of flames. I aim it all at her pompous, self-righteous, arrogant face. I hit her in the face and then again and again and again. I let it all pummel her until I see her body fall and then I drop to the ground sobbing. She coughs up blood, and I hear her heartbeat slowing. She extends her left hand out toward Meghan. "Eva-ge-line... I'm... sorry... I... love you... please, don't...hate...m-" Her head slumps as her lifeless hand falls to the ground.

#####

Chapter 23: Silver

Alana

"Did you hear that?" my Nathan asks.

I listen to yells, gunfire, and screams of anguish. I nod. He looks around before ushering me forward.

The sounds of battle grow quieter and quieter behind us. I hope everyone else is faring well...but I feel her...my daughter...I look to my right...to my husband...our daughter is just ahead, near the center of this floor. We approach a pair of doors.

"I smell her on the other side," our Nathan whispers.

"I sense her there as well," I reply. He looks at me, and those gorgeous honey and emerald eyes drink me in again. "We have to save her," I say the words repeating in the back of his mind.

He nods. "Remember what we promised." I nod as a shiver runs up my spine...are my dreams...my nightmares coming to prophetic fruition? Will I regain my daughter at the cost of my husband's life? I feel his every emotion as if they were my own. He doesn't care...he would gladly lay down his life for me or her...because we are his world. We are the longing that his heart has held since he was a child...to have a family...to have people who love him unconditionally.

"I love you," he whispers.

"I love you so very much," I return with tears in my eyes. His hand moves through my hair just before he pulls me in for a kiss...a kiss that says every emotion he's feeling right now...that all-encompassing love expressed through passion. We part...far too soon like most of our kisses.

"Ready?"

"Of course."

He nods and takes the door handle on the right as I reciprocate with the left. We pull the large ornately decorated wooden doors and open them. We step into a bright room with my grandfather, Anaras, standing in the center. He wears a white suit, as usual, but has a sword at his side.

"What an unexpected surprise," he says with a sneering sort of smirk moving across his lips.

"We've come for our daughter," Nathan says with a bit of a growl in his voice.

"You have her, don't you?" I ask, while drawing my sword.

"Of course, he does," my Nathan...our Nathan says, brandishing that massive blade of his as if it were a small stick.

"Of course, I do," he replies clasping his hands in front of his stomach as he turns to his right. He takes a step away from a waist-high white pillar with a matching bassinet on top.

I step forward without even giving it a thought, and my Nathan catches my wrist. "Don't," he whispers. "If you go over there without a plan, he'll kill you...and then he'll kill me, and all of this will have been for nothing." I nod and return to my original position.

"The mongrel is smart," Anaras says, undoing the buttons on his coat. His lips purse in a surprised way.

"My husband is brilliant," I snarl. "He's already devising a strategy that will allow us to reclaim our daughter and defeat you." My eyes slowly move through deep blue to silver, and I can feel the shift in my husband's eyes. "Do you understand me, grandfather? My husband and I are going to kill you and take our daughter away from this nightmare."

"Oh," he says, slipping his jacket off his left shoulder. He nods slowly while repeating the action with his right. "If I were a lesser being, in the face of such formidable enemies and after such a...conviction-filled threat, I would truly be frightened." He extends his jacket at the tips of his fingers to his right. He drops it, and I can't help but feel that he's doing this all as an act of intimidation. As if to say that we aren't a threat to him. "Fortunately for me..." He takes hold of the saber at his side and pulls it from its sheath slowly. "...I am me..." He extends his arms to his sides and issues a bow. "...I have nothing to fear, least of all, from my half-breed granddaughter and her mongrel husband."

"Well, it's really gonna piss you off," our Nathan says. "...to know that you're going to die at the hands of a half-breed and a mongrel." I smirk. Nathan looks to me. *Do it.* I nod and dive into his mind that is wide open to me...I plunge into darkness only to emerge in a snow-covered field with sparse barren trees in the distance. A bitter wind howls and despite knowing this is a product of my husband's mind, I shiver from the intense cold.

"Love," Nathan calls to me. I turn to him with his golden eyes with emerald encroaching at the edges. Approaching me from his right, but at a distance, is a wolf with amber colored pupils with black in place of the white portion of its eyes.

I smile because even with the weeks of practicing this particular maneuver...this is the first time his two halves have been this clear to me. I extend a hand to each of them. "Come." Nathan approaches me confidently and for the first time, his skinwalker half does the same. I caress my Nathan's cheek with my right hand, while rubbing the wolf's head with my left. "So soft," I breathe as the fur moves between my fingers. The wolf looks up at me, and I see silver reflected back. "Calm." The wolf tilts into my hand as his eyes drift closed.

I come back to my Nathan and feel the fiery skin beneath my palm. "Warm," I hum absently. He smirks…that roguish smile of his still does things to me…things that…

"Later, my love," he breathes, placing his hand on top of mine.

I nod. "Focus," I say as his eyes drift closed. I close my eyes and slowly bring my hands together, pulling each of them with me until my hands are grasping a single being. I open my eyes to silver reflected back at me over honey and emerald with black replacing the whites…his skin darkens a few shades, his canines and incisors grow longer, sharper, his nails turn black and extend, and his body becomes thicker, more muscular…impossibly sexier.

"Later," he rumbles in two voices.

"Promise?"

"Anything."

"What have you done?" Anaras asks as I return to the world around us. I look at Nathan, who now looks exactly the way he did in my mind…I don't feel that same fury coming from him that normally overtakes him when he takes this form. I only feel calm, focus, and love…

"Ready?" he asks in his dual voiced growl.

"Always."

I raise my sword near my chin, holding it horizontally with tip pointed at Anaras's heart. My Nathan lifts his and holds it vertically with a bit of a tilt forward…defensively.

"Ready?" I ask this time.

"Steady," he returns.

"Go!" I snap and run to my left as fast as my legs will carry me. Nathan does the same, going to the right. I reach my grandfather first…opting to attack from behind him. He holds the sword over his shoulder…covering his back at an angle…the target of my attack. KLANK! My silver blade bounces off his that seems to be made of a steel-silver alloy. My Nathan appears in front of him before the sound fully reaches my ear. He brings his sword forward and parries Nathan's attack.

He comes back to me as I stab at him. He blocks and slashes at me while pushing off. I lean back and see several strands of my hair go flying. I rise just in time to see him engage Nathan again. He blocks Nathan's latest attack with his saber aimed downward, then drives the weapon outward and toward the ground, cutting my Nathan's leg. My Nathan hisses and stumbles back.

I swing at Anaras's head. He tilts his head to avoid the assault and then stabs at me. I abandon following through on my next strike and leap back to avoid his. My Nathan comes back with a descending slash. Anaras raises his weapon above his head. The blades collide, and the ground beneath Anaras crumbles.

I take the opportunity to stab him in the back. He disengages with Nathan as my sword pierces his shirt… Kl-klink! …the blade strikes his skin and slides off, going to the right.

"HAHAHA," Anaras chuckles. "It was fun, humoring the two of you." He pushes off with his right hand, using his sword to drive Nathan back a step. He rises, while throwing his left forearm back, knocking my sword away. He completes the turn and backhands my Nathan in the side with his left fist.

"NATHAN!" I shriek as he goes flying.

"WORRY ABOUT YOURSELF!" Anaras rumbles, driving his sword toward me. Our blades collide, and he pushes me back a step. His silver eyes meet mine. "No more mongrel to protect you! What will you do now?" I grit my teeth as he pushes me back another step. "I won't just cut your throat…or break your neck…no…this time, I'll remove your head."

"No," I groan. "You won't…" I focus with all my strength…physical and mental. "Datio!" I raise my index and pointer fingers up to my mouth. "Convenisti mecum! Perago!"

Suddenly, I'm plunged into a world of pure white. "By the first," Anaras says in a language that isn't English, but I understood every word. "I didn't think you possible of this…being this strong…" He looks at me. "…you should know that no matter how long we're here…less than a second would have passed out there."

"Sometimes one second is more than enough," mother says behind him.

He gasps and turns to her. "Anara," he whispers.

"Hello father."

His eyes move from her to me and back again. "This is a trick. This isn't…"

"You know the touch of my silver eyes as surely as you know mother's," mom says. "You know this is a memory that I implanted in her mind given the visions she gave me of the future," she adds, motioning to me.

"How are the two of you this powerful?"

"Love," we reply at the same time. "I did everything I did for my daughter," mom says.

"I will fight any enemy…even you, to protect mine," I add. Mom smiles.

"It should've been Adamar," Anaras moans, turning back to mom. He lifts his trembling left hand and points at her. "It should've been Adamar, who died and not you."

"I knew your plan father," she says walking over to him. "You are what you always have been." She takes his left hand. "Selfish to a fault...even when you know being selfless is for the best."

"You were my daughter."

"And I always will be," she says, just before she kisses the back of his hand. "But I can't let you take my granddaughter." He snatches his hand away and steps back. "I love you."

"I love you too," he whispers.

"I wasn't talking to you," mom replies. Her silver eyes dart to mine. "This is the last time you will see me...but know that it all has been leading to this moment." I frown as she takes Anaras's sword arm. She pulls him closer, driving the sword through herself.

I gasp. "MOTHER!"

"This will give you the time you need," she says as blood seeps from the corners of her mouth. "Tell my granddaughter," she says, gripping Anaras's arm tighter. "...I love her more than she'll ever know...just like you."

I gasp and inhale in the real world. Anaras stands...frozen...staring at his sword... I run to the bassinet and grab Anara. I focus on moving faster than I ever have before and run toward the door.

"You won't make it!" Anaras snarls, and his eyes have gone over to distraught, crazed even.

"Operite nos in velamine mendacii," I mutter quickly and concentrate on making him see five different versions of Anara and me.

"That would work on anyone else on the planet, but me!" he snarls driving his saber directly at my right eye.

KLANG! His blade rebounds off the flat side of my Nathan's blade held defensively over him. The force of the blow was still enough to drive him back into me. I stumble but manage to steady my legs under me and secure Anara to my heart.

"How is she?" he asks, his increased muscle mass having diminished. He's covered in slowly heeling bruises and blood trickles from the corner of his mouth. "Love?"

I sheathe my sword so that I can hold Anara with both hands. I tilt her back, and she opens her eyes. She looks at me and smiles while moving as if trying to reach for me, but the swaddle won't let her. "Fine," I breathe. "She's fine. We just have to go."

"If you think for one second," Anaras says, stepping in front of the only door. "I'm going to let you or the mongrel leave with that child, you are sorely mistaken."

"Any other exits?" I ask.

"No," he groans. "As I just found out, the hard way, the entire room is covered in stone…at least three feet thick."

"So, our only way out is through him?"

"Yes," Nathan says, peering at me…silver reflects off honey and emerald, and he sparks with a realization. "Anara."

"I have her."

"No, your mother…"

"What?"

"…it's a good plan," he adds, gripping is sword tighter. "He even showed you where to strike."

"What are you…?" I feel it before I can even ask and well before he has any hope of answering. "ABSOLUTELY NOT!" I snarl.

"We don't have a choice, Love…" He groans. "…with the exception of Angela, anyone else who enters this room will be a liability that he can exploit or worse turn against us."

"…but…I can do it," I gasp, as my dreams come back to me, repeating the message that this is it…this is the moment that I lose my husband.

"No, you can't!"

"Yes, I can!" I weep.

"No, you can't," he says again. "You're carrying the baby."

I look down at our daughter cradled in my arms. "I am carrying the baby, aren't I?" I weep. He nods. "I love you more than anything in this world."

"You two are my world," he returns as tears stream from his eyes. "Ready?"

"Steady," I sob, although my voice was anything but.

"Go," he snaps and vanishes. I catch it as soon as he lets it go.

"SUCH A MAD, RECKLESS DASH!" Anaras growls as my husband goes into motion with his attack. Anaras's sword explodes out of my Nathan's back. I swallow down the scream that feels as though it's going to burst out of my chest. "What is this?" Anaras snarls. "Where's your sword?"

I sprint forward as fast as I can, dragging the massive thing behind me. "HERE IT IS!" I snarl, bringing the blade forward…aimed at his eyes…the only vulnerable part of his body. He gasps and tries to pull his sword free, but my Nathan holds the weapon in place with both hands. My husband smiles as blood flows from the corners of his mouth.

"DAMN!" Anaras growls and abandons his weapon with his left hand. He reaches up and catches my Nathan's claymore with his bare hand. "ONE DOWN!" he growls in a boastful way.

"ONE TO GO," I return, releasing Nathan's sword, leaving Anaras shocked for a moment. I draw my sword, pull back, and stab him in his left eyes before he can recover.

"ULK," is all he manages as blood spurts from his eye socket and seeps over his cheek. He releases his weapon and Nathan's falls to the ground with a KLUNG! Anaras stumbles back...as I withdraw my blade. "I should've..." His remaining eye rolls back in his head as he falls onto his back with a thud.

Nathan falls, and I drop my sword in favor of catching him, hand cradling his head. "Love," he mutters. "Love...d-d-did we...?"

"We did," I sob. "She's safe..." He nods staring into my eyes. The world freezes around us...and then life leaves his eyes....and I cry...I cry because my prophetic dreams have come to pass...I have my daughter...but the love of my life is gone! Anara's cries join mine as I cling to her as if she were a life raft.

#####

Jamie

"Hunh," I groan as I hit the floor…hard.

"Jamina," Quincy says, wrapping an arm around me.

"What just happened?" I ask as he pulls me to my feet.

"We were moved," Tony says, offering my glasses to me.

"Thanks," I breathe, staring up at him. I slip my glasses back on, and he barely holds my gaze for a full second. I want to ask him how he's doing so badly, but he has made it more than abundantly clear that he doesn't want to talk about Shay or what happened to her. I feel it though. He's in agony…he finally finds someone who loves him, just him…and she's stolen away from him in an instant.

"Where are we?" Quincy asks, looking around, staring over my head.

"Not sure," Tony replies. "It's almost pitch black in here…"

"It is?"

"You're looking at the world through a hunter's eyes, Jamie," Tony says. He pulls the bowie knife from behind his back. "I don't see Sarah. She was with us, right?"

"Yeah," I respond.

"There's a door," Quincy says, moving toward it and pulling me along with him. He gives the handle a jiggle. "Locked." He wrenches the handle, and with a metallic groan, the lock snaps. He pulls the door open. Tony steps up to the door and lifts a finger between us. Quincy nods, and Tony peers out the door. He looks left and then right. He comes back and nods before stepping out. Quincy gives me a gentle shove and follows me into a dark hallway…and I instantly make the comparison to the room we were just in. It's definitely not nearly as dark as the closet or whatever we just stepped out of.

"Damn," Tony complains.

"What?" Quincy asks before I can. "Oh," he groans a moment later. "Damn."

"What?" I snap.

"Did you hear?" a voice says from down the hall.

"What?" another guy repeats my question.

"We're under attack…most of the other squads have been hit."

"Is it bad?"

"All of the Alpha's people have been engaged."

"Then…"

"HEY!" a new voice snaps. "YOU TWO! We're under attack. The witch needs all of us guarding her, at least, until the rune she's working on is finished."

"Sir!" they snap in unison and then three sets of footsteps move away from us.

"The witch?" I ask as a tremble moves up my spine. Every time I think I'm ready…I'm not. Every time I see her, I swear I'll be able to handle it this time. I never am…even when I was furious at her for ki…for ki…for what she did to Rais. I don't think I could have done it. No matter what, at the end of the day, she's still my… "…mom."

"Yeah," Quincy and Tony say at the same time. I look at Quincy and then Tony. "Are you…?"

"…okay?" Quincy finishes what his brother started.

"No." I tremble. "But when has that ever stopped me before?"

"I love you," Quincy whispers and kisses me on the temple.

"I know you do, and I don't blame you," I say as my stomach rolls.

"What?"

"What what?" I ask Tony.

"I thought I heard…" He stares at me with focus so intense, I'm surprised he's not burning a hole through me. "…never mind." He starts walking, very quietly. "Let's go."

We make our way down the hall and come to a four-way intersection. I can't help thinking that not only does this hallway look like a hospital, but with the pine scented cleanser lingering in the air, it smells like it too.

"So," Tony continues. "How are we going to do this?" He throws his hand out, sweeping over each of the three directions.

"Like this," I reply, right before I let out a gentle wave of spirit magic, using my echolocation. I nearly choke when I realize just how close she is to us.

"Jamie?" Quincy calls me.

"This way." I motion to the right and start walking. Tony quickly takes up the spot ahead of me, moving in a little bit of a crouch, hand on his knife. Quincy follows behind me, keeping watch over his shoulder.

We reach a corner, and Tony extends a hand to me, halting me. He holds his finger to his lips. He holds up two fingers and then points to the corner. I nod. He signals his brother and then to the right, and then to himself and to the left. Quincy nods this time.

Tony counts down from three, and they both vanish on one. There's a thunk and then another thunk. Then there are two heavier whoomphs like two people falling. Quincy peers around the corner, gives me a 'come on' hand. I follow him. We approach a pair of double doors with two unconscious vampire hunters on either side of it. Tony holds an offering hand out to the door.

I extend my hand toward it. With a gentle wave of spirit magic, I realize, "She's in there!"

Tony takes the left door's handle, and Quincy grabs the right. I raise my hands and nod to them. They return the gesture. They look at each other for a moment and then nod. They swing their doors in at the same time and rush into the room in a blur of motion.

"Fulgur," Tony snaps with a literal snap of his fingers, hurling lightning at the nearest guard on our left.

"Flamma!" Quincy barks, throwing a line of fire at the one on our right.

Both vampire hunters fall, one unconscious, and the other, trying to put out the flames that are covering his arms and back now. We push forward toward the center of the room…toward my mom standing in the middle of a large circle.

"You're early," she says in a blasé fashion, still staring at the massive rune.

"Extermino!" I snap, throwing my hand out to her. A fireball rushes toward her, but she doesn't even look at me…am I going to? Is it…?

"Defendo!" a man's voice calls, and my fireball strikes a translucent blue shield, between mom and me.

"Ventus!" a woman shouts, and a burst of wind rushes toward us.

"Capio!" I call and hold praying hands out in front of me, aimed at mom. The wind sweeps across my conical shield, decreasing the impact on me and my magic.

"She's a smart cookie," a woman with pixie cut red hair says, stepping out from behind a pillar on my right. Judging by her voice, she was the wind magic user.

"I'm impressed," a tall thin man with wavy brown hair says, stepping out on my left.

"Don't be impressed," mom says absently. "Get them out of here!"

"Don't you mean, kill them?" a tall muscular man draped in hunter's gear says. He has short cut salt and pepper hair, nearly shaved on the sides. He wears a long trench coat like Sera, but he also wears that light body armor that I saw on a few of the hunters who kidnapped me.

"You may be the Order of Ezekiel's Alpha," mom says, surveying the rune she's standing on. She's dressed in all black again, but at least it's not the fetish corset over leather. "…but I follow Eden's orders only."

"Hmph," the man grumbles, cutting dangerous eyes at mom.

"But you're welcome to try to kill them if you think you can." I gasp on that one…and mom doesn't even notice. She pays me no attention, whatsoever.

"Good," the man, this Alpha, says, stepping away from her. He pulls a pistol from his hip and pulls back on the slide, making sure the first bullet chambered, as dad would say. He points it at me.

"Fulgur," Tony snaps, and Alpha bends backward to avoid the lightning strike.

"How'd he…?" the startled witch says, staring at him as her friend, the tall thin guy, glares over his shoulder at him.

"It doesn't matter, witches," the Alpha says, standing up straight. "He's going to die, here and now." He aims at Tony and barely manages to defend against Tony's knife pressed again the gun's trigger guard. "What the hell are you?"

"The man who's going to murder you," Tony returns and kicks the Alpha, sending him flying. He vanishes a moment later.

"Aaaaahhhh," the woman on my right shrieks as flames cover her entire back.

"Jamie!" Quincy shouts, coming to a rest, standing over her. "GO!" I nod and run forward.

"NO, YOU DON'T!" the man roars extending his hand to me. "LIRO!"

The floor starts to crumble beneath me as I try to pour on some of that hunter's speed like dad and Amira have been trying to teach me.

I inhale deeply as the world slows around me. My right hand glances off the Crescent Moon Pendant, and I feel some of the magic from the Philosopher's Stone draw away. Good, if I didn't use the stone, this would suck. I half-turn to him in stride.

"Circumaggero," I murmur and bring my forearms together with upturned fists. Bits of concrete and linoleum knit themselves back together underneath me as the floor beneath him starts to crumble away.

"Wha…?" is all he manages, before he falls to the floor below…or, at least, I hope there's a floor beneath us.

"VENTULUS!" I hear from the right as the world speeds up to normal levels around me. The witch, still with fire clinging to her back, extends her hand toward me. Damn! She's got me…I'm not practiced enough as a witch/hunter to pull that move off twice.

"CAPIO!" Quincy snarls, extending his hand out near hers as wind sweeps up around them. He creates a shield in front of them…that effectively blocks her wind. I didn't know you could use a defensive spell like that.

"Thank you, babe!" I mouth to him.

"You're welcome, baby!" he mouths back.

BANG! And suddenly, the world turns gray around me…except the streak of crimson now coming from Quincy's left hip.

Alpha and his gun tumble to the side a second later. "You'll pay for that too!" Tony snarls, raising his blood-spattered knife above his head.

"You should be so lucky, you mutant-freak!" Alpha returns, pulling his knife. "I was aiming for his heart!" Tony and Alpha clash again as soon as the latter reclaims his feet.

"Quincy!" I breathe, turning to him as my feet snarl to a stop, kicking up loose linoleum chips and bits of concrete.

"Keep going!" he growls, dropping to one knee…my heart drops with him…as his hand snaps to his wound.

"Ventus!" the woman beneath him bellows, aiming her hand at him as best she can. Quincy grits his teeth as he lifts off his feet and goes fly.

"YOU!" I growl.

"Me," she returns, rising to her feet, hair and shoulders still smoldering. "Did you think this would be easy?" She lifts her right hand.

"No," I breathe. "I just didn't think anyone would be stupid enough to side with them…besides my mom, I mean."

"I heard that," mom says absently.

"I don't care," I snap. And just like that…I don't. I don't care anymore…this has to end…and I'm going to be the one who ends it, before anyone else…anyone I care about…gets hurt.

"VENTULUS!" the woman bellows throwing both hands out toward me this time.

"Ventus," I bark, sweeping my hand to the left, deflecting the tornado she sent my way with matching wind.

"Liro!" the man says, while crawling out of the hole I put him in.

"Capio!" I say, extending my left hand to him. Tiny bits of concrete fly at me and bounce of my shield like little stone bullets.

"How long can you keep this up, girlie?" he asks.

"Longer than you," I say, while etching a triangle with the tips of my finger on the shield. Suddenly, rocks stop pelting the shield as the man groans and falls with several spatters of blood flying away from him.

"What the…?" the woman says as I stop feeding my wind spell and turn the shield toward her. I then etch a square around the triangle already on this shield. The ensuing tornado thrown back at her toss her like a rag doll. She collides with the wall behind her and spits up blood before she falls unconscious. Or I hope she's unconscious.

"Well done, baby girl," mom says, giving me her full attention. "But as you can see, I'm done…now Eden's consciousness will start filtering through this tower, drawing strength from all the souls of Edenton as well as the places of their previous falls, and the ritual will begin."

"You're going to turn Nathan and Alana's daughter into a monster!" I scream at her.

"I do what I have to do. I told you, baby girl. I strayed from my purpose once, and I refuse to do it again."

"Then I guess, I'll have to do the same," I reply, marching toward her. None of it seems real for a moment...she throws a fire spell at me, and I deflect with wind. Water and I use earth. Wind and not only do I keep the earth shield up, I hurl it at her. She avoids it thankfully...yeah...thankfully.

The strange part is...that with every spell, I remember her sitting me down and patiently teaching me...her impatient daughter...her daughter, who always seemed as though she wanted to crawl before she could sit up. To walk before she crawled...and to run before she walked...

It's as if I were speeding toward this moment and no matter how much I want to...I can't do it...I can't kill her. I can't pull the trigger. I can't murder my own mom...even with her hurling a lightning bolt the size of a skyscraper at me... The image of Quincy protecting me from that woman's wind spell passes through my mind. ...but maybe...

I grab the Crescent Moon Pendant with my left hand, while extending my right hand to her. "Expugnationis!" I say as if it were a much shorter word and quickly draw a triangle, a square, and octagon on top of it. Mom gasps as the protective bubble surrounds her, not me, but continues holding both hands up as if she were about to cast a spell.

I sigh and walk up to examine the rune, she created... "Oh no," I breathe, because it's not the rune she created...it's the rune she must've already activated before I even got here.

Mom rests her palms against the shield. "You're too late, baby-girl."

"I see that."

"You're still gonna try and stop it somehow, aren't you?"

"Yep. I have to. You were always too good at making runes. With this design, no matter what happens, Eden's consciousness will still be filtered into Anara."

"Yep." She looks at the shield. "And you know, I have to stop you stopping me."

"Yeah, right," I breathe absently. "You know as well as I do that shield won't dissipate even if I stop feeding it magic and that it's practically indestructible."

"I know, baby girl. Flamma!" she says, opening her hand.

"Mom!" I shriek turning to her in horror as she holds a flame in her right hand. "You can't! You know what kind of shield that is and what will happen to you, if you do it."

"I have to, baby-girl…" I shake my head, tears filling my eyes as she shakes hers with tears filling hers. "…know this…" Her hand trembles as she raises it to an attack position. "…everything I've done…all of it…I've done because I love you…" She nods. "I love you so much, and I always will."

"Mom don't!" I weep, pressing my hands against the shield. "We can-" She purses her lips and shakes her head, before mouthing, 'Goodbye, baby-girl.' She releases the fire, and the second it comes into contact with the shield, the interior of that space becomes an inferno repeating in on itself, constantly increasing the heat.

"NO!" I scream, slamming both hands against the shield's exterior, but of course, it's no good. Nothing can get through this thing…not even me. I fall to my knees. The fire finally fades and there's nothing inside the shield anymore.

I sigh and wipe my nose. "I love you too, mom." I look at the rune beneath me, starting to glow. "But not enough to let this slide." I grab the Crescent Moon Pendant and quickly etch a triangle in mid-air, I surround that with a square, a pentagon, a hexagon, and finally a heptagon and then begin using both index fingers to create a circle around the seal floating in mid-air.

"Jamie?" Quincy calls, still clutching his bloody side. "What are you doing?"

"What I have to."

"You can't!" Tony barks. "That will."

"Expugnationis!!!" I shriek and then wrap my arms around myself. Quincy and Tony run to the edge of this even larger shield. "I'm sorry. This is the only way…even if we break the rune, it'll still…" I look at my stern and studious Tony and then my flirty and funny Quincy. "…I love you so much."

"Then don't leave me!" Quincy pleads.

I nod. "Tell my dad…and Amira…and-and Alex…" Quincy shakes his head. "…you tell 'em."

"Please," he whispers, clutching at the shield.

"I'm sorry," I mouth back as the seal takes effect, and I'm hit with a torrent of power…it feels as though something is wrapping around my heart…squeezing it…and then, I don't feel anything… a little dizzy, I mean… everything fades to white…and I…

"Waaaaahhhhh….waaaaaahhhhh…waaaahhhhh…."

Is that a baby? Am I being reincarnated? What's goin-

#####

Chapter 25: Birthright

Alex

"I can't believe I'm here!" I say, while shoving a hunter down by his semi-automatic weapon. I'm honestly a little surprised, considering that he's almost as strong as I am. If not for Nate's training, this probably would've gone the exact opposite way.

"I love you too, cousin," Kai says, avoiding the knife of another hunter before snap-kicking him to the side of the head.

"You know what I mean," I say right before I headbutt the guy in tactical gear, shattering his goggles. He groans as blood spurts from his left eye. Oh, I hope I didn't… Never mind, he just opened his eye. This time I punch him in the face driving his head down to the ground, knocking him unconscious. "I mean, I followed Gwen so that we wouldn't get separated!"

"Believe me, I understand, pet!" Gavin growls, while batting one of the hunters away. "At this point, even I'm worried about my sister!"

"Worry about yourself!" Amira says, driving the butt of her sword into one of her fellow hunters to the point of lifting them off the ground.

"Huh," Gavin grumbles as three more hunters run toward him. Blue flames renew all around him, starting from his shoulders and moving down to his hands. "How many of these guys are there?" he says while using huge, flaming fox paws to swat the three hunters away.

"Too many," Sora replies as she claws the vest off one of them.

"Smell them!" The leggy vampire with the long red hair says just before she vanishes again. She's fast even compared to us…even compared to Nate. Thinking about it…I wonder how everyone else is doing…how Gwen's doing. I can't think about that now or I'll freeze up worrying about my wife. I sniff, and all I get is human… A little superhuman, but human, nonetheless.

"Ugh!" Kai moans as he withdraws from the female hunter he was fighting while pulling her goggles away.

"What?" I ask. Before he can answer, the smell hits me. It smells like roadkill that's been left in the sun for way too many days…after being fished out of a sewer. I turn and see vacant, white-on-white eyes staring out from under the riot gear of the girl with grayed out patchy rough skin… I guess I should've said the ghoul Kai's mixing it up with.

"It seems they're trying to crush us with sheer weight of numbers, mago!" sofu says, while mirroring Gavin with the huge flame paws over his hands.

"Or," that black woman who was with Amira's mom starts. "They're trying to make us doubt ourselves…mixing daemons, monsters, and undead in with the hunters, knowing that we're trying not to kill the hunters, even if we wouldn't hesitate with the creepy crawlies."

"Now, that's just playing dirty," Jamie's dad says, standing back-to-back with Tracy. They extend pistols, firing pretty indiscriminately considering we're trying not to kill the members of their organization.

"Aren't we supposed to be trying to spare as many as we can?" that gorgeous dark-haired woman with the French accent repeats my thought, while tossing a hunter over her head as if she were throwing away an empty soda can.

"We are…," Tracy says, tucking one of her guns under her arm, while reloading the other one. She flips and repeats with the other. "…and it's a good strategy, sir!" She glances at 'Duchess,' I think I heard that redhead vampire call her, and resumes shooting. "I'm running low on rubber bullets…it won't be long before we have to break out the real stuff and then go hand-to-hand."

Considering how many shells Mr. Baggett and Tracy are going through, I should be glad that somehow the doors kicked us out to the parking lot…complete with the wolves' and vampires' armored vehicles to duck behind.

"The sun's going down," a black guy in a really expensive looking suit says. I wonder what his deal is. He smells a little like Nate, but not quite.

"What's that mean?" Gavin grumbles.

"Vampires," says a white guy in almost as nice a suit. He also smells like Nate…but not nearly as close to his scent as the other guy. They must be wolves because they don't smell like skinwalkers.

"HOW DARE YOU?" Stefana shrieks with her flaming sword extended in front of her. Oh no…is that another fairy on the ground in front of her… bleeding…and is she squaring off with a third fairy…?

"Alex," Sora says over my shoulder with a little bit of a rumble to her voice. "Isn't that the fairy who burned you in Nanbu? Right after your wedding?"

My teeth gnash and oddly enough, I feel like my skin's on fire…especially the spot where she burned me. "Yeah," I growl back and hunter's step over to Stefana.

"Alexander!" she bellows, never taking her eyes off the fairy across from her. "Get my sister to safety!"

"But…"

"Do it," Amira says, extending her katana in front of me…the flat side closest to me, sharp edge aimed at the ground. "This is fairy business," she adds as her eyes meet Stefana's. They both nod, just before Amira vanishes again.

"Alright," I say, pulling the redheaded woman away as best as I can, without damaging her wings any more than they already are, without moving her body any more than absolutely necessary, and without getting blood on me. I pull her behind the black SUV with Nate's scent all over it. "GAVIN!" I yell as soon as we're away from them and behind cover...but, still keeping Stefana and that other fairy in sight.

"What, pet?" he asks, appearing out of a burst of blue flames, opposite me. "Oh," he humbles himself. Sora appears behind him, to watch his back, as blue flames start to cover said back. Kai moves over to cover mine. Gavin pours his healing blue flames over the fairy.

"YOU KNOW IT SHOULD'VE BEEN ME!" that brunette, mousy-looking fairy who burned me screams as she uses a glowing maple leaf like a knife against Stefana's sword. Oddly enough, it holds the burning weapon off like it's made of steel.

"MY SISTER EARNED HER PLACE, ARIELLE, AND MORE THAN THAT SHE WAS DEEMED WORTHY BY OUR MOTHER...," Stefana shouts back, while swinging her sword...I guess, because the only way I know she's still attacking are the metallic clangs that ring out, the tiny flames that fly away with every sound, and the fact that she has Arielle on her backfoot. "...OUR MOTHER, WHO YOU MURDERED, YOU UNGRATEFUL BRAT!"

"Damn," Gavin grumbles. I look at him as the flames vanish from his body all at once.

"Wha...?" I start to ask, but I don't have to. The look on Sora's face as she puts her hands on his shoulders says it all. I look down at this fairy...who gave her life for the cause.

"You spoiled, arrogant sow," Stefana rumbles, as her sword begins to glow beneath the bright, yellow-orange flames. "...you've taken another life from the fairy kingdom!" How did she know? "Stolen another sister from me! For that, I will never forgive you!"

"Forgiveness? Do you think I want something like that from the likes of you? I was meant to rule the fae realm...I was meant to rule all fae...I alone perfected healing magic...to the point that I could use it as a weapon!" she snarls with a little spittle flying away and the craziest crazy-eyes I've ever seen as she pulls out another glowing maple leaf. "Becoming the Fairy Queen is my birthright!"

"Whatever you have to tell yourself, traitor," says a huge woman with short red hair right before she swats the 'traitor' away with a mace that looks like three rakes welded together...and made of steel instead of plastic or aluminum.

"Abbie the Seventy-fifth?" Stefana says.

"Stefana the Seventh," Abbie returns with a 1000-megawatt smile and a two-finger salute...her pointer and middle...not two middles. The smile comes down instantly when she looks past Stefana and in our direction. "They got big sis, huh?"

"Yeah," Stefana replies, stealing a glance in our direction.

"I guess that's really the way of things, huh?" Abbie says.

"It is so," Stefana says, sounding stiffer, stuffier than I've ever heard her.

"We might as well go out with a bang!" Abbie returns, renewing her smile and raising her mace.

"I don't plan on going out at all," says another woman...no, fairy landing on the other side of Abbie. This one is tall and curvy like Stefana, but with almost as much muscle as Abbie. Her skin is the color of milk chocolate, and her hair is long and wavy with a medium reddish-brown coloring.

"Jeania the Eighth," Stefana calls her calmly. Jeania just nods in return.

"Three against one!" Arielle snarls from somewhere. I peek over the hood of the SUV...we're winning...I couldn't tell before because I was in the thick of it. There are a lot more 'hunters' on the ground dead or in handcuffs than there are us super naturals around. "It's begun!" Arielle snarls as the ground beneath us begins to glow with bright red lines moving in various directions. "Our master will be revived soon!"

"Not soon enough!" Stefana declares.

"Because you won't live long enough to see it," Abbie adds.

"For we are our mother's vengeance!" Jeania says, pulling a long, thin sword from her hip.

"Then come...and face your deaths, 'sisters!'" the maniac replies.

A fire gap opens closer to her...and a short Chinese man...and his clothes are definitely an indicator of his ethnicity, rises from the burned-out marking. Crazy Pants smirks, still staring at her 'sisters.'

"It seems the sun went down just in time, sister," he says with his arms folded neatly behind his back.

"Indeed," Arielle says and with so much viciousness that even the little guy raises an eyebrow to her. "Now, help me slaughter my sisters and then the rest of these..."

"I don't t'ink so, Xiao!" that redheaded woman says, bringing a blade across the Chinese guy's midsection as Amira comes across his shoulders with her katana. "Now, t'is feels familiar," the vampire lady says, keeping her eyes low.

"I don't even wanna know," Amira replies.

"I-" is all this Xiao guy manages to get out before... I nearly retch. ...his head falls off and then his body falls off his legs before any of him even reaches the ground.

Arielle stares at the woman and Amira with huge eyes and a quivering, lower lip. "T'at's all t'e mercy traitors deserve," the redhead says.

"A quick death?" Amira asks. A nod is the only answer she gets. "You sound like my mom." They smirk at each other. "Working with vamps…good vamps, might not be so bad."

"Likewise, good hunter." They nod and vanish.

"We won't make this fast," Stefana says, bearing down on Arielle, surprising her entirely. She removes her 'sister's' left arm before she can even react. She shrieks in pain and actual foam starts gathering at the corners of her mouth. "That was for my sister, your new queen."

That new fairy, Jeania, slices up her back, removing her wings…and surprisingly, she screams even louder as tears fall away, and she drops the leaf she was still holding. "That," Jeania growls, towering over her. "…was for our mother, your former queen."

Crunch sounds out as Abbie brings her mase across Arielle's left knee, driving it into her right and dropping her instantly. She groans and tries to catch herself on both hands…but she only has one. Her head thuds against the ground. "And that," Abbie says, draping her mace over her shoulder. "…is for our brother and future king, Tibal, ya traitorous cow!" She spits on her.

"No!" Arielle shrieks. "I should've been queen!" she cries, trying to pull herself away from her sisters with her remaining hand. Six snaps sound out and six fairies…every one of them with a weapon in hand…appear in front of her. She swallows a lump, staring up at them as tears and snot run down her face.

I duck behind the car…because I get the feeling that if Xiao being cut up nearly made me puke, then whatever's about to happen to her…I definitely don't want to see.

My phone starts to vibrate and thank God, because answering it will hopefully distract me from Arielle's screams. "Hello?"

"Alex," Gwen weeps.

"Gwen!" Gavin appears next to me and then sofu and obāsan. "Are you okay? Where are you…? So that we can…?"

"Alex!" she cries. "…it's Meghan…"

"Meghan…?" I gasp as I realize why she's crying.

I stand and meet Gavin's eyes. He frowns, and I shake my head.

"Damn," he growls as Sora buries her face in his chest.

"Gwen," Kai whispers. She makes a noise that tells me she heard him.

"Kai," I start, expecting him to try and crack a joke to make the situation lighter. "This isn't the time for…"

"We're here for you," he says and sounds the sincerest I've ever heard my cousin sound. "Whatever you need, we're here for you. Your family has your back."

"Hello?" that white guy wolf in the really nice suit says answering his phone. "Angela, where are you…? Are you okay?" That redheaded vampire appears in front of him and stares at him with fear in her eyes…right Angela's her sire, I think. He looks at her and nods. She sighs in relief. "And is Natavius speaking Spanish?" He pauses. "Mexico City?! How did you get to Mex-" He bows his head, and his eyes become serious. "No," he moans. "Unfortunately, our limbs don't grow back…and if you didn't get him to someone to reattach it almost immediately, I'm sure it already…" He rubs his eyes with his free hand.

"Hello?" that really well-dressed wolf says. "Alana, were you…?" His eyes lose all their focus. "Okay…" His expression buckles as he drops to his knees. "NO!" he roars and punches the asphalt, destroying the part right under his fist. The part that's not glowing…in fact, none of the ground is glowing anymore. "NO!" he growls and then emits a noise like a whimper.

"Nathan?" the other wolf says as the redhead wraps her arms around him, holding him tight.

"Nate," I growl…and I think I missed whatever Gwen said next. Wait, where's my…?

"Yeah," Gavin rumbles into my phone against his ear. His eyes move from me and over to the two wolves, who're both bawling their eyes out and releasing intermittent howls. "…we have other…casualties…" His eyes go over to Stefana and the other fairies who are now, carrying their fallen actual sister away…I don't even wanna know what happened to the traitor.

"Tony?" Kai says, answering his phone. "Why are…?"

I gasp…and everything becomes numb all at once…because there's only one reason Tony would be calling Kai. "Jamie…?"

#####

Midnight Princess Epilogue

Angela

"How many...?" Alana breathes. She stares at the overcast sky outside her bedroom window. She's taken over my room again...and again because her heart has been destroyed because of Nate. This time it absolutely wasn't his choice...actually, given what she told us after a while...yeah, it was his choice. At least this time, I completely agree with his choice. It's the same choice I would've made in his shoes...it's the same choice she would've made.

"How many members of my family will I have to bury?" She swallows a lump and shakes her head. "How much of my life will be torn away from me?"

I open my mouth to respond, but there's nothing...not a single thing in my head...not a word of comfort that I can offer her. Nothing will ever make this make any sense...let alone make it ok-

"Listen to me." She turns to me with silver tears moving away from her matching eyes. "Since this insanity started, you've lost your lover...your cousin...and your best friend...all within a little over a year of your life being completely turned upside down." I shake my head slowly. "I don't know how you're still standing," she says, walking toward me with open arms.

"Lots and lots of therapy," I say, reciprocating the hug. I pat her back. "It's just too bad prescription drugs don't work on vampires!"

She huffs a laugh. "This is why you were his best friend." We separate, and she stares into my eyes. "I'm going to need that levity in the days...weeks, and months to come."

"Anything you need, Alana," I return, taking her hand. I kiss it and hold it to my heart. "Anything."

A gentle knock comes from the door. "T'e car's here," Raven says and even she looks as if she's cried her eyes out.

"Thank you," Alana says, moving over to Anara sleeping in her carrier. I'm kind of glad she's asleep. She'd be bawling her eyes out like her mom otherwise. "Does...?" Alana pauses. She frowns and cants her head to the left. "Does she look...larger...perhaps, taller to you...than she did this morning?"

Raven and I rush over to her side. I frown because she looks exactly like she did this morning. Raven and I exchange a glance behind Alana's back. I shake my head, while shrugging. "No, dear," Raven says, returning to her original posture. "I don't believe so."

"Ah," Alana purrs. "It must be me then." Her palms press firm against her stomach as she inhales deeply. "I will have to be mindful of that."

"You don't have to be mindful of anything," I say.

"Not today, ya don't," Raven agrees.

Alana nods as fresh tears fill her eyes. She collects Anara using the handle for her carrier. "Let's go."

We make our way down to the car, waiting at the curb. Richard stands next to the door holding an umbrella, even though the rain let up. "Richard," Alana breathes, standing next to him.

"I was there when you met, miss," he says, sounding stodgier than usual. "I should be there when you…" Even his lower lip quivers, and he bows his head. Alana wraps one arm around him, and he reciprocates. She climbs into the car. Raven pats his arm and then follows Alana.

"It's been a helluva year, hasn't it, big bro?"

"Yeah," he says and looks up as if trying to keep tears in his eyes. I rub his forearm and then climb in behind Raven. He closes the door, and we're on our way.

We pull into the cemetery, and it's easy to tell where we're headed. If not for the crap load of fancy cars lining the parking area, the concert level crowd would probably be a dead giveaway. The car stops, the door opens instantly, and a scent that makes my still heart want to move wafts into the car. I reach out and take Natavius's hand…his only hand…and he pulls me into his arms…well, arm. I tremble…because it just came crashing back into me like a wave. Meghan's gone…Nate's gone…Jamie's gone…we won, but we've lost so much along the way.

Natavius pulls me away from the door as Richard takes Anara from Alana. He then helps her out. Then Raven.

"We'll leave the carrier," Alana says in a monotone voice. "…since she's awake." We all look at Anara, just as her gorgeous light brown eyes open. She inhales deeply and looks at us as if she's about to say something. I smile, and she smiles back. She tilts her head back and looks at her mother…and her expression crumbles instantly. She wears a sour face and shuts her eyes tight. "Come here, my love," Alana purrs while pulling her from her carrier. This has got to be agonizing for her, trying to keep her emotions even while her own heart is breaking. She stops and looks at me. "Could you…?"

"Yeah," I breathe, taking Anara from her. She makes grabbing motions for my face.

"Gah, gah…," she says, staring at me, while holding my face. Her eyes flash silver for a moment, and I feel as though she just asked me a question…about Alana.

"She's fine," I whisper to her. "Or she will be." Anara inhales deeply and rests her head on my shoulder as she suckles on the side of her fist. We walk toward the crowd that parts for us…some wear sneers, others with sad expressions, and a few with actual sympathy.

"Alana," a woman with dark red hair, full pale lips, and perfect olive skin says, stepping into the aisle. "I know you don't know me...but I've been a friend to Nathan for many years."

"Clarissa," Alana says in a way that suggests they may have met before, but I doubt it. "...of course, Nathan spoke fondly of you and the kindness you showed him when he returned to the States after..." She inhales deeply and nods. "...thank you for your kindness."

"Of course," Clarissa breathes, before tears start to spill from her own eyes. Alana continues, and we follow. She stops when she reaches the first row and acknowledges her pack...Scowly-I mean, Christopher and his wife, da or my sire-father, Vance, one of my best friends, Kyra, who's holding her son, Calvin, and the wolf I fell for pretty hard, when I didn't think I could anymore. He must have taken the long way around, using his speed. How can vampires and wolves get this close after hating each other for centuries?

I lift my eyes as Christopoher hugs Alana...that's how...her...the Midnight Princess, now the Midnight Queen...I give Anara a jostle because she's the Midnight Princess now.

Alana moves to the far side of the casket and half-turns to me. She makes a beckoning motion, asking me to follow, and I do.

Alana steps up to the lectern. She grips it tightly, staring at the Bible resting there. She lifts her eyes...and stares at the coffin laid out before her, not daring to look at the picture of Nate beside it. I make the mistake of looking at it and shiver instantly. The tears start falling, and I can't stop them.

Alana looks at me and smiles, before returning to face the other mourners. She takes a deep breath. "My Nathan," she says finally. She lifts her eyes, glowing bright with silver. "Our Nathan," she adds a moment later. "I say 'our,' because that was the beauty of my husband. He suffered..." She pauses and pants like a marathon runner. "...so much throughout his life. He felt abandoned...he felt betrayed...feared...he felt as though he were hated even." She swallows a lump as silvery tears move down her face. Her hands tremble on the dais as she shakes her head slowly. "But somehow, he never let that change him...not at his core. He was always a kind soul. He always wanted to protect those close to him. He was always ready to lend a hand. And always wanted to be of use.

"In the end, he died for the one thing he wanted most in life...the one thing we both wanted most in life...he died for our family." I lean closer to her, and she reaches out to caresses Anara's cheek, causing her to coo while leaning into her mother's touch.

"Little known fact," she picks up again. "My Nathan and I met at the tip of a sword...the tip of my sword..." She pats her stomach. "...buried in his hip." She huffs a laugh. "He'd just saved my life, and the first thing I do in return, I stabbed him." A low rumble of laughter moves through the crowd.

"He was the first wolf I'd ever met…and that moment was only the start of a much wider world…" She huffs and weeps, her lower lip quivers. "…that you opened up for me, my Nathan."

She shakes her head feverishly. "I will never stop appreciating you for showing me that there was more to this world than I had ever seen before. I will never stop being grateful to you for the way you reached out and touched my heart. And I will never…ever stop loving you for gifting me our daughter, or the sacrifice you made to ensure her happiness."

She holds her hands up to her lips and then touches the casket. "Mon petit loup," she whispers as more tears move down her face. "My love…my world…" She reaches out and puts her hand on Anara again. "…you were the best father she could've ever asked for, my love."

Alana steps forward, placing both hands on the casket now as if it's the only thing holding her up…and I don't know why, but I move with her. I feel like she needs Anara by her side.

She shivers and more tears spill over…can't believe I caught that because I'm bawling like Anara is too. "…and you were a far better husband than I could have ever wished for…" She sniffs, and a shiver stills her lower lip…but it quivers as she tries to speak again. "…and the world will be forever dimmer…without you in it…" She falls to her knees, clutching at the earth. "…I miss you with every part of me…with every fiber of my being I will continue to…for the rest of my days…and I long for the day that we are reunited in the hereafter, my love."

She forces herself up and looks out to the crowd again…and everyone…every single person, wolf, witch, and vampire alike…is on their feet.

"Thank you all for coming…my Nathan…our Nathan, loved you all." She moves around the casket and straight into Raven's arms. Maggie and Duchess are there to pat her on her back…and probably help hold her up…I think her legs finally gave out on her. I don't know why mine haven't.

Richard and Christopher help Alana, move back up the aisle toward the parking lot. I turn to the cemetery attendant and nod. He goes to the little device at the top of the casket and engages it. The casket begins to sink as he removes the flowers from the top.

"I can't put into words how much I hate burying my best friend," I mutter. "I'm gonna miss you so much, Nate." I bounce Anara on my hip. "But I promise you…this little girl will know how much she was loved…and how much she'll be loved for the rest of her life. I promise you that."

"Yah, yah, yah," Anara says, shaking her fist at the sinking casket.

I make my way over to Raven as Da kisses her on the cheek. "She's gon' ta need us." I nod and frown. "Wha…? What is it?"

I bounce Anara on my hip again. "This might sound crazy…but I think she is a little heavier…even from when I took her at the car." Raven frowns and stares at her niece, who returns her stare with silver eyes that have tiny green and gold flecks intruding on the silver.

#####

Fox Fire Epilogue

Gwen

I sit behind the family on the second row with Stephen. Meghan's mom had asked Stephen to sit with the family, but he had declined. I can feel his sorrow and the pain he feels for not being able to protect her. He's wearing thick sunglasses since we're outside, but I know it's more to hide the puffiness of his eyes. He's not crying now, but he's shed so many tears. I know he wishes Alex were here…so do I, but I know he's needed in Edenton.

I fidget absently with my wedding ring, looking at the stones. They glitter, reminding me of that first shopping spree we went on. The one that cost me a ton in chore money but gained me a real "bestie."

I haven't even known Meghan all that long, but she's left such an impression on me. We went through so much together. I try not to crinkle the notes in my hand since I find my hands are sweating, trembling, and curling under as if they want to hold something, grab onto something…anything.

It shocked me when Mrs. Powers asked me to do the eulogy, but she told me I was, "Literally, the only person who ever really knew Meghan." I had been hesitant until she pulled the "Meghan would've wanted you to" card. I'm just glad there are fewer people here than at graduation.

I look at the beautifully carved marble crypt where Meghan will be entombed. It looks so cold and final. I shiver staring at it, thoughts of Meghan going anywhere alone…even to her grave are a hard concept for me to grasp. Then again, she went from always having an entourage of lemmings with her to spending all her time with just Stephen or me.

In almost stark contrast are the elaborate floral arrangements crowding the casket. They're so vibrant and alive…just like Meghan was. And not just as a living being, I mean…everything about her seemed vivid and lively. Her gorgeous hair, those brilliant eyes, her smile…invigorated entire rooms…possibly entire towns at a time. I do know that for me Edenton will forever be darkened by her absence.

As everyone takes their seat, I feel a hand on my shoulder. Turning around, I see that Gavin has taken a seat in the row of chairs behind me. I had thought that he would be going with Sora to Nathan's funeral. "She was my friend," he says simply. "She called me on my sh…stuff." He nods. "I'm gonna miss her." The corners of my mouth turn down, because I would've never expected Gavin to be so…contrite. "And if you tell anyone I said that I'll kill you." I smile.

I fight the impulse to jump up and hug him. His lips form a line, and he pats me on the shoulder again. I can tell he doesn't really know what to say beyond that, but him being here means more than anything he could say. I reach my opposite hand over to grab his. He gives mine a squeeze.

"Gwen?" I hear from the row in front of me. I turn back to Anne Powers, Meghan's mom. "We're ready for you, dear," she says.

I exhale a deep breath. I take in a deep breath and try to breathe out the overwhelming sorrow I'm feeling from everyone gathered. Stephen pats my arm while continuing to look forward.

I head to the front of the assembled group and try not to think about Meghan's lifeless body in the closed casket behind me. I shudder thinking about her body on the ground that night…

I look out at the assembled and see Mrs. Powers, one of her hands gripping her boyfriend's hand, and the other hand gripping Angela's mom's hand. Angela sits stoically next to her mother, but I can feel that this is hard for her too. Gavin gives me a nod, and I can feel even more sadness than he hinted at coming from him.

"Thank you, Mrs. Powers for the honor of speaking today. Meghan Powers was an incredible friend. She chose me to be her 'bestie,'" I say, adding air quotes, "when I was the awkward new girl. 'Nice shoes,' was the first thing she said about my little pink shoes with purple piping. She was like a ray of sunshine. Anyone who knew Meghan knew she had a magnetism that drew everyone too her."

I see Mrs. Power's eyes twinkle at this statement.

"Everything Meghan did, she did fiercely. She was a warrior. That included friendship, love, and taking care of those she cared about. She did it all with style and grace, usually while wearing heels and a cute little dress."

There was a small spattering of laughter at this.

"I couldn't have asked for a better choice of a best friend…and she chose me."

There are more words on the page, but my eyes are too blurry to read them. I nod and mouth a, 'Thank you' to everyone before walking up the aisle of chairs. I turn the corner to stand out of sight before I lose it. I wrap my arms around myself and lean over from the pain of her loss. I don't hear him walk up, but I allow Gavin to pull me forward into a hug. He lets out a sigh, and I just cry into his chest.

#####

Fiery Witch Epilogue

Alex

Everything in me wants to scream or kick something...or go running through the woods. Okay, so that last one's the skinwalker half of me, but I could definitely go for a run. Anything to get rid of this feeling...this nervous empty feeling. Like my nerves are all on fire, but at the same time, like something's weighing my body down. I hate this...I hate that you're not here to tell me how stupid or maybe even, normal that the way I feel is.

I feel like it should be raining...why isn't it raining? Tears move down my face like rain though. Damn it, it should be raining. I can only imagine what Gwen's going through in New York. I can't believe we lost Nate...and Meghan...and...and...I tremble, and that dull ache moves through my head again before going down into my chest, making my whole body feel heavy.

It's kind of like when my dad died...I had my mom still...and parents are supposed to go before kids...right? This...this just feels wrong though...not that it felt right with dad, but this... We were supposed to grow up together...like become adults together...get married...well, her get married...and then have kids and let our kids play together...grow up together. We were supposed to grow old together and be those old friends with funny, quirky inside jokes.

"Thank you," Tony says to the reverend, while shaking his hand with both of his. Did he just slip him a couple of bills? I know the Blackshears wanted to keep her passing a secret, but hush money?

"You said that there was nothing you could do!" Jamie's dad snarls while pointing at Quincy's chest. Amira struggles to hold him back which is surprising because I know she's a lot stronger than him but at the same time is completely understandable because...it'd be pretty hard to hold me back too in his shoes. If I didn't know how easy it was to lose somebody during that mess, I'd probably be going off on them too. The elves lost their first...Titania. Twee said that she was the strongest of them...and she fell. Just like Jamie...just like Nate...just like Meghan.

"WHY DIDN'T YOU SAVE HER? WHY DIDN'T YOU STOP HER?" He glares at Tony. "OR YOU? YOU WERE BOTH SUPPOSED TO BE IN LOVE WITH HER AND YOU JUST LET HER DIE! YOU LET BOTH OF THEM DIE!"

It sucks for everyone all around... I look to the right of Jamie's tombstone and see her mom's.... It's really gotta suck for Mr. Baggett. He lost his oldest daughter and his estranged wife on the same day... Hell in the same fight, I couldn't even imagine if something were to happen to Gwen let alone our daughter.

"We'll talk…later," Tony says, putting special emphasis on the word 'later.' I still hate that guy. He always seems so cold, so standoffish, but now it's even worse. You would think that if anyone would be crying over Jamie's death, it would be the two of them. It's bad enough that Quincy's not even crying, and he was her boyfriend, but Tony, he doesn't even seem broken up about it like Quincy at least does.

I kneel next to Jamie's grave and collect a handful of dirt from the side. The smell of freshly overturned earth, way too much lacquer, and Jamie, smelling just like she did the last time I saw her…alive, wafts up the six feet as if it were right under my nose. I can't even rightly put into words how wrong it feels that she smells the same…like exactly the same…the only difference is I'm not getting hints of her breath with her breathing. She's not the same though…she's not breathing…and there's no heartbeat either.

"I'm gonna miss you so much, little sis," I say, while sprinkling the tiny granules over the casket…the words my wife makes me remember. I huff a laugh…because it isn't just her that makes me remember things. I hear Jamie in my head, reminding me that 'my little sister' is a few weeks older than I am. "Yeah," I sigh. "But I was talking about height…Shorty." Two tears fall into the grave, falling on her casket. I tremble. "Especially now," I weep as it sets in that that's my best friend down there…in her grave.

Suddenly, a pair of arms wrapped around me at the neck. Amira pulls me in and holds onto me really tight, before she rocks us gently. "I know it's selfish," she starts, whispering in my ear. "But I wish I had at least a fraction of the time that you had with her."

I pet her arm with my right hand while holding her wrist with my left. "It's not selfish," I reply. "Your sister was the best, and there's no two ways about that. Honestly, I wish you had gotten to spend more time with her too. 'Cause even knowing her since I was four, I still want more time with her." The two of us laugh, which turns into shivering chuckles, which turns into tears. Her other arm wraps around my midsection as if trying to steady herself and not me. I stand pulling her up with me. I turn and wrap both arms around her as she starts to bawl in a way that I never would've imagined the girl beheading vampires in Nanbu capable of.

Her mother is there a second later to take her off my arms. I pass her over as gently as possible, which is also something I would've never imagined attributing to Jamie's badass half-sister.

"I'm so sorry for your loss, Alexander," her mom says from behind those huge sunglasses. I nod and mouth, 'Thank you,' just before her full attention returns to Amira. "We should go," Sera says, bundling Amira up. Her daughter nods, although the tears haven't stopped flowing. They stumble away, as Amira's legs seem to repeatedly give out on her. I look around, and Mr. Baggett is already gone, too.

I turned to Quincy and Tony, who're standing at the foot of the grave staring into it. "Are you sure she'll be safe down there?" Quincy asks as if she's still alive.

The younger brother leans into the older. "The interior of the casket is lined with protective runes, shielding enchantments, and a few disguising charms that should ward off anyone who might come looking for her."

Quincy groans as his right hand moves down his face, pulling the stubble and baggy eyes down a bit before they return to their regular positions. "Is all this…any of this really necessary?" he asks, glowering at his younger brother while throwing his upturned palm out to the hole where 'the love of his life' rests.

"You know that it is," Tony growls as a response with a stern expression. "…and you know why that is!" he adds with even more tension filling his voice. My eyes narrow, because I can't help but feel like they're up to something. This feels way too much like when they attacked us because of Bethany.

Tony's eyes dart to me and then back to his brother. He holds a calm down hand out to him as his own face loses some of the hard edge. I can't help noticing that the usually neatly trimmed and clean-shaven Tony is sporting longer, slightly unkempt hair and a few days five o'clock shadow. Thanks for that expression, dad. Still have no idea what it means, but whenever you would use it, your facial hair looked like his.

"Perhaps," Tony starts again in an even lower whisper than before. "…we should discuss this further in private…back at the manor."

"No, no," I say storming over to the two of them trying to keep the beast in check, because even with the thoughts about my dad, he's still circling the cage. "Please go on acting like two heartless a-holes, while your friend and your girlfriend lays dead literally at your feet!"

"Alex," Quincy starts in a somber tone extending his own calming hand toward me. "You don't-"

Tony, who is closer to me, staring me down, steps even closer. He's practically in my face at this point. "We have been watching over McCabe witches," he grumbles, hunching his shoulders up at me. "…since long before you or your father were even born, boy," he barks, like a dog with a warning growl behind every word.

The wolf's breathing in my ear, urging me not only to bark back, but to bark louder. Even the words he's using piss me off because he's finally sounding like the old man that he actually is. He pokes me in the chest. The wolf snarls. "Don't pretend that you have any idea how we are feeling in this moment."

I…maybe, the beast…maybe, both of us punch him in the face, dropping him on his back. I move to stand over him, and Quincy moves to protect his brother. I retreat a step and point at Tony. "Just so you know…" I renew my point for emphasis. "…that's how I'm feeling…'in this moment.'"

I turn to walk away before he can even get to his feet. I hear shuffling, and the sound of clothes being grabbed. I peer over my shoulder at Tony still trying to rush me, and Quincy trying to hold him back.

"Let it go, little brother." He moves around him so that he eclipses, yep, another Gwen word, his younger brother. "Let it go."

"Unhand me!" Tony barks, pushing his brother and gaining separation between them. Quincy does, and Tony straightens his ruffled suit, eyes still blazing with anger toward me. He smooths back his hair before adjusting his tie.

"Sir," a guy in an orange vest asks, standing nearby.

"Go ahead," Tony says in a stern tone while throwing his hand forward in a sort of chopping motion. The guy nods and then repeats it with another guy in a vest standing a short distance away. This guy brings over a wheelbarrow full of dirt. They work together to dump it out into the hole…on top of Jamie.

My phone starts vibrating. I take it out and answer before I even look at it. "Hey, Gwen," I moan.

"You sound how I feel," she replies.

"How are you feeling?" I ask. She huffs a sigh. "I mean, I know how you're feeling…but I know you were also queasy this morning…before you took the fire gap."

"It comes and goes. I think I might be coming down with something," she breathes. "It might be…" She breaks off, and I can practically hear her lower lip tremble as she fights back tears.

"Are you back yet?"

"No, I'm still in New York…Anne…she seemed to need the support." I nod because I can imagine she's feeling about the same way that Mr. Baggett is. "Gavin, Sora, and I will fire gap back after the wake."

"Gavin and Sora?"

"Yeah," she replies. "I was just as shocked as you are, but he said they owed her whatever that means."

"You said…" I don't know how to say this, so I'm just gonna say it. "…that she took a hit meant for you, right?" She moans a yes. "Gwen…we're married…kitsune marry for life. Meghan not only saved you…she saved me t-"

"I know," she snaps, cutting me off. "I'm sorry," she says, sounding as if her hand is covering mouth. "I'm sorry, I didn't mean-"

"I know, Fox Face. I know."

"How was...Jamie's...?"

"Intimate would be the best word for it," I reply. "The...Blackshears insisted on it being just family...apparently, I barely made the cut." She makes a questioning noise this time. "I also...might've...punched Tony...again."

"Alex, you didn't."

"I did." I peer back at the burial site and lean against the red pick-up truck mom planned on surprising me with at graduation but copped early because of my marriedness. "I think the Blackshears are up to something again."

"What do you mean?"

"Why would they forbid anyone but immediate family from coming to her funeral? Why would they line her casket with all kinds of magic crap to keep people away?"

"Alex...witches, especially ones as powerful as Jamie is...was...continue to be a source of tremendous power, even in death."

"Really?"

"Yeah," she replies. "And the more people who know Jamie's dead, that's the more people we have to lie to about how she died...the more likely it is that someone will start digging...figuratively and possibly...pos... Oh God!" The phone sounds as if it hits the ground.

"GWEN! GWEN!"

There's a rush of air moving past the phone a second later. "Pet," Gavin says in a calm voice. "I don't know what you and my dear sister were talking about, but...she's now vomiting into a bush and my bride-to-be is tending to her." He groans. "Aw, now she's vomiting too."

"That's it," I rumble. "Open a fire gap, I'm coming to New York."

#####

www.ingramcontent.com/pod-product-compliance
Lightning Source LLC
Chambersburg PA
CBHW070503200726
48293CB00007B/2358